and your little friend into the basement," he says as he shoves his cock away, adjusting it just right, and zips up his jeans, looking delirious and satisfied. I smirk, knowing how good of a job I had done. Seriously, what a bargain—for him.

His lip quirks up playfully as he meets my eyes, and he asks, "Maybe we could make this a regular thing?" He looks so hopeful with a gleam in his eyes.

Cute.

I grin at him, trying to hold back a face of utter disgust. "Don't hold your breath," I tell him arrogantly as I roll my eyes and adjust my sheer black long-sleeve top with a lace bra underneath that makes my boobs look perky, making sure to tuck it back into my skirt.

He huffs and shakes his head with immediate disappointment on his face before walking back into the club and angrily opening the door, rushing to get back to his security position at the popular club known as Th

CW01498471

FRAT ROW

KRISTA TURNER CLARK

Cover Design: ArtistaGrafico
Editing & Formatting: Deliciously Dark Editing

Paperback ISBN: 979-8-9994195-0-7
E-book ISBN: 979-8-9994195-1-4

This is purely a work of fiction. Names, characters, places, and incidents are
created by the author or used fictitiously.

❀ Formatted with Vellum

TRIGGER/CONTENT WARNINGS

Forced orgasm; Blindfolding; Sodomy; Choking; Primal Play;
Captivity; Humiliation; Sex Club; Thoughts of suicide;
Whipping; Sex Slaves; Degradation; Kidnapping; Drugs;
Imprisonment/Tied up against will; Wax play; Spanking;
Dildos; Pussy Slapping; Anal Stretching; Physical Scars; Anal
play; Human Sacrifice; Cages; Blood Drinking; Cults; Blood
Mutilation; Mental Abuse; Extreme BDSM; Rituals; Sexual
Assault; Starvation; Forced Oral Sex; Dehydration; Forced
threesome; Physical Abuse; Drinking of Urine; Sleep
Deprivation; Chains; Sexual Abuse; Beatings; Sex Trafficking;
Talk of Mental Scarring; Extreme Torture; Physical Scars;
Branding; Lacerations; Sex Machines; Forced Birth Control; Sex
Toys; Breath Play; CNC; Flogging; Rape; Human Auction

**Disclaimer. This book is dark. Consider this a broad blanket
trigger warning for any possible trigger you may have.
Continue at your discretion.

AUTHOR'S NOTE

$1 from each book sold, in either the Kindle version or paperback version, will be donated to cities in need of **inclusive playgrounds**.

Inclusive playgrounds are for all children with different abilities, allowing them to play together in a safe and inclusive environment.
It goes far beyond your typical playground and considers the needs of children with broad cognitive, sensory processing needs, physical, and our neurodivergent community.
The equipment is adaptable for all children, featuring sensory activities and providing easier access for wheelchairs. Examples of easily accessible surfaces include rubber mats or artificial turf.
There are many sensory activities, such as sensory panels with varying textures, sound-making panels, and visual aids. More ground-level activities, which allow children with mobility challenges to engage in.
They are very colorful, with a variety of textures to create an inviting environment for all children. Additionally, they offer greater safety than regular playgrounds.

Bringing awareness to this is a huge passion of mine. Overall, this is extremely beneficial for every community.

The mental health of parents is also a benefit; being able to go to an outdoor, safe, and accessible environment for their children allows them to connect with other parents and have play dates.

DEDICATION

To my pitch-black readers who love the darkness as much as I do.
This one is for you.

CHAPTER ONE

CASSIDY

The alleyway I'm in is pitch-black, and it looks like the emergency flood lights have been knocked out, probably on purpose because of all the shady shit going on out here. There's only one door into the club, and we are right beside it. There is just enough light to see the outlines of our sweaty bodies, but enough darkness to conceal us from onlookers. It's just us out here. The cracked and uneven pavement is digging relentlessly into my knees, the loose gravel sticking to them and causing a stinging pain. I'll feel the soreness tomorrow, hopefully with minimal cuts.

Lucky fucking me.

As I cup his sticky balls—no doubt due to sweat from being in South Florida—with my left hand, the tip of his cock glistens with the salty pre-cum and hits the back of my throat over and over, with his hands wrapped around my neck, not letting up on the roughness. His musky smell overwhelms my senses. I gasp for air while tears mix with the mascara running down my face, but this guy keeps thrusting at a fast pace. I try to focus on swirling my tongue underneath his cock; most men enjoy it. It's very sensitive, but with him thrusting so hard, it makes it almost impossible.

This is my favorite part—the moment of complete euphoria from bringing a man to his climax. When they lean their heads back and their mouths open wide, groaning loudly, not being able to control the sounds coming out of them, I can tell the down-the-spine tingling is starting, which happens right before a mind-blowing orgasm.

If there is one thing I know for sure about myself, it's how well I can suck dick. It's the complete control that gets me off—the power. But tonight isn't about my pleasure; it's about ensuring he gets his. When it comes to anything sexual, women hold all of the power. It's just how you use it to your advantage.

Some women love diamonds around their necks; I love hands.

"Goddamn, Cassidy," he groans as he releases and jerks himself forward, hitting the back of my throat, making sure I swallow every drop he has to offer.

After sucking down every single drop, making sure none of it hits my heels, I lick my full, swollen lips like it was the best five-course meal so he thinks I enjoyed myself and stand. I pull my black leather skirt down, run a hand through my chestnut hair a few times, trying to look as though I didn't just get my face fucked, and wipe the mascara from my face, removing some of the concealer that makes my hazel eyes pop. Wiping the inner corners of my water lines, I pull out the compact mirror from my purse and reapply mascara.

Fuck me.

With my hand on my hip, I look him straight in his eyes with utter confidence rolling off of me. "A deal is a deal," I say to him, trying to catch my breath like I just ran a damn marathon since I made him come quicker than the time it takes to tie your shoelaces.

"Give me 10 minutes to get back to my post, and I'll let you

CHAPTER TWO

CASSIDY

Everyone who attends Miami University knows about this notorious club, whether you are part of Greek life or not. It is owned by the hottest fraternity on campus, Alpha Chi. If you're a man, even if you aren't Greek life affiliated, you want to befriend the brothers in Alpha Chi because everyone knows they are constantly surrounded by the most beautiful women on campus. If you are a woman, you want to date a brother who is in Alpha Chi just so you can have access to the club and the outrageous parties they throw at the fraternity house. Rumor has it that they host a lingerie and boxers-only party, one of the biggest events on campus, which is a paper invitation-only affair.

It also doesn't hurt that they have contacts for the best drugs if you're into that sort of thing. Cocaine, weed, meth, pills, Adderall, you name it. They have the hook-up with all the best dealers around town.

Even when I was in high school, I was familiar with *The Dungeon*. It was all anyone talked about because it was so forbidden for anyone underage, and the mystery surrounding it piqued people's interest. This is the holy grail of places to be if you're someone, especially a Miami University student. The club is exclusive; you can't just walk up and expect to get in, even if you were to flash the bouncer a couple of hundred-dollar bills. You have to have some kind of connection. My connection tonight is the security guard I just gave a blow job to. I overheard him talking at the bookstore on campus about working there while attending school, and I promised that if he could get my friend Blair and me in, I would make it worthwhile for him. Like I said, it really doesn't take much when you use sex to your advantage.

The club is absolutely packed tonight, considering it is the last night of 'freedom' if you are rushing a sorority, which I am. Fraternity and sorority rules are entirely different. I am talking about totally opposite ends of the spectrum. Fraternities essentially have no rules during the rush period, whereas sororities adhere to a strict set of them. When you are trying to join a fraternity or sorority, it is called rush week. You go to all of the different sorority and fraternity houses on campus and talk about yourself for hours on end. You are essentially trying to sell yourself and explain why you would be a good fit for their organization. It's pretty superficial, but I'll do anything to get in, even give one of my kidneys. So the rules are, if you are rushing a sorority, you aren't allowed to drink alcohol, do drugs, or even be on any kind of social media; they call this being 'dry.' I call it pure torture. Talk about being bored to tears.

My mom was a sister at Zeta Kappa Phi, so I'm not really nervous about this entire rush experience. She has talked about it consistently since I started high school, preparing me to rush and expecting me to rush her sorority. She has told me multiple times that it makes your college experience infinitely better, and it's easier to make friends and excel in classes because the chances of one of your sisters either being in the same class as you or having already taken the class are high, and they can help you.

As if I would rush anywhere else at Miami University. Zeta Kappa Phi is the best sorority on this campus. Not to sound too cocky, but I'm not unattractive either, and that helps their image, especially when it comes to wanting other women to join. My mom was even the treasurer of her sorority, so she has a lot of influence when it comes to who gets bids. As she is still heavily involved as an advisor to past, present, and future treasurers, they can vent about how hard it is, and she can explain how it works.

It is rare not to receive a bid if you have connections, but it does happen, and you have to be a complete social outcast or have an extensive juvenile record for them not to accept you. They do background checks and even go as far as checking if there is any written documentation of insubordination from the high school you attended. Like I said, they don't just let anyone in.

Blair, who has been my best friend since the first day of sixth grade, is rushing alongside me. I still remember meeting her as if it were yesterday. On my first day of middle school, I was scared as shit to be late to one of my classes, so I decided to carry all of my books so I wouldn't have to stop at my locker since my next class was in a completely different building. I was rushing down the hallway to my next class with my handful of books, and some asshole kid purposely bumped into me hard enough that my books scattered everywhere, and I fell to the floor. Panicking, I began crawling and picking them up while other students stepped all over them. Blair saw this happen from her locker, rushed over to me, pushed the guy while calling him a prick, and hurriedly helped me pick up my books.

I knew from that moment I had to be her friend, so I thanked her and immediately asked her what her name was and what her next class was. It just so happened to be where I was headed— science, which turned out to be our least favorite subject at the time. She had this charisma about her that you just gravitate toward; it really didn't matter who you were; you were sucked into her aura. She had this effect on the girls in our school, teachers, cheer coaches, and even parents. Blair has always been fearless, while I've been the opposite, more observant of situations and cautious by nature.

Since that day, we've been attached by the hip while going through life's milestones together, including puberty, getting braces, glasses, first dates, first kisses, losing our virginities, and we were even on the high school cheer team together.

Currently, we are roommates in an apartment off campus for just the first semester of college. Since we aren't officially Zeta Kappa Phi sisters yet, we can't live in the sorority house, which is ultimately our plan. As soon as the fall semester is over, we plan on moving into the sorority house and sharing one of the dorm-like rooms with an adjoining bathroom. It's not ideal, but at least our sorority house is somewhat updated; some of them have communal bathrooms. Honestly, I wouldn't even consider living there if that were the case with our house.

Sharing has never been one of my strong suits. Could you imagine sharing a bathroom between four girls? That would be a complete nightmare. I don't vibe with petty drama over things, such as misplacing someone's makeup brush. Additionally, a huge rule that you have to follow when living in the house is no sleepovers with guys. They are allowed in the common area but not upstairs near the bedrooms. I heard that a sister tried to sneak her boyfriend in at night when everyone was asleep, and she was immediately kicked out. So when it comes to trying to get laid, I'm going to have to get pretty creative or hope he has a place we can go to.

But living in the house has its advantages. You find out about all of the events first and get to be involved in the planning of them, know all about the drama surrounding the executive board and other sisters before everyone else, access to the best tutors, first to place your orders with the private chef that lives in the house as well and receive the invitations to the best parties that are thrown at all of the fraternity houses before everyone else.

We just have to abide by the rules and make it through the rush week new member period, which is also the entirety of the fall semester. However, I've heard that some legacies are initiated faster than others and don't have to wait until the end of the semester.

The only thing that bothers me is this whole dry period, especially before classes start. Don't they know this is the week you want to get the most hammered when there are no responsibilities at the moment?

I would also like to start fucking my way through Frat Row and get with a brother from every fraternity house. I heard you get a badge for achieving that, and I plan on getting mine.

They torture us like this because they think there will be less of a chance that the girls who are rushing will be able to talk to other rushes or even people who aren't rushing. No secrets are supposed to be exposed, and if they learn that you told someone, you are immediately kicked out of the rush process, no questions asked, and you won't be able to rush the following year. Since some of us are legacies, we know more than the average person rushing, so honestly, the whole thing is bullshit. Things like initiation and other rituals aren't known to Blair and me. My mom never shared even the slightest detail. They are intended to be shared only with initiated sisters.

It's a complete week of hell, especially for someone like me. I would call myself more of an introvert than an extrovert. Blair brings out the extroverted side of me and always has. Another rule is that we aren't allowed to go out to bars or clubs even if we don't drink. We can't even grab lunch or dinner at a restaurant in case we run into other girls who are rushing and could be tempted to talk about the process.

So, it looks like it's a week of DoorDash and Uber Eats for me and Blair; I'm not going to complain about that since neither one of us can cook. I'm honestly surprised Blair can boil water or turn on a stove.

I'm already annoyed at the thought of this upcoming week

and the number of times I'm going to have to repeatedly open my mouth and use my voice to the point of losing it, which most people do. There's event after event, but at least I'll have Blair at the end of the day to laugh through the pain and exhaustion.

I couldn't imagine rushing alone and not having anyone to vent to about the entire process. Plus, every day has a different theme, so you have to dress accordingly; otherwise, you'll look like an oddball. I'm almost positive they write your name down because there's a rumor that they have some kind of point system.

After straightening myself up in the alleyway, I smile, happy with the way I look. With my head held high, I take in a deep breath of fresh air and make my way toward the door that leads back into the club. Thankfully, it is dark, and no one notices me. Looking around, I search for my best friend. Of course, knowing her and her promiscuous, sultry ways, I'm willing to bet she's dry-humping a random guy—or multiple—on the dance floor. We pre-gamed in our apartment before we got here, downing a few shots of Fireball, so I know she must be at least a little tipsy, if not leaning more toward being on the drunk side. That could only mean one thing—loud and flirty Blair comes out to play, and it is a sight to behold since she is only 5'3" and has a don't-fuck-with-me attitude. I roll my eyes thinking about it and how many times I've had to coerce her into leaving a party, bar, or club. I always make sure to form a quick mental list of all her great qualities and why I love her, so I don't lose my cool. I try to be as patient as possible, knowing it's just the alcohol taking over the way she acts.

It's so dark in here that you can barely see your hands and feet right in front of you. The walls are painted black, and there are neon strobe lights on the ceiling. The DJ is in the corner, playing music so loud that you can barely have a conversation or think clearly. So many shady things happen in this club that it would make your head spin. You could essentially fuck or have an orgy in the middle of the club, and no one would see you, and if they did, they wouldn't bat an eye. I heard it's allowed, and if anything, the employees love a good show, just like everyone else here. I push my way toward the dance floor, bumping into a lot of people and apologizing more times than I can count. I'm attempting to get to the dance floor in the back right corner of the club that I saw when we first arrived.

Yay for muscle memory!

The club floor is made of dark gray concrete, while the dance floor features outdated laminate with scuff marks, which you can kind of see if a strobe light hits it. My eyesight is already dreadful, so while feeling for the change in flooring, I stumble in my five-inch heels but recover quickly.

I spot Blair instantly. She's gorgeous, with platinum blonde hair, blue eyes, tanned skin, and a body that men—and women—fantasize about. Tonight, she is in her strappy light blue dress that barely covers her ass with matching heels that lace up to her mid-thigh. I've always been jealous of her shorter height. I'm 5'7", so most of the time, I tower over a majority of men when I wear my super high heels.

In true Blair fashion, she's not dry-humping one guy but sandwiched between two guys and dancing to Jack Harlow's new song. Both the guys dancing with her and those surrounding her are absolutely mesmerized, just praying for a turn and salivating over her. She never notices all of the attention and genuinely couldn't care less. She's always ready for a good time, and it doesn't have to be for a long time.

Quickly, I snag her tiny elbow, pull her over to the bar, and whisper excitedly where only she can hear, "Listen, I figured out a way into The Dungeon's basement, but we have to go right now."

CHAPTER THREE

CASSIDY

Blair's eyes turn into saucers with disbelief, and her jaw hangs open. She knows, like everyone else, it's next to impossible to get access to the basement, and the people who have been down there don't ever discuss what it's like. Of course, this made me want to find out for myself even more, and I'm towing my best friend with me in these shenanigans, as always. Since we met, we've given our mothers gray hair.

She quietly squeals, "Let's go, skank, lead the way!"

She forcefully shoves one of the drinks she has into my hand, our favorite—vodka and club soda. Not shockingly, she had a drink in each hand while dancing. I'm sure one of her dance partners was more than happy to supply her with more alcohol. I down it as swiftly as possible, tasting primarily vodka, not soda, and it instantly calms my nerves.

She reaches for my hand, and we set off toward a door located behind the bar that blends in with the wall. It has a black knob and a vintage-looking key lock, which tells me not many people have access. It's so concealed in the wall that you'd have to know about it already or be purposefully looking for it. The area in front of the door is always guarded by at least two security guards, who appear as inconspicuous as possible. But even partly tipsy, I can tell they guard one area and never leave their posts. Sucking off the security guard earlier definitely paid off since he told me where to go and is letting us into a place few people have ever been.

The security guard I had my special time with earlier is standing by the door. He winks at me with an overconfident, smug look on his face, looks around, turns, and punches in a four-digit code, the door cracking open just a few inches. He hurriedly opens it enough to slide through and gestures to us with two fingers to quickly follow behind him.

There's a small black booth completely blacked out with the most miserable-looking man I've seen here. Maybe I would be, too, if everything was black. This part of the club is so quiet you could hear a pin drop. The lighting is dim, likely to conceal the identities of people entering and exiting the basement. There are four people ahead of us, and I don't even bother looking at them because I don't want it to seem like this is my first time. I do try to look at what the man is collecting, and it's definitely not coats or umbrellas.

"No cellphones allowed past this point, so hand them over." Another guard comes out of what feels like the wall, making me jump with his raspy voice.

It's a cellphone check booth, which makes sense since I've never seen any pictures of this place online. He pulls out one of the many plastic boxes, and there must be at least fifty or more phones in it. He passes us cards to fill out so they can be returned to us later. We fill them out, and he tapes them on our cellphones, tossing them into the box.

"Straight down the stairs, you can't miss it." He smiles maliciously like he can sniff out first-timers.

Blair and I look at each other quizzically, and for a moment, we kind of second-guess this decision. My body is buzzing; I'm not sure if it's the alcohol or the tension of feeling unsure about this whole decision.

"I'm getting kind of nervous now," I blurt out.

"That's just excitement for the unknown. If we aren't into it, we'll give it a solid 15 minutes and then just leave as fast as possible," Blair whispers to me.

I clamp onto her arm for dear life, and we start to descend the dark stairs that are lit by dull yellow Victorian lights all the way to the bottom, with a deep forest green railing on both sides. The wallpaper is made of black velvet, making it even more eerie.

When we reach the bottom of the stairs, my jaw falls open, and it feels like we've entered Narnia's wardrobe because this is entirely different from what we saw upstairs.

The first thing I notice is the archaic, gothic-looking cages hanging above our heads, which are chained to the ceiling, and the swings moving back and forth. There must be over twenty of them spread out around the room, which is the size of a large warehouse. My feet move on their own, pulling me forward as I squint upwards to get a better look at what is inside the cages and what is making the swings move back and forth. To my utter horror, there are naked women in each of the cages swinging on the swings with the only piece of clothing, if you can even call it that, being a black lace lingerie mask.

They are nude. *Nude.* I try not to stare at the scene before me, but it's hard not to. I've never seen anything like this before.

Some of them are holding on to the sides of the cage, swaying their hips to the music, and you can see their boobs bouncing freely and their vaginas on full display, rubbing themselves against the cages. Others in the cages are standing there with frightened looks in their eyes, cowering on one side of the cage and hugging their knees to their chests. The women on the swings move their legs back and forth, and they have detached looks on their faces.

Gradually taking in the rest of the room, I notice half of the room has private black booths full of men in business suits who are either snorting cocaine or smoking cigars, talking in hushed tones to one another at their tables. In the back, there are three stripper poles with women performing naked again, and the men are barely paying any attention. In the middle of the room is a U-shaped bar, and Blair leads us tentatively over there. The chairs are a deep purple velvet, and we slide them out and take a seat, scanning the room and feeling utterly uncomfortable, except for the tingle between my legs. Showcasing your sexuality like this is so different from how I grew up. Sex wasn't talked about in my household. It was like it was taboo and forbidden. Secretly, I love being in and around this kind of scene.

At the bar, there are five female bartenders who are also waiting on the men in the booths. They are wearing black lace teddies and black lace masks with black stilettos.

"What can I get you both to drink?" one of the bartenders says sweetly, placing napkins in front of us.

Blair responds, "Vodka and club soda, please, and make it two."

This place is packed, predominantly with men. Even at the bar, the other seats, except for a few, are taken.

Blair looks at me, grinning devilishly. "I can't believe you got us in here."

"Honestly, me neither. There are barely any women in here besides maybe two in the booths next to some of the men," I say, finally seeing some other women here.

"This place doesn't feel right; it feels like some illegal underground business, and we definitely stick out," Blair whispers to me.

"I'll go to the bathroom, and then we can make our way out of here. I'm not sure we want to get caught up in this type of crowd," I respond.

I ask the bartender where the bathroom is, and she points to a small hallway I hadn't seen before behind the stripper poles.

I jump off my seat. "Be right back, whore, don't move from this seat." I wink at her and smile, crossing my fingers that she doesn't fucking move.

Blair smiles and rolls her eyes while she takes a huge sip of her drink, flicking me off.

As I make my way to the dark hallway with dimmed lights, it's creepily quiet, and something feels off-putting. The hairs on my arms rise, and I get goosebumps, suddenly feeling freezing cold. I almost bolt back to the bar, but my bladder wins out. I have to pee so badly, and there's no way I can hold it.

There are multiple black doors down this long hallway that seem to go on forever; I check one of them, and it's locked, so I assume all of them must be locked. There are peepholes in the middle of them of varying heights, all in a straight vertical line. They don't look like bathrooms at all, so I keep walking and frantically look for any sign that says 'bathrooms.' Curiosity finally gets the best of me, and I hesitantly approach one of the peepholes and press my hands on either side, trying not to put too much pressure on the door so no one hears me. I'll just take a brief look and then make my way to the bathroom.

There's no harm in just looking. It's not like I'm opening the door.

CHAPTER FOUR

CASSIDY

I blink rapidly, willing my eyes to adjust to the dimly lit room. On the right side of the room are more whips and chains than I can count, all different sizes, hanging from the wall. Below is a selection of dildos in every size and color on a small table. This must be some sort of sex room or type of sex club.

My eyes venture over to the middle of the room, where I see a king-size bed with four tall posts and a black fitted sheet. My mouth drops open, and I gasp. On the bed is a woman with her legs and hands chained to the bed posts but with enough slack from the chains so she can be on all fours naked with her glistening pussy and ass on full display. She is blindfolded with her head facing the wall behind the headboard with a leash tightly around her neck that a man is roughly pulling on, making her head bend at an odd angle. Spit and drool fly out of her mouth, and she gags while he thrusts, showing no mercy while she deep-throats his cock.

At the same time, another man is fucking her ass so violently while pulling on a silver chain as he thrusts all the way in and out. He groans, and I now see the silver chain is hooked to nipple clamps. She's moaning so loudly I'm surprised I didn't hear her while walking through the hallway. I feel myself getting wet, and I am so turned on. Finally, the guy that was fucking her mouth pulls out, and streams of cum jet out all over her face. He releases the leash and gets underneath her body, placing his head directly under her pussy. He lifts up and starts feasting on her clit and hole, tongue fucking her. She's shaking now; her orgasm is obvi-ously close. The man fucking her ass finds his relief and cums inside her. Some of it dribbles out, and he catches it with his fingers and stuffs it back in her hole, then gives her ass a loud smack. She lets the orgasm take over her, screaming and writhing while she rides the man's face.

I stumble backward in shock, almost tripping over my own feet.

There is another threesome taking place in this room with three men. One man is on his back with his head hanging off the edge of the bed and has a black chain collar around his neck, while another one is fucking him so hard the bed seems like it could break as it rocks back and forth while he grips the chain. A third man with pierced nipples stands in front of the man being fucked, forcing him to deep-throat his cock.

Not able to hold back anymore, I reach up under my skirt and begin to rub my clit back and forth; I know how to quickly get myself off. I'm so wet already and so turned on by the sight of this. I can tell I'm close.

The guy on his back moans loudly while taking cocks in both of his holes. Everyone is in sync with each other, and animalistic noises fill the air.

In a frenzy, I start flicking my clit faster while putting more pressure on it, whimpering quietly because I am about to come. I find my release at the exact moment they do, and shivers wrack through my body as I watch both guys pull out and come all over the guy lying down. They're breathing hard, sweat shining on their faces. Suddenly, they take their fingers and spread their mixed cum all over his stomach, putting it in their mouths and turning to each other to share deep kisses.

This is what must be going on in all these rooms. I'm intrigued and want to come back or at least stay a little longer, but I know Blair is waiting on me, and before she gets sucked into one of those booths, I turn away, a little flushed in the face, and practically sprint to find the bathroom.

I fling open the bathroom door and notice that there are only two huge stalls, and both are empty, thank baby Jesus. I pick the furthest stall and pee faster than I ever have in my life. Afterward, I make my way to the sink and wash my hands. I look around and notice that the bathroom matches the basement's Gothic, all-black aesthetic. Even the wallpaper has the same black velvet with intricate designs. I lean down to splash some water on my face to cool down from how hot what I just witnessed was.

As I look back up from the sink, I startle when I see a woman standing beside me in the mirror. I didn't even hear her walk in. She stands there and washes her hands in the sink beside me. The gloves she was wearing are placed on the side of the sink, and I glance over and notice a number on her wrist I can't really make out because it's so small. It starts with an eight. Confused, I shrug to myself. Some people have a lucky number or a number that means something to them. She is decked out in a dominatrix outfit: leather boots, a leather one-piece that is thong-style, showing off her curvaceous ass while also hugging all her curves and the same lingerie mask as the other women working here. She slips her gloves back on and starts applying red lipstick. She looks magnificent, and I can't help but gawk at her.

She arches her eyebrow at me, catching my eye in the mirror, and asks, "I can tell this is your first time here, right?"

"Wow, is it that obvious?" I ask sheepishly, looking her in the eye.

Her eyes look lifeless as if her soul has been completely removed from her body, and this is just a regular night for her. It instantly gave me chills and a bad feeling in the pit of my stomach.

"Take my advice and get out of here as soon as you possibly can, and don't ever come back," she says angrily and then abruptly leaves the bathroom as if she is scared of something. I gape at her in shock while rapidly drying my hands, not even caring that the paper towel didn't land in the wastebasket, and I scurry out of there.

CHAPTER FIVE

CASSIDY

Bewildered by what just happened, I head back to the bar to find Blair thankfully still sitting in the same chair I left her in. We need to get the hell out of here without drawing too much attention. Not surprisingly, she ordered us another round of drinks. I slide into the chair next to her and snatch my drink, swallowing the entire thing in one gulp and taking the woman's advice to get out of here as quickly as humanly possible. Decisively, I face Blair. Catching her eye, I say in a panic, "We need to go back upstairs right this second."

She must have seen the crazed look in my eyes because she instantly nods and says, "Lead the way, girl; let's get out of here." She jumps up so fast and doesn't even bother to finish her drink.

We link arms as we try to avoid attracting any unwanted attention, heading back for the stairs that lead up to the club. I hold my breath until we reach the top of the stairs, seeing the booth where our cell phones are. The line to retrieve them is long, and my hands are sweating while I fidget impatiently, worrying someone is going to pull us back downstairs. After waiting for what feels like an eternity, we retrieve them, walk back into the club, and head straight to the dance floor. I let out the breath I had been holding until we got through the door and let relief wash over me.

Blair, no doubt feeling the side effects of the large amount of alcohol she has consumed, throws her head back and starts moving her hips to some song I've never heard of, but she figures out the beat fast. I reach for her hand, laughing, and join her, moving my hips back and forth to the rhythm. I'm not as good a dancer as she is; however, that doesn't seem to matter as plenty of lingering eyes are focused on us.

The relief swimming through my mind from getting out of the basement in one piece sends me into oblivion mentally. I let go of the racing adrenaline coursing through me and let my body flow even more than I normally do dancing.

"This is out of character for you," Blair yells over the music.

"It's our last night of being spontaneous and wild," I yell back at her, grinning mischievously.

"Well, dance your heart out, babe," Blair responds humorously.

After only a few minutes of dancing, I have this feeling that someone is watching me. Spinning around swiftly, not wanting to look too obvious, my eyes instantly lock with deep blue eyes that remind me of a storm brewing in the sea. The most gorgeous eyes I have ever seen. This man looks like a sculpture Michael Angelo carved himself, with the ripples of muscle showing through his red V-neck shirt. His medium build with wide shoulders and dark brown hair looks like something out of a magazine. I would guess his height to be at least 6'3".

Pure perfection. I glance down and see him wearing tight jeans with white Jordans, drooling at the sight of him. He has style as well?

Jackpot.

He is surrounded by a few guys who are clearly engaged in a deep conversation, but he isn't paying them any attention. His eyes never left me as soon as he spotted me, and haven't since we locked eyes. It's as if some kind of dark possession has taken over him, giving me a deep, sultry look while taking an aggressive sip of his beer.

My skin heats as he continues to stare at me as if he is picturing me with my clothes off and fucking me roughly. I can't deny I'd be completely into that.

I feel daring, knowing rush starts tomorrow and then school directly after. My first semester is full of hard classes. I don't have time for men or dating of any sort. I prefer one-night stands anyway; commitment isn't really for me.

Moving myself behind Blair, we begin moving our hips in sync with one another. Since I am taller than her, I always dance behind her. My hands go to her small waist, gripping each side. She arches her shoulders back into me while rolling her body in one single motion seductively, entirely overcome with the music. The club is so hot, and we are both glistening with sweat. The mysterious guy's eyes start to darken, and his jaw instantaneously tightens with outrage as if he can't just sit in the shadows anymore and watch other men leer at me.

After a few moments, I can tell his self-control doesn't win out, and he places his empty beer on one of the small high tops scattered throughout the club and starts stalking over in my direction.

CHAPTER SIX

TYLER

I'm staring at one of the sexiest girls I've ever laid eyes on, with her chestnut hair, curvy body, and toned legs. As soon as I saw her walk onto the dance floor, I knew I had to have a taste of her. Her friend is dancing with her, but there are plenty of guys eye fucking them, lined up and waiting for a turn with either one. Arrogantly, I stalk right up behind her and glare at the guy grinding on her, daring him to say something as I shove him away. He stumbles back and leaves the dance floor quickly, not even looking behind him.

Stepping behind her, I place one hand on her hip, possessively holding on tightly as she moves her body against mine. Grinding to the music, she moves her ass over my semi-erect cock, teasing me. To be honest, I was already horny as fuck watching her dance with her friend. But now, having my hands on her body and feeling her thong through her tight skirt, my dick is begging for some kind of release. I have always considered myself a decent dancer and can sense she enjoys dancing with me.

She tosses her head back to gather her hair and put it to one side, and the smell of it invades my senses as I inhale deeply; damn, she smells like lavender and honey; I am intoxicated.

My other hand finds her other hip, and after a few moments, I glide one of my hands up the side of her body, over her arm, and up her neck, applying pressure to her throat just under her jaw and leaning her head back. I tower over her, using it to my advantage to control her, and growl in her ear, "I need to know your name, and then I want to know every fucking inch of your body." My hand slowly dips down, feeling the curve of her breast and lingering there, watching her nipples harden and her thighs squeeze together.

She lifts her chin gradually to the side and peers up at me with her doe eyes that I know are anything but innocent, and in a throaty whisper with her lips lifting in one corner, she says, "Cassidy Matthews; your turn."

"Tyler Chase, but tonight, you can call me yours," I whisper in her ear.

We continue to dance to the song, and my fingertips graze all over her body, slowly exploring all of her curves without putting too much pressure on her skin.

Unexpectedly, she turns around to face me and wraps both of her arms around my neck, her breasts ever so slightly skimming my chest, and pulls the back of my neck toward her face so that we are at eye level. I can feel her hot breath as she breathes heavily onto my lips, faintly open, barely touching mine.

My patience gives out, and I wrap my hands around the back of her head and pull her into me, pressing my tongue to her lips and forcefully pushing it into her mouth. She meets my tenacity as our tongues intertwine, tasting each other and exploring each other's mouths. Soaking in every bit of each other, my hands slowly caress her lower back until I reach her ass, and with both hands, I give it a hard squeeze and aggressively pull her up toward me. Her legs willingly wrap around my torso as she melts into me.

Suddenly, she breaks the kiss and licks her lips, looking completely stunned but hungry for more. I'd be lying if I didn't say I feel the same way; I need to get her clothes off as fast as possible and feel how wet she is for me.

"Do you want to get out of here?" she asks hurriedly.

My eyes round in disbelief, but smirking, I say, "Hell yes, baby, lead the way."

Who the hell are you, Cassidy Matthews, and how am I already willing to do whatever you ask?

CHAPTER SEVEN

CASSIDY

Do I enjoy sex? Yes, who the fuck doesn't? That's like saying you don't enjoy a cup of coffee in the morning.

Have you ever met someone who said they hated orgasms? I haven't, but if someone told me they were just 'nice,' I'd have to question if they were being fucked properly. When you elevate out of your body and lose complete control over what it is doing and what is coming out of your mouth, that feeling is like no other. I feel sorry for women who never experience it at least once in their lifetime.

With all the stress surrounding rush week, I, without a doubt, need to let off some steam. While some people do physical exercise or drugs, I love to be dominated, called a good girl, and get fucked until I can't see straight. I want to feel soreness between my legs the next day so I can be flooded with exhilarating memories from the night before.

Someone as sexy as Tyler Chase, what more could a girl ask for? *Literal eye candy.*

He seems to know his way around a woman's body, and he's definitely gifted in the below-the-belt department. I could feel it as I moved up and down his length on the dance floor.

Can you blame me? I need length and girth for complete satisfaction.

You can learn a lot about someone on the dance floor by the way they move their hips. It makes my body tingle thinking about what his moves are like in the bedroom.

"Let me find my friend Blair and ask if she's okay and if she wants to stay here. If not, we can share an Uber back to our place," I tell Tyler deliriously.

You could say I'm past tipsy right now, and I couldn't care less.

I swear this man hasn't taken his eyes off of me from the moment he saw me, and he's probably thinking about what I sound like when I climax. If I'm being honest, I am guilty of thinking the same thing about him. The anticipation is killing me.

Finally, I find Blair dancing with a random guy; she is wasted and way past the point of making responsible decisions. Her dress is pulled so far up that I can see her white lace panties that leave nothing to the imagination.

Feeling protective, I rush over to her and pull her dress down as far as it will go.

"BRAD!" she yells at me.

Confusion is written all over my face, and I say loudly, "What?"

She drives her pointer finger on and off his chest roughly and yells, "This is Brad. Brad, this is Cassidy." She rolls her eyes like she doesn't understand why I was confused in the first place. Yeah, she's plastered, beyond inebriated.

Brad doesn't look like he gives two fucks who the hell I am. He already has tunnel vision and is set on getting laid tonight. He is blatantly captivated by Blair and is obviously mentally calculating how fast he can get her to himself and rip her clothes from her body.

Gently reaching for her arm and pulling her close to me, I whisper where only she can hear, "I'm going to head back to the apartment. Do you want to come or are you good here? I'd prefer it if you came back with me. You don't know this guy."

She looks behind me and notices Tyler, inspecting him from his shoes to the top of his head, making it very obvious she is checking him out.

Grinning so widely that you can see all of her perfect white teeth, she yells, "Damn, bestie. I'd want to get him home and undressed as soon as possible, too!" My cheeks turn red, even though she couldn't be more correct.

Ding, ding, ding, we have a winner. Thanks, Blair, for stating the obvious.

I grin at her wickedly. Laughing, she snags Brad's sleeve and whispers something in his ear, which only they can hear, like an inside joke. They both grin naughtily at each other with a flicker of sexual tension between them.

"We're coming with you guys; we can split an Uber," Blair declares.

Blair whips out her phone so fast that it practically falls out of her hand as she begins clicking away, and she somehow success-fully orders an Uber that accommodates us all.

Tyler reaches out to place his hand on my hip and presses his face against my neck, deeply inhaling my scent as he works his way up to my earlobe and bites it softly.

I close my eyes, and a thrill shivers through my entire body— that's my spot. Then, he begins walking beside me as our small party heads outside to where the Uber is waiting for us.

Blair tugs on Brad by the collar of his shirt, acting like she can't get there fast enough, pressing her body roughly against his and rubbing herself all over him.

We all barrel into the Uber like we have no patience, which, let's be honest, died in the club. It's a 4Runner with only three seats in the back and the passenger seat. Brad climbs in first, with Blair jumping in his lap and straddling him, leaving two seats for me and Tyler. The Uber driver rolls his eyes as if this happens all the time and turns down the AC to cool the car. I'm thankful after sweating on the dance floor.

Tyler begins sensually brushing my hair behind my shoulders. He wastes no time, peppering me with kisses from my jawline down to my collarbone and pulling my shirt down. I allow him access.

Then, he brushes his fingertips above my breasts, which are pushed up and practically hanging out of the lace bra I'm wearing.

I let out a soft moan, needing more of him. He pulls back and briefly makes eye contact with me as if asking for permission, and after I nod, he starts nipping at my neck harshly and licking the spots he's bitten. Even though the pain and pleasure feel great, there will be bruising and marks all over, but I don't even care.

This man. I am so turned on, and we haven't even taken a single piece of clothing off.

My hand slowly runs down in between his legs to explore and feel him with my fingers, and just as I thought, his cock is huge and bulging through his jeans.

I quickly send up my thanks to baby Jesus.

The Uber driver needs to floor the gas pedal because I'm salivating at this point. Seriously, I don't care if he has to break the law while driving; I'll give him an extra tip. The driver turns up the music, which happens to be R&B from the 2000s. Frankly, I don't blame him. The sex noises coming from all of us must be annoying—or turning him on; who knows. People are freaks these days, so I'm guessing it's the latter.

Blair is moaning so loudly like she's never had a dick before in her life. She is either giving the performance of her life or actually enjoying it. I can barely pay attention because my hands haven't left Tyler's body.

As we pull up to our apartment complex, Blair and Brad basically fall out on top of one another while getting out of the car, laughing hysterically as they do so. Then, they practically sprint to our apartment, Blair holding her heels in her hands so she can keep up with Brad.

Tyler, being a complete gentleman, lets me out first, but not without me noticing him staring at my ass. He shamelessly watches me walk in front of him for a minute, and I sway my hips enticingly, loving the attention. All of a sudden, he jogs up beside me and quickly pulls me toward him. I am flush against his body, breathing heavily and feeling our body heat radiating from us. He puts his hand on the back of my neck, grabbing my hair and slightly pulling back so I'm forced to look up at him. My lips part, and our eyes lock on each other, and I see something dark and playful in his. He bites my lip hard to the point I lick it, and that metallic taste overwhelms and excites me. Then, he kisses me, our tongues dancing back and forth with our teeth connecting at some points, sharing the blood on my lip. He's loving it. I push him back abruptly and reach for his hand again, leading him to my apartment on the second floor.

Blair was kind enough to leave the front door unlocked and somewhat ajar, not even bothering to close it. We enter my apartment silently, grinning at each other. Of course, Blair is already in her room with the door shut, moaning Brad's name so loudly that our neighbors are definitely going to complain tomorrow. I swear that girl wastes no time.

Leading Tyler to my room, which is on the opposite side of the apartment, thankfully, we enter and shut the door.

He casually looks around, taking in my bedroom, which is scarcely decorated because I don't plan on being here long. There's a bed, a dresser, a desk, a nightstand, and an average-sized TV.

I'm leaning on my desk, waiting for him to make the first move.

Lastly, he looks over at me, narrowing his eyes and finding his prey for the night. His eyes darken with a cocky smirk, and his eyebrows are slightly raised. He notices a candle and lighter next to my bed and immediately lights it.

The lights in my room have an automatic dimmer. He doesn't even make a move to turn them off.

So, he's that kind of guy. He wants to watch.

He takes a seat in my desk chair, backing it up a little from where I stand, and turns it toward me.

"Take off your shirt," he growls at me from the seat, leaning back into the chair and resting his arms on the armrests, seemingly owning the room and in complete control. He strikes me as very dominating, and I enjoy relinquishing dominance and submitting to his every demand.

Slowly, I inch it up over my head with a sinful grin on my face. My thighs clench with anticipation, and I feel myself already slick with desire.

"Now, your skirt." I unbutton the back and shimmy out of it, kicking it to the side, standing now in only a navy lace bra and thong from La Perla and my heels.

He takes his time looking longingly at me, starting from the bottom and working his way up to my eyes. Urgently, he stands and takes off his shirt, next unbuttoning his jeans and pulling down his boxers. His hard cock springs free. His body is free from any hair, allowing his abs and V-cut to stand out on his immaculate frame.

As I eye fuck his entire glorious body, drooling over his nakedness, he begins stroking himself and rubbing his thumb over the tip of his cock, spreading the pre-cum all over and lubing himself with it.

"Spread your legs and rub your clit over your thong," he commands.

I do exactly what he says, and as soon as my fingers touch my sensitive bundle of nerves, I throw my head back. The instant pleasure consumes me and starts building.

He walks up to me, and I can see him mentally calculating where he wants to start. Finally, without hesitation, he stands in front of me, and all I feel is his body heat radiating off of him, breathing on me in slow, agonizing breaths. He bends down and puts his face between my legs, taking a deep breath and inhaling my scent, driving me absolutely crazy. He lazily licks the outside of my panties and then bites it, causing a sharp pain to thrum through my pussy.

His hand moves in between my thighs roughly, and his fingers push my panties to the side as he slips one finger inside and slowly moves it in and out. This waiting is excruciating. A whimper slips from my lips, and I can't help but imagine what is going to happen next, but I also love the unknown.

"You're soaked, baby. Tell me how badly you want my cock in this tight pussy," he says huskily.

I don't say anything, totally immersed in the satisfaction racking through my body.

"Use your words, or I'll punish you; I'll take you over my knee and smack that ass until it turns red with my handprint," he growls at me.

"Badly," I pant. Words forming together seem impossible right now. He's unimaginably good at this.

His thumb begins to skim over my clit while he slips another finger inside of me, still thrusting them in and out, curving perfectly and hitting my G-spot. Moaning again, he stands up and captures it in his mouth, and our tongues deliciously play with each other, sucking and pulling. Just when I feel a wave of pleasure, he stops and takes a step away from me, edging me to insanity.

"Take off your bra and panties, then crawl to the bed with your ass in the air so I can see you spread out and ready for me. Then, I want you to position yourself on all fours with your head facing the headboard. I want your knees spread far apart and your head touching the mattress with your face to the side. I want to see that needy wet cunt and swollen slit," he harshly demands.

I take my panties off first and then gradually unhook my bra. My nipples are so hard and sensitive. He sees them and lets out a panting noise while biting his fisted hand, holding himself back from devouring me.

I do as he says, and I crawl at a snail's pace so he can get a good view. Then, I get on the bed and in the position exactly as he ordered me to do it.

I really wasn't expecting him to have the self-control of a saint, but the excitement of it sends chills up my spine, not knowing what will happen next. I am so turned on that there is nothing this man could ask of me that I probably wouldn't do. I want him so badly, I feel it everywhere.

Feeling the bed faintly dip, I know he's on his knees directly behind me; I feel his cock brush back and forth against my ass and rub over my pussy. Then, he leans back and smacks my pussy hard enough that my body moves forward a bit, and I try to hold back the moan, but it escapes. He spanks me there again, and I know I'm wet because I can feel it dripping down my thigh.

"I thought I wasn't getting punished," I huskily say.

"Oh, baby, this is nothing compared to the punishment I have planned for you," he says casually.

Quickly, he pulls on my clit and suddenly shoves one finger inside of me, thrusting back and forth fast and hard; using my wetness as lube, he uses his other finger and slips it in my back hole, thrusting harder, and he keeps this going until my legs are shaking and I can't take it any longer. I'm rocking my body back and forth, fucking his fingers with my body, shamelessly begging for more.

He leans down and whispers in my ear, "Such a needy little slut."

He takes his fingers out and starts softly circling my clit, and I can barely hold myself up, writhing around so badly I am about to combust. Then his weight on the mattress moves, and just when I am about to come, I feel this hot, stinging sensation above my ass, dripping slowly down my back and making its way to my shoulders before stopping. It's the wax from the candle he lit earlier.

I scream out as the different sensations hit me all at once, and as my mind jumps from almost orgasming and feeling the burning from the wax, he blows on it. He's mixing pain with pleasure and edging the fuck out of me. He flips me on my back, and his mouth finds my clit, and he starts sucking hard and lapping up my wetness like he can't get enough of it in his mouth. He pulls my clit into his mouth and sucks hard, and then tongue fucks my pussy until finally I explode. It feels like my soul levitated out of my body, and I ride out the utter bliss as I lie there dazed. I collapse on my bed, completely speechless. He gets off the bed, walks into my en suite, grabs a towel, and cleans off my back. Wow, this man is into aftercare, which is rare and kind of sweet.

I roll over to my side with my elbow propping me up and look up at him, the bed sheets halfway off my body with my boobs on display. He's still hard as a rock, and I lick my lips hungrily, absolutely satisfied.

He flips me on my back forcefully, takes hold of underneath the top of my arms, and pulls me over to the edge of the bed to the point where my head is hanging off, his cock directly above me. "Suck it like a good fucking girl," he says in a guttural voice. My thighs clench together again like I didn't just have the best orgasm of my life. But when he talks to me like that, I know I'm instantly wet again. I open my mouth, and as soon as I do, he shoves his cock in all the way to the back of my throat, and I immediately gag. He doesn't let go of both sides of my head; all I can do is taste the pre-cum as he thrusts harder and deeper, fucking my face relentlessly. Saliva begins to drip down my cheeks and into my eyes, and I try to blink it away. He plugs my nose, and my throat opens voluntarily. He pulls out completely, allowing my lungs to expand for mere seconds, and then he continues fucking my mouth harder than before, groaning and throwing his head back.

"That's my good fucking girl; swallow my cock whole; you look so beautiful like this," he growls and runs his fingers through my hair, pulling it toward him, wanting me to go to the hilt of his cock at every thrust.

His hands drop to his sides, and he pulls his cock abruptly out of my mouth. I roll to my side, gasping for air, choking on my saliva. He doesn't waste any time and slides back onto the bed where my feet are. He spins me to my side, hikes one of my legs up as far as it will go, bending it like a fucking flamingo, and rubs his cock up and down my wetness before vigorously shoving his cock inside. He reaches up and twists one of my nipples. I clutch the side of the bed with one hand, and the other is around his neck while he ruthlessly fucks my pussy. Then, very swiftly, he holds on to my hip while rolling his hips, hitting that spot so deliciously. His hand reaches around to my clit, and his thumb connects with it, massaging it back and forth while still fucking me.

My eyes roll into the back of my head as that tingly sensation works its way down my back, and I come all over his dick while screaming his name, my legs shaking uncontrollably. "That's it, scream my fucking name," he yells as he thrusts in and out a few more times. Then, without warning, he pulls out, shooting cum all over my stomach and breasts.

He smiles maniacally. We are both panting hard, speechless, and sweaty.

Tyler swings himself off the bed, goes into the bathroom to grab another towel, and cleans me up gently. Both of us are dripping with sweat. I sit up and move slowly toward my bathroom mirror to see the damage. My makeup is tear-streaked with whatever was left from my eyeliner, and mascara runs down my face, so I grab another towel and wipe my face. My hair looks freshly fucked and tangled.

No words. I can't form a sentence right now. Those were the best two orgasms I've ever had, and I own one of the more expensive vibrators on the market.

I'm surprised they are still working as much as I use them.

I go back to my desk chair, bending down, reaching for his

clothes, and tossing them directly at his chest, urgently wanting him to leave.

Sighing, I say, "That was a good time. I have an early morning, so I trust you can see yourself out."

Surprise immediately flickers in his eyes, but he quickly masks it. He smirks at me with one eyebrow lifted. "Wow, I feel used, and being kicked out after sex is a first. Women usually beg me to spend the night with them."

"I don't spend the night with guys I've just met." I roll my eyes at him, annoyed.

"Oh, so you just fuck them without condoms then or even questioning whether I'm safe. Got it." He winks at me.

"It's nothing personal; you were great. I would give you an 8/10." I shrug my shoulders.

He chuckles. "The way you were screaming my name, I'd say you're lying. You had the time of your life."

He starts getting dressed. I ignore him and turn away from him, heading to my bathroom. I turn on my shower and poke my head out. "You remember your way out, right?"

Shaking his head, snickering, he says, "Pretty sure it's the same way we came in."

"Okay, well, have a good night then," I yell at him, jumping in the shower as I hear the front door shut. I smile to myself as I think about the mind-blowing experience I just had. This college is so big that the chance of me ever seeing Tyler again is slim to none.

CHAPTER EIGHT

CASSIDY

The front door of our apartment slams, and I jolt upright in my bed, looking around in confusion at first about where I am since we just moved in. I slept like the dead, a totally dreamless sleep. If this is how you sleep after incredible sex, sign me the fuck up. Usually, I need sleeping pills since I suffer from insomnia and can never lie still.

Typically, I'm a night owl.

My phone pings twice in a row. I rub my eyes, grumbling, and reach over on my nightstand for it. I squint at the screen, letting my eyes adjust to the light from a massive hangover. Naturally, the texts are from Blair.

Blair: Rise and shine, skank.

Blair: Come to the school cafeteria; let's get breakfast, compare dick sizes, and then head to the assembly. 😅

Grinning widely while rubbing my face, I quickly text her back.

Me: Give me 15, you whore!

Stretching my arms over my head while yawning louder than necessary, I move achingly and get out of bed, stumbling to my bathroom. Confronting it head-on, I go straight for the mirror to see what I'm working with today, which is honestly a lot.

My vagina feels like a train ran through it.

Scanning my reflection, it is confirmed I look well and thoroughly fucked, with a bit of bruising around my throat and nipples. Rubbing my fingers over my chest and across my nipples quickly sends a shiver straight to the middle of my thighs. I'm going to need the more expensive makeup in my collection to cover this up today. I highly doubt any sorority sisters would like to know how much I enjoy being roughly dicked down. Although, as far as rumors go, they would love to hear it. It would undeniably make this day more bearable.

Making a fast, last-minute decision, I brush my hair, trying to get the knots out, slick it back into a high ponytail, and apply some light makeup, including a full-coverage foundation on my throat. In a rush, I brush my teeth while peeing.

I silently curse to myself because I remember today is the longest day of the sorority rush. Closing my eyes, wishing the day away, I think about what exactly sorority rush week is going to entail.

There are five days total, with the sixth day being bid day. On the first day, you must visit every house and engage in a polite meet-and-greet, chatting about absolutely nothing of importance. They know ahead of time that we are legacies. They hang our pictures up, talk about us in-depth, and vote on whether we receive. They are hoping that we automatically pick them, as it makes it easier for a mutual decision, and they don't have to work as hard selling themselves to us and why it would be a great fit.

Sometimes, even though it's rare, girls will choose other sororities where they have no familial relations to guarantee their entrance. It is much harder this way, especially at a huge college like the University of Miami.

Being a legacy, I'm part of the minority. Statistically, over one-third of people who rush are legacies. Legacies are individuals in your family tree who were members of the same sorority; it's essentially your golden ticket in, and you must have a handwritten letter from a former sister with their badge number, stating that they are vouching for you.

Blair and I only have our eyes on Zeta Kappa Phi. Our mothers were in the same sorority but attended different colleges. We've always talked about it since we were little about how we were going to go to the same college and be sorority sisters.

It has been our dream to be here together.

Throwing my head back and huffing like a toddler having a tantrum, I do a quick peek through my closet, deciding on something to wear. I'm going for the 'I want this, but I'm not desperate' look. They are going to want me more than I want them.

Not to be arrogant, but they would be lucky to have me. I was heavily involved in sports and extracurricular activities in high school, in addition to volunteering at the local animal shelter.

I love dogs; if someone says they don't, then run for the hills; they aren't normal.

Ultimately, I settle on a white ruffled stretch satin midi dress with thin straps and small pink flowers from Anthropologie. It shows off every curve I have while looking somewhat sophisticated. I pair it with white strappy sandals with low heels. Also, I put a ton of sunscreen on, trying not to miss a single spot that isn't covered. Today, there will be tons of walking outside. The sun is unforgiving, and this Florida heat is deadly. At least I'll get my steps in today, so there's that.

As my mom has always said, first impressions are everything. I reach for my wristlet and my phone, mentally double-checking that I have everything, and head out the door. I lock the front door and check to make sure it's locked a couple of times because you can never be too safe, and then I head straight to the cafeteria to gossip with my best friend.

Since we live off campus, I jump in my navy Mazda SUV and play my favorite album, Midnights, and right away, I feel better, convincing myself that today is going to be a good day.

CHAPTER NINE

TYLER

Waking up, I hear the most annoying noise, which happens to be my alarm. I sluggishly get out of bed, run a hand through my hair, which is sticking up in every direction, and shake my head slowly, testing how bad the hangover actually is. It's bad. I walk toward my shower and turn it on. While waiting for the water to heat up, I grab a towel, smiling to myself and thinking about last night, and it instantly makes me hard.

I jump in the shower, feeling the warmth hit my head and run down my face; the sensation is heavenly. Today isn't that important of a day. It's the first day of rush, and you're bombarded with questions, almost like a job interview, which I find hilarious since we're all only eighteen. Who the fuck has that much job experience? I mean, how much of life have we lived at this point?

Then, the rest of the week is pretty laid back, just hanging out with the brothers, playing video games, and drinking games. The brothers have convinced the advisors that this is bonding and how we really get to know each other. Completely different from the sorority rush.

Today, I'll do the meet and greet with all of the fraternities, and then for the rest of the week, I'll be with Alpha Chi. That is the only fraternity I can imagine myself in. My father and grandfather are legacies, so it was always known in our household that this was the fraternity I would rush to become a full-fledged brother.

Pumping some soap in my hand, I grip my dick and start stroking it back and forth. I place my other hand against the wall, watching my hand move the way I like it, all the while thinking about Cassidy taking my cock so well last night in that pretty little mouth with those doe eyes innocently staring up at me.

What is it about this girl? She was up for anything sexually, and I would be willing to bet she doesn't have any hard limits or believes in safe words. I think what turned me on the most was her kicking me out. Unbelievable. A girl I had just pleasured multiple times kicked me out after she got hers.

Oh well, I love a challenge, and she's a puzzle I want to solve.

She'll be catering to my every need in no time. Mulling it over, I can't recall anyone who can resist my charms, especially women. Girls were all over me in high school, willing to do my homework, make my lunch, carry my books, and walk me to my classes; you name it, they did it.

Moaning through my release and painting the shower floor with my cum, I finish washing up and step out onto my blue bath rug. Drying my hair off with a towel, then the rest of my body before wrapping it around my waist with my chiseled abs on display, I brush my teeth. Looking at my hair, I decide to slick it to the side, not really giving a shit.

Sauntering over to my closet, I select a light blue and red plaid long-sleeved button-down and tan golf shorts. I tuck in the shirt and get my Prada belt, putting it on. Slipping on my brown drivers, I grab my wallet and head for the front door. My stomach growls hungrily, and I suddenly realize that I don't remember the last time I've eaten, and this hangover isn't going to fix itself. I guess I might as well head to the cafeteria for a quick breakfast since I don't know when we'll be able to eat next. I think they provide water in between houses so we don't faint from the heat, but that's it.

It seemed like a good idea to walk there because my apartment is right beside the university, but this heat in August is scorching. As I enter the cafeteria, I instantly recognize some older brothers in Alpha Chi. They wave me over to come sit down with them. Speedily grabbing an everything bagel with a side of cream cheese at one of the buffet areas where they serve food, I go directly over to their booth, sliding in smoothly as I shove the bagel in my mouth.

"Hey guys, you ready for today?" I ask nonchalantly, not knowing how brothers conduct rush week since everything is a secret.

"This is my favorite week of the semester; we get to mess with the recruits," one of the brothers, Jamie, pipes in, propping his leg on one of the chairs next to the booth.

"We take this week very seriously," Archer states with his eyes narrowing on Jamie. Archer is the president of Alpha Chi, and he glares over all of the brothers, daring them to disagree with him.

He seems very uptight and not at all talkative, so I strike up a conversation with Jamie about the school's football team and how this season is looking with the new offensive coordinator. We also talk about what players we are looking forward to seeing out on the field in the scrimmage next week.

Lo and behold, I happen to look over Jamie's shoulder, and to my shock, I see Blair at another booth texting on her phone without a care in the world.

Smirking devilishly because I know who could be just around the corner, well, really hoping, I get up and tell the guys I'll see them later.

Sauntering up to the booth where Blair sits, I say, "I'm amazed you could even get out of bed this morning when you could barely walk last night."

She looks up with a look of disgust and squints her nose like I'm dirt on her heel, then recognition hits her, and she glowers at me. "I'm surprised you even got your dick touched last night."

And just like I anticipated, Cassidy slides into the booth with so much self-assurance. To anyone else, it would be a turn-off, but I'm mesmerized. With her yogurt and granola in hand, she doesn't even look up while she delicately swirls her tongue along the spoon, unaware I'm hovering over the same table. She doesn't notice me until she puts her food back on the table and looks up, startled by my presence, and I can tell she really thought she would never see me again.

I'm going to ruin her, and she'll be my undoing.

CHAPTER TEN

CASSIDY

When I walk into the cafeteria, my eyes immediately find Blair. It's like a sixth sense when you've been best friends and inseparable since elementary school. If my jaw weren't attached to my face, it would have fallen on the floor when I saw who was sitting next to her.

Fuck. Fuck. Fuck. Think Cassidy, think.

Unfortunately, I have no choice but to walk over to my best friend and my one-night stand, who looks mouth-wateringly gorgeous. The minimal effort look makes me positively feral for this man. Begging has never been a weakness of mine, but he has the power to make me squirm in my seat as the dampness between my thighs has me actually considering it as I imagine him hoisting me up and fucking me savagely on this table in front of everyone.

Exuding calmness and complete control over my facial expressions, I look him directly in the eye. Then I move over, trying to get as far away from him as possible, where I'm practically sitting on Blair. Plastering a displeased look on my face, I roll my eyes, hoping he moves along from our table as hastily as possible.

"We were just talking about you, beautiful, and how I got my dick wet last night," he says, a lust-filled grin appearing on his face.

Coughing up my water in disbelief at how he would even have the audacity to be so forward with me in public, I glare at him, willing him to go away.

What a way to start your day.

Wasting no time, he squeezes into the bench in the booth directly across from us.

"Pick a different booth to sit at and fantasize about me; it was a one-time thing," I hiss at him.

Shrugging, he whispers to me, "But I haven't stopped thinking about those delightful noises you make while screaming my name. Cassidy Matthews, you'll be my undoing by the end of the semester and, therefore, mine." His eyes darken, and a possessive look crosses over his face.

Blair and I swivel our heads, trying to comprehend how ridiculous what he just said is, and burst out laughing hysterically as tears form in our eyes.

"As cute and amusing as this is, Cassidy and I have an assembly to attend, and we can't be late. Honestly, I very much wish we could stay so you could entertain us more with your captivating charisma," Blair cuts in while snorting.

"Oh, you girls are rushing? Me too," Tyler states, giving off a superior demeanor as he leans back and opens his legs in a more relaxed position.

I'm dumbstruck. Of course this good-looking panty dropper is rushing.

"Yes, and we have to get a move on; see you!" I say in a bitchy voice, completely dismissing him as I collide with Blair, nearly pushing her out of the booth.

His eyes roam over my body one last time. "There's no need to worry. I will, without a doubt, be seeing you later, Cassidy," Tyler says simply with a rise to his voice.

Shaking my head with my face masked in irritation, Blair and I jog as we leave the cafeteria and head to the gymnasium, where the sorority rush assembly is occurring.

As we walk in casually, we notice hundreds of women talking excitedly about Rush Week and expressing interest in which sororities they are interested in. Naturally, it is overwhelmingly loud due to all the commotion.

Tables are neatly arranged and already set up; each one has a flag containing the first letter of your last name. This is the definition of organized chaos, as schedules are snatched up with women wondering where they are going for the day. All of this is timed accordingly so that there are enough sisters to talk to the recruits one-on-one. It's a science that requires months of preparation. Blair and I separate since her last name is Underwood. Since we were kids, we have loathed our last names being so far apart.

The lines wrap around the entire gymnasium, and we have to fight our way through the crowds to reach our designated line to obtain our schedules. Then, we reunite outside to compare and see if we are assigned to any of the houses at the same time.

"Out of the twelve sororities, it looks like we only have three that will be at the same time," I say, whining annoyingly.

"It's not like we'll even get a chance to talk to each other anyway," she snaps back, annoyed about it as well.

As usual, Blair is factual and straight to the point, disinterested, and not thrilled about having to fit all twelve sorority houses in one day, hoping you arrive promptly at your assigned time.

Plastering a smile on my face, I look at Blair and say, "We got this, and it will be over before we know it."

Beaming, she says, "Not much longer, and we will officially be sisters!"

Nodding my head and squeezing her hand, we head in different directions.

There is no problem finding Frat Row, also known as Greek Row; it stands out from any of the buildings on campus. All of them are white, and they have a Georgian architectural style with the Greek letters of the sorority or fraternity on the front.

I look forward to seeing Blair tonight so we can gossip about all the other sororities as we curl up on the couch and eat sushi.

If you are unlucky and get assigned to a sister in one of the houses that is long-winded, you have to sprint to the next house on your schedule. If you are late, most of the time, they let you in, but I've heard from other sisters that sometimes they lock the door, and you are screwed since you must visit every single house.

Determined, I whip my hair to the side and get to work on mingling with all of these girls.

Day one is full of downright misery.

CHAPTER ELEVEN

TYLER

The first house I arrive at is a fraternity I have heard of, but it isn't as popular as Alpha Chi. Upon walking through the front door, I am greeted with a pat on the back, and a beer is pushed into my hand, which I gladly crack open. The beer cools me down since the weather is already a staggering 90 degrees outside. Recruits and fraternity brothers must wear metal name tags with their first and last names, as well as any current position they hold; this is intended to make conversations less awkward. Nerves are running high, and it's incredibly easy to forget the name of the person you are talking to. I mingle politely with one of the brothers, considering that chances are high that I'll see him around campus. I part ways as soon as humanly possible, my eye on the ultimate prize—Alpha Chi.

Essentially, that is how the day goes, house after house. Really boring and draining. Finally, I reach Alpha Chi, which turns out to be my last house.

Go figure.

As I'm staggering in, a few of the older brothers wave to me or shake my hand. Touring the house ensues because they know I'm a legacy, and they greatly want me to join. As I stare and memorize every aspect of the house, we stop at the huge composite photos of the past initiated brothers. I find my dad in one with a huge smile on his face, looking handsome in a suit. He has perpetually said this was the best time of his life, especially as college became closer for me. Reliving the memory of last night with a salacious smirk on my face, I slick my hair back. I can't help but think my father was definitely right.

Luckily, these girls in Miami are wild, but I have only one girl on my mind at present.

The fraternity house has three stories, and it has been on campus since my grandfather rushed and became an initiated brother. The second and third floors are where the brothers live. The first floor is a recreation area where the offices of the executive board are located.

Somehow, I have stumbled upon the back half of the house, which, for some reason, is clearly off-limits. With a tense feeling in my gut, I notice a long hallway that is barricaded off by an antique-looking gated doorway. My dad never mentioned this part of the house, probably because this could be used for the initiation ritual that deems you a brother. Shrugging off the uneasy feeling, I continue to roam the house. Unsurprisingly, the house contains everything you could likely need with no expense spared—brand new TVs, furniture, the newest electronics, and a chef on call.

I hang out at the house for a bit longer, knowing with confidence I'll be a brother soon enough. After talking incessantly to the executive board, trying to make a good impression and not wanting to leave, I say goodbye to a few of the brothers and then slip out the front door. Overcome with weariness, I'm ready for a long, hot shower and to collapse onto my bed.

CHAPTER TWELVE

CASSIDY

The day goes by agonizingly slow, and by the end of it, I want to pluck my eyes and ears out from my head. Physically, I can't muster another fake elated answer to one more question about my high school experience, the extracurriculars I was involved in, or what I did over the summer. Interestingly enough, while I was at Zeta Kappa Phi, I didn't have to pretend how eccentric I was to talk to as many sisters as possible, and the tour of the house feigned a lot of interest for me. It is the only part of the day I can actually recall without cringing, probably because it was the best part. Imagining my mom living and walking through the house had me grinning from ear to ear. I cannot wait to be part of the sorority life. All I have ever seen or heard about it is how you make friendships that last a lifetime and make some of the best memories in your life.

After such a long day, my body is sagging in relief, picturing my bathtub filled to the top with bubbles and sinking all the way in, consoling my aching feet. I cringe, thinking about how much sweat my dress endured. I'm positive it needs dry cleaning. I head back to my apartment as quickly as my feet will allow, and as soon as my key hits the lock, I sigh with contentment as Blair greets me.

"How was everything?" she asks tiredly.

"As predicted, boring as hell," I groan.

"At least tomorrow we only have to visit six houses instead of twelve. What did you think about Zeta Kappa Phi?" she says with a yawn.

Beaming, I tell her, "Oh my gosh, Blair, it's perfect."

"I thought so, too." She nods her head rapidly.

Since we visited all twelve houses today, uninterested in eleven of them, of course, we still had to write down our top six sororities that we think are the best fit for us. Likewise, the sororities write down who they would like to see back, and if it matches up, that will make up your schedule for the next day. Naturally, we don't find out until the morning when we go to the gymnasium again. Rumor has it that all of the sororities are up painstakingly until well past midnight, discussing the recruits at length and voting.

"I'm headed directly for a bath to soak until I turn into a prune and then to bed," I announce.

"Girl, me too, sounds like heaven." She sighs, running her fingers through her hair.

I blow her a kiss. "Goodnight, lover," I say as I sluggishly drag myself toward my room.

Strolling into my room, I start the bath and add some floral-scented bath salts and bubbles. I sink into the warmth and scrub away the sweat, my mind drifting to Tyler. A deep sensation grows in my abdomen as I replay last night in my mind, and my hand instinctively moves between my thighs. Spreading my legs wide enough where each knee hits either side of the bathtub, I skim a finger across my clit. Burning arousal travels through my body as I begin to circle it exactly the way Tyler did, closing my eyes and envisioning him. Sinking two fingers into myself, I begin fucking my hand, rocking back and forth. Then, I pull my fingers out and touch my clit. I lean my head back and shamelessly moan Tyler's name, coming in the bathtub. Coming down from the high, the relaxation takes over, and after soaking for a few more minutes, I hop out of the bath, reaching for a fluffy white towel and drying myself off. Turning toward my closet, I pull out my most comfortable pajamas and head directly to my bed, flopping on top of it. Grabbing the remote, I click a few buttons and turn on a mindless reality show, and sleep finds me immediately.

CHAPTER THIRTEEN

TYLER

Unlike sorority rush, I received a bid that night. I got to spend the rest of the week with Alpha Chi, my fraternity, simultaneously chugging beers and playing beer pong, video games, and watching porn or a homemade video on a projector one of the brothers recorded with a girl who clearly didn't know she was being filmed. Having your own homemade sex videos is a rite of passage here, and sharing them at chapter is thought of as a normal thing. If you video yourself banging a girl from each sorority, you obtain a special pin on your sash when you graduate, and only our fraternity knows what it means. Yes, it is someone's job to keep up with it and track this kind of shit. Trust me, it's not a hard position to fill.

You're surrounded by cocky and horny guys; they are basically foaming at the mouth to get their hands on any of the homemade videos. Share any of this, and the fraternity will rain hell down on you. Recruits who don't make it into the fraternity keep their mouths shut.

It doesn't matter if you are a legacy or not. If you are a new member of a fraternity, you are going to get hazed. Everyone is assigned grunt work, and you're expected to do anything the older brothers instruct you to do. You're dropped if you say no without a second thought. My dad prepared me for this part of becoming a new member and told me some of the stories of things he had to endure.

Making it through hazing is essential to being an initiated brother of any fraternity. We'll only be new members for around a month of absolute hell.

Here's to hoping they don't ask me to do any illegal shit. I desperately want to be a brother, and I know I'll do whatever they ask of me. Thankfully, my dad told me about what might be coming and what I might be asked to do. One of the first things is having to chug a ton of alcohol and go swimming in the school fountain at night, fully nude.

Then, we have to memorize the current top hit songs and sing them to other sororities. Carrying books for older brothers is expected and easy, and the same is true for taking notes for them in every one of their classes. That's all beginner-level hazing.

One of the things my dad had to do was steal a crest flag from one of the other fraternities without getting caught. Quite honestly, I don't know how he pulled it off with how heavily locked the Greek houses are.

Unless they tell me to, drinking and going to bars is out of the question. You must have your phone on loud at all times, especially at night, in case a brother needs a designated driver to pick them up.

Fraternity brothers drink considerably; for some, it's their whole personality.

As if this wasn't enough mental suffering, we are also expected to wake up at four in the morning and run along the beach for miles until they tell us to stop, all the while chanting our fraternity's songs.

If you cannot keep up with the group, you are forced to stop and swallow about a fourth of a bottle of vodka in large gulps. Afterward, you have to race to catch up with the group, and if you puke, a brother will oversee you doing push-ups, sit-ups, planks, and anything else they can think of until they decide you can stop.

Breaking you is their ultimate goal. Dropping out means that you don't have what it takes to be a brother.

They need you to think you've earned it when you become a fully initiated brother. Hazing is frowned upon at any college, but no one says shit because you're a brother now, and you would risk your fraternity getting kicked off campus.

By the end of the week, they hand me and fourteen other guys an invitation cordially inviting us to become members of Alpha Chi.

I accepted right away. The happiness that surges through me because I don't have to be anyone's bitch anymore is unmatched.

Now for the initiation.

CHAPTER FOURTEEN

CASSIDY

The week flew by. Since we visit fewer houses each day, the conversations were much longer, and I was running out of stuff to talk about. The sisters seemed over it as well. When we reached the third day of rush, there were four houses we needed to visit. On the fourth day, there were three houses. Finally, on the fifth day, known as Preference Night, there were two house events to attend. The attire was a black dress and black heels. This was where we had the most intimate and lengthy conversation with one sister at a table, almost like a date, where you sit across from one another.

I headed home after preference night with one of my houses being Zeta Kappa Phi. I had a huge grin on my face knowing there was no possible way I wouldn't get a bid from them to be a new member.

It's Saturday morning, and I'm wearing my cutest scalloped

Lilly Pulitzer shorts with a matching top and sneakers, sitting with Blair for coffee in the cafeteria.

"Are you nervous?" she asks me with a shaky breath.

"Blair, there's nothing to be worried about! Zeta Kappa Phi is both in our top two, and best of all, we are legacies! We got this in the bag," I tell her as I shrug my shoulders with a confident smile on my face.

"Come on, let's go get our bids!" I squeal as I jump with excitement on our way to the gymnasium, which is decorated with all of the crests of the different sororities.

A bid is a formal invitation to join a new sorority, complete with your full name, their crest, and motto. It's legit and something you keep forever.

If you receive a phone call the night before, they try to break the bad news to you as best they can, letting you know you didn't get a bid. This is to make sure you don't show up the next day expecting one.

Imagine if they didn't call. How fucked up would it be to show up and not have a bid while other girls around you are crying and screaming? I could never show my face again.

One of the girls on the executive board of Greek Life, who approves everything from events to homecoming and philanthropies, stands up with a megaphone and shouts, "Go!"

In a frenzy, we snatch our envelopes that are taped underneath our chairs and tear them open, and there it is in all its glory—my invitation. I read over it twice because this is such a surreal moment. At the very top in calligraphy, it states with infinite precision, "Cassidy Marie Matthews, you are cordially invited to become a new member of Zeta Kappa Phi," with their crest at the top and signed by the current presiding president.

I spin my head over at Blair. We gawk at each other as we overlook each other's invitations, confirming that we are both accepted into the same sorority. Staring at the invitations in disbelief, Blair whips out her phone and takes a selfie of us teary-eyed and happily laughing and hugging.

After taking the picture, it occurs to us to send it to our moms and post it all over our social media accounts, considering we can now reactivate them.

Now it's time to 'run' home to Zeta Kappa Phi, hence the sneakers, where we will spend the day getting to know the sisters.

Blair and I take off, clasping hands the entire way to the sorority. Several sisters are jumping up and down, holding signs with our names on them; the rest are swarming us ecstatically, welcoming us as new members. The sisters holding the signs have volunteered to be our 'buddy' for the day and show us around to get us accustomed to how the sorority is run and introduce us to other sisters.

While being embraced by other sisters beaming at us like we just won the sorority lottery, I take notice of about thirty new members.

I spent the day having lunch in the house kitchen alongside all the sisters, learning some of the sorority chants and the overall history, which includes famous celebrities who are also Kappa Zeta Phi members.

Now, all there is to do is to make it to initiation in one month. Previously, my mom told me they try not to haze because they don't want anyone to drop out. Most of the time, there are still mundane tasks you are required to do, such as carrying books to classes for your sisters or picking up their dry cleaning.

Quite honestly, being a new member of this sorority is the best in terms of hazing. Rumor has it that another sorority has new members sit on the washer and dryers at the house entirely bare. If part of your body jiggles, they circle it with a permanent marker, and you have to lose the weight before initiation, or they drop you.

After lounging and watching TV, I decide to call it a night before Blair, so I head back to our apartment. Classes start next week, so I'm excited to head back to our apartment and relax and hang out all weekend. While driving through the streets hazily, I daydream about becoming a sister.

Pulling into the parking lot, my phone suddenly pings, and a text message comes through.

Unknown: Congrats on becoming a new member of Zeta Kappa Phi! They obviously needed a new poster girl to recruit more members.

I look around the parking lot, confused and on high. Is someone watching me? I bite my lip, contemplating whether I should text back or not. I quickly try to think of who this could possibly be. Shaking my head, knowing I'm overreacting, I speedily type out a reply.

Me: Who is this?

Unknown: Your favorite one-night stand.

Rolling my eyes, I text back.

Me: How did you get my number? Something on your record you'd like to share?

Tyler: I am a certified stalker when it comes to you 😌 and I have more than a few connections.

Me: Well, I hope you got the fraternity you wanted.

Tyler: I did. You're looking at a new member of Alpha Chi.

Me: Congrats to you, too, then.

Tyler: What are you doing tomorrow?

Me: I'm busy.

Tyler: What about tomorrow night?

Me: You're never going to give up, are you?

Tyler: Nah. You should give in sooner rather than later. Kind of like how fast you spread your legs for me...

I laugh to myself silently.

Me: I'm available after 7:00.

Tyler: I'll pick you up at 6:50.

Me: It's not a date. I'll be eating dinner beforehand.

Tyler: I'll surprise you 😉 I'm going to skip dinner since I plan on feasting on your delicious pussy.

A tingly sensation runs through my body, thinking about the last time Tyler touched me. He seems unpredictable in that area, and it is drawing me in. After always being so routine-based and organized my entire life, it's nice to let someone else take control and tell me what to do, especially in the bedroom.

A smile cracks my lips as I head up to my apartment. I grab a book I've been reading while I wait up for Blair. When she gets home, we chat about what we loved during our fun-filled day and then head for bed.

Sunday morning comes faster than I'd like, and I throw on some yoga pants with a matching sports bra. The only plans on my agenda for the day are running errands, picking up some last-minute school supplies, and catching up on laundry.

Tyler is at the forefront of my mind, and I can't help how my body writhes, thinking about him touching me. Clenching my thighs together and straightening up, I focus on the task at hand—

laundry. Aggravatingly, I throw load after load in and fold a tremendous amount.

Time seems to slowly creep by. After an internal battle with myself, I begin getting ready earlier than I should, while listening to some workout music to keep me up after a tiring day.

Around six o'clock, I recheck my makeup, essentially redoing it because I don't like the colors I chose in contrast to my tanning skin. Then, I make sure every inch of my body is covered in lotion since I shaved everything.

Going to my closet, I lay out the lavender sundress I recently bought at Zara and pair it with some nude sandals. As I try doing something with my thick hair, I decide to leave it loose, not wanting to bother with it any longer, reminding myself this isn't a date, and I do not need to put much effort into my appearance. Turning around in front of my floor-length mirror with a sly smile plastered on my face, knowing he'll be the one doing any kind of begging.

Just like he promised, at exactly 6:50, there's a loud knocking at my door. My heart is thundering in my chest as I take a deep breath and, as slowly as possible, walk over to the door.

Is this guy wearing me down? He's already gotten under my skin.

Clutching my small, crossover Gucci bag and keys on the hook beside the door, I open it.

Wagging his brows with one hand on the side of the door, he looks me up and down and whistles.

"After tonight, you won't be able to keep your hands off of me," he says as he winks at me.

Warmth spreads between my thighs instantly because he's right. Standing in front of me with a Lululemon T-shirt and black jeans, he smells like I could swallow him right up. I shake my head, knowing he clearly put minimal effort into himself tonight. His muscular torso is outlined by the shirt, and the way the light-weight material wraps around his biceps has me biting my lip to keep the drool in my mouth.

"You're one to talk; you haven't stopped thinking about me since you first saw me." I giggle with a knowing smile.

His eyes roam over me, and with a throaty whisper, he says, "Not only have I not stopped thinking about you, but I haven't stopped fantasizing about your body in every position possible while tugging on those perky nipples with my teeth."

My eyes widen, and my mouth drops open, trying but failing to mentally overpower his lewd remarks. Nothing comes to mind. *Nothing.*

Pushing my way out the door, my shoulder knocks into his side, and he smiles wickedly at me.

I slam my door shut and huff as I speed-walk to the parking lot, and he jogs up beside me.

Threading his fingers through his brown hair, he asks me cockily, "Are you ready for a night with one of the most eligible bachelors in the city?"

My footsteps falter as I come nose to nose with him. "Good thing you have a big cock to match that even bigger ego."

I start to walk away to who knows where since I don't know what car he drives, and he yanks the back of my neck, pulling me close. I can feel the stiffening of his cock as his other hand snakes up my thigh, and he purrs in my ear, "This cock is going to be buried so deeply inside you you'll be moaning my approval."

My body betrays me as I lean back into him, breathing him in and drawing out the heat that radiates from his body.

Wrapping himself out of the hold he has on me, he points to his car, a gray Chevy Tahoe, and my face must look shocked because he says, "Were you expecting something flashier?"

He opens the door for me, and I step up on the side railing and slide into the seat, ensuring my dress isn't exposing too much of my legs. Then, I buckle my seatbelt.

Getting into the driver's seat and pressing the ignition button, Tyler looks at me as I say, "Expectations never meet my reality."

He chuckles and starts backing out of the parking space.

Feeling the black leather begin to cool on this hot night, I look behind me and am amazed by how decently clean he has kept it.

If I were in the dating game, this is a box I would want checked.

Grinning handsomely, he states, "As previously discussed, I hope you already ate since this isn't a date."

Flirting back with him, I respond, "Sitting across from you at a table while making meaningless small talk isn't really my thing."

His eyes darken deviously.

"Good to know you're a cheap date. Hang on tight, sunshine; you'll be begging in no time." Then he connects his phone to the car, and it continues playing the Apple radio station he was listening to earlier.

Other than humming to some of the songs, we sit in comfortable silence for a little more than twenty minutes, stealing glances at each other and silently communicating consent for anything that is about to happen.

The sexual chemistry brewing in the car is building and is going to explode in a luscious way.

"You look ravishing; I've said that in my head about a hundred times," he says with a sultry tone barely above a whisper. "All I keep thinking about is what you taste like." He licks his lips.

Heat ignites in my lower abdomen as I stretch my body, slightly whimpering, imagining his head between my thighs.

I glance over at him, about to say something just as fiery back, when I realize the car is slowing down, and we are pulling into a beach parking lot by Indian Beach Park. There's not a car in sight.

Picking a corner with no streetlight above it, he unbuckles his seatbelt, leans his seat back, and gestures with his finger, calling me over to him.

Climbing over the console, I straddle his lap, facing him. I can feel his erect cock beneath me as I rub myself over it. He skims his fingers down my arm until his hand is underneath my dress, and he seductively hooks my panties to the side and dips a finger inside me, coating his finger in my arousal. Drawing out his finger, he smears it across his bottom lip, then shoves it into his mouth, groaning at the taste.

"Open," he growls, then slides the finger into my mouth. "Suck."

I deep-throat his finger and my eyes roll into the back of my head, moaning around it.

His gaze clings to my skin as his eyes begin to darken.

"Have you ever come in a car before?" he asks as he grinds against me.

"No, but this better be a night I remember," I whisper back.

He captures my lips in his, sucking, nibbling, biting, and tasting my exposed skin. I yank his hair, exposing his neck so I can bite and lick it continuously. My head is spinning with need. Just as quickly as he latched onto my lips, he lets go.

More. I need more.

Clenching the back of my ass under my dress, he rubs himself roughly against my dampness.

Unabashedly, I moan into his mouth. He sticks one finger inside me while his other hand pushes the strap of my dress down. He works my nipple free of my strapless bra and tugs on it hard with his mouth. He licks around my nipple and runs his teeth gently over it. My senses are on fire as my body registers the feeling.

Sinking another finger inside me, he finds the perfect rhythm, and my stomach coils as I feel that familiar ache. Gasping from the pleasure, I throw my arms around his shoulders and start riding his fingers. Nuzzling my throat, his thumb barely touches my clit and is moving in those delicious circles.

Trembling from the need to come, he hikes my dress up over my thighs and tears off my panties.

"Go to the passenger seat and lean it all the way back," he murmurs to me, wrenching his lips from mine.

Obediently, I crawl over to the seat, knowing this man has me in the palm of his hand and that I'll do anything he asks of me.

"Do you trust me?" he asks.

My heart rate speeds up as I nod.

"I need your words, Cassidy," he says sternly.

"Yes, I do," I whimper.

"Turn over and hold the headrest with both of your hands and hike that dress up. Arch your back so I can see that pretty pussy and ass."

I do exactly as he says, looking back at him and waiting with anticipation. After a stretch of silence, he has me practically salivating for him. I hear him slide his belt out from his pants with measurable quickness, and he handcuffs my wrists to the silver poles that separate the seat from the headrest.

Moving behind me, he holds on desperately to both my thighs, stretching them as far as they will go. He buries his face into me and licks and sucks lightly on both of my holes, lapping up my juices and rubbing his tongue up and down. I'm going to collapse at any moment. "Tyler, I need your cock now."

Feeling him fumbling around with something, he reaches around and gives immediate attention to my clit. I hear something squirt out from a bottle, and I turn around and notice a small bottle of lube. I lick my lips greedily.

He slips a finger into my tight ring of muscle using the slickness from between my thighs, working his way in slowly, massaging inside both walls, letting me open up for him.

"Oh my god." I'm panting as he glides another finger into my back entrance, fondling my clit faster and pinching it every so often.

Barely able to hold myself up, I see stars as that rush of pleasure works its way down my back and releases, and I come down my legs. My words are a mumbled mess. He holds his fingers in place while I transport to another universe, shuddering all over.

Wasting no time, he gathers up my wetness with something rubbery as he slaps it across my thighs. Swiveling my head back to see what it is, I recognize a small flesh-colored dildo.

My eyes widen in confusion. "This is going in your ass while I fuck that tight cunt until you come as you scream my name, baby," he declares while studying me and lifting up the dildo with a devious grin.

He maneuvers the dildo inch by inch and circles my clit with his fingers at the same time, and my eyes flutter as my body twists at the sensation. He smacks my ass and pussy firmly, and the dildo moves deeper inside me. My gut clenches as I let out a cry of shock.

He shoves his dick inside me forcefully, not giving me any time to adjust. My head begins lolling back at the feeling of fullness. Pushing himself all the way to the hilt, he starts thrusting manically, drawing his dick all the way out of me each time while the dildo hits me deliciously, intensifying the waves of pleasure rolling over me.

"Don't fucking stop," I breathe heavily, barely getting the words out of my mouth. My body seizes up once more as my muscles contract and spasms make their way through my body.

"Your body surrenders beautifully while I'm inside you," he whispers huskily.

That sends me toppling over the edge, and I gutturally scream out his name, taken aback by the sounds I'm making.

Seconds later, he finds his release, shooting his cum inside me and mercilessly gripping my upper thighs as a roar escapes his mouth.

Goosebumps flood my skin as my orgasm rocks through me. "Come all over my cock, baby. I want to lap up your pleasure afterward."

Both of us are glistening with sweat and breathing rapidly. We don't move for a minute, catching our breath. Bending his body on top of mine, he clasps my face and kisses me needlessly, both of us lust-drunk and satisfied.

Tyler ends the kiss and begins caressing my shoulders before moving all the way down to the dildo. He grips it tightly and gently pulls it out of me.

"If you move, I'll punish you," he states, almost like he's daring me to. He flips on his back and squeezes his head between my shaking legs, and true to his word, licks my thighs first, then he makes his way to my wetness. He swallows every bit of our mixed cum. My body recoils because of the extreme sensitivity, but that spurs him on further. Plunging his tongue into both of my holes, he hums with appreciation of the taste on his tongue.

When he finishes, he slaps my ass, and the sting lingers.

Moving back into his seat with a lust-filled gaze mixed with a knowing smirk, he says, "Alright, well, I better get you home."

Quickly, he unbuckles my hands, and I turn around and straighten my dress, running a hand through my hair. Putting his legs in his pants and his shirt on seamlessly, he grabs my hand and delicately kisses the back of it.

Grumbling, I state, "It wasn't a date."

"Hungry? Will going through a drive-thru still not make a date?" He slyly grazes his eyes over me.

"Oh god, a juicy hamburger with fries sounds orgasmic." I moan, my mouth watering, rearing my head back.

"I think you may need another orgasm; you must not have had your fill," he says, chuckling.

"Food can be quite the experience, too." I smile at him.

He puts the car in reverse, and we veer back onto the road with horrible traffic, which is typical for South Beach.

Never asking for my preference, he drives up to one of my favorites, the Shake Shack. When asked for our order, he takes control again, ordering us hamburgers, fries, and large milk-shakes. Control must be a common theme for him. Pulling out his card, he pays and hands me my bag of food, and the smell alone makes my mouth salivate.

Tyler finds an isolated parking spot. Ripping my package open, totally famished, I dig in and take a larger bite than I probably should have, leaning back and exhaling loudly at how the delicious flavor meets my tongue.

"So, where are you from?" he asks nonchalantly.

I look at him wearily, hating small talk but semi-interested in his answer. I shrug my shoulders and state, "Boca Raton, so not too far from here, you?"

"Miami, born and raised." He beams, then continues, "Are you ready for your initiation?"

"Yes, I've heard it's not that bad," I say indifferently. "How was yours, or is it coming up?"

Uneasiness invades his eyes, and he lays his burger down on the console, zoning out as his mind goes elsewhere. After a minute, he snaps out of it. "You're looking at a soon-to-be brother of Alpha Chi," he states monotonously.

Unfortunately, I could see myself falling for this guy, tossing out my personal rule of no dating. I side-eye him and consider all of his qualities—he's handsome, fucks me into oblivion, he's smart, appears to have his head on his shoulders, and he is in Greek life like me, so we have something in common.

"Congrats on that! Will you be moving into the fraternity house?" I say excitedly, trying to change the tone in the car.

"We don't get a choice. We have to move in; it's in the bylaws. I'm moving in next Sunday, right after our first week of classes. You know, you could help me move in. I could use the motiva-tion." He makes eye contact with me, his gaze conveying a look that suggests he is up to no good.

One of my lips quirks up. "Yeah, sure, why not?"

"Still not a date, right? he says seriously, looking over at me.

"Let's call it a half date," I tell him, scrunching up my face, asking myself what the hell I'm doing.

"I knew I'd wear you down eventually. Whether you like it or not, Cassidy, that pretty little cunt really likes the way it grips my cock." He aggressively takes a bite of his fry before adding, "And I'm charming."

I squeeze my thighs together, willing my body not to respond to his dirty mouth, but I'm unsuccessful.

"Don't get your hopes up," I tease him, playfully slapping him on the arm.

Finishing up our meal, he drives me back to my apartment

while thrumming on the console and sneakily stealing glances at me.

He parks and turns off the car, comes to my side, and opens my door for me. Ever the gentleman, another unexpected trait that has me absolutely feral for this man. Jumping out with adrenaline still running through me, he walks me up to my door.

"You're quite old-fashioned when it comes to knowing how to treat a girl." I smirk at him.

"I'm just trying to impress you. I'll pick you up next Sunday, bright and early," he cheerily states.

"You better bring coffee and food," I yell back demandingly while he walks back to his vehicle, not looking forward to waking up early on a Sunday.

"I'll bring donuts. I know a place that makes the best donuts you've ever had," he yells as he raises his arms, widening them.

"It's a—" I catch myself, biting my lip.

"Damn right, it's a date." He rushes back to me, lightly touching my cheeks and resting his hand on my neck. With his thumb on my jaw, he leans down and kisses me affectionately. Then, he saunters off down the stairs, whistling to himself.

I stare at his firm ass until I can't see him anymore.

Unlocking my apartment door, I head straight for the shower to rinse off and then flop on my bed. I fall into a deep, dreamless sleep, perfectly satiated.

CHAPTER FIFTEEN

TYLER

Initiation

After doing a few bullshit hazing things to become a brother, the day I've been waiting for has arrived. I walk to the school library, which is open on weekends, but it's a ghost town with some over-achievers like me there. I have my books in my hand, a backpack slung over my shoulder, and I'm leisurely walking, not wanting to start on my math homework.

For some unknown reason, call it instinct, I happen to glance behind me, and a black SUV swerves wildly in front of me on a sidewalk, nearly hitting me. Several things cross my mind. First, this is illegal, and second, what the fuck?

A chill runs down my spine; fearing for my life, my feet kick into gear as I make a run for it. I drop all my things and sprint toward the library, expecting someone to at least see me and help.

Three men emerge from the car in full black attire, complete with gloves, masks, and even shoes. My calves are burning as I pick up speed, not comprehending what is happening.

Latching onto the door, I open it, about to yell for help, when one of them tackles me. Pain fires through me as I grunt out, landing hard, and he quickly places his hand over my mouth.

Methodically, the other two zip-tie my legs and hands together, securing them where they are cutting into my skin. Hauling me to my feet, one of them shoves some type of material into my mouth to keep me quiet. Fighting them, I shout, but only muffled sounds come out. They easily overpower me, but some-how, I manage to elbow one of them in the face, and his hands come off of me, reaching for it.

"You fucker," he growls.

With a terrifying gaze, they drag me back to their car. One of them holds the duct tape up and undoes it in front of my face, ensuring I see it.

Turning from side to side with a terrified gaze plastered on my face, one of them slinks behind me and violently covers my head with a canvas bag, fastening it with a tie on the bottom.

I lose my vision and my voice, leaving me with only my sense of smell and hearing. Dread and frustration form inside me.

Hovering over me, I hear them burst into a fit of laughter. Sweat beads on my forehead, profusely falling into my eyes.

Only a moment passes before two of them grip me hard and toss me into the back of the trunk. I hit my head harshly, grunting in agony.

Panicking, I try to calmly take deep breaths, stubbornly not wanting to pass out. Gasoline overwhelms my nose as my body rolls back and forth, colliding with the top when we go over a bump.

I try to time the drive to decipher how far away these guys are taking me from campus. If I get the chance to escape, I need to know the distance.

After driving for a while, the car starts to slow down, and if my calculations are correct, we are about twenty-eight to thirty minutes from campus.

Unexpectedly, the car suddenly comes to a complete stop, and I'm thrown forward in the trunk. Shouting as loud as I can, two of the guys haul me out of the trunk, placing their hands underneath my armpits, dragging me helplessly again to an unknown destination. Hearing my shoes scrape across dirt and gravel indicates that we are in the middle of nowhere.

Suddenly, the ground shifts a bit higher, and I'm struck by cool air coming from an air conditioner. I'm inside. I instantly detect a type of incense that overpowers my nose. They carry me down an extensive number of stairs, and I count them as we go. The air temperature changes, and it becomes colder.

I cringe at the thought that it's, without a doubt, a basement. After reaching the bottom, the canvas bag is torn off my head. My eyes take a while to adjust to my surroundings and what I see before me.

Hundreds of candles are scattered around a dungeon. Water is leaking in certain places, so we must be significantly below ground. People surround the area, wearing black robes attached to black hoods with skull masks. I can only assume they are men. Each of them has a familiar emblem on the right side of their chest. It's of my fraternity, Alpha Chi. Realization shakes me to my core—this is initiation.

Standing, waiting in silence, there have to be over a hundred men before me with their heads bowed. Finally, I made it here after years of my dad talking excessively about the brotherhood. He never mentioned this part; unless you are an initiated brother, you are forbidden from talking about it with others.

Briskly observing that there are fifteen other initiates near me, I notice that I am the last one to arrive.

Instantaneously, the room of hooded figures separates into two groups, and they back up against either wall, shoulder to shoulder.

At the very end of this manmade passageway is a woman lying naked on a king-size bed and blindfolded with both of her hands chained up far apart from each other, her legs spread and displaying her cunt.

Taken aback by the sight before me, knots form in my stomach, and I try to hold back the vomit. What in the actual fuck?

Hooded figures step behind us, subtly cutting our zip-ties. I glance at the other initiates' faces, all of them looking appalled.

"You will remove all of your clothing this instant," a deep voice commands, and I can only assume the voice belongs to Archer.

Hesitating for a moment, I hear rustling around me as the other initiates remove their clothing. Startled, I finish taking off my clothes, and another hooded figure sweeps in and collects all of it, including our shoes.

"Next, you will form a line in alphabetical order by last name." Archer condescendingly gestures to where the line should start.

The brothers hold their hands over their mouths, trying to hide their snickering over what is about to happen.

"After the line is flawlessly straight, you will begin the elephant walk," Archer continues with a deranged look on his face, being the only one we can currently see.

The snickers grow louder. Forming the line, which, in my opinion, could not be straighter, it leads in the direction of the naked lady lying on the bed.

"This woman knows the ritual in its entirety and has volunteered to be our plaything and human sacrifice. She is not being forced or held against her will; she knows this must be done," Archer continues confidently.

This has to be some demented ass joke. There is no way someone would willingly volunteer for this. I call bullshit.

"Each of you will be required to fuck one of her holes—mouth, cunt, or ass—whatever is your preference." He shrugs. "Her pleasure needs to be avoided, but you need to find your release, and when you do, you may come wherever you wish."

"That is where the elephant walk comes in. While waiting your turn, you will obediently clasp the dick behind you and jerk him off, preparing him to fuck her." With his hand gripped into a fist, he brings it to his mouth and chuckles.

What? Horror and shock engulf us as we turn our heads, staring at one another. Never in my life have I put my hands on another cock, let alone jacked one off. Now, it's a requisite for being initiated as a brother. How am I ever supposed to look at them after this without embarrassment flooding through me? Is this some sort of sick and twisted bonding technique? No wonder this is never talked about.

Unfortunately, I end up located in the middle, jealous of the fucker who is first because he won't have to participate in this line for long. Do they really expect us to do this? Hopefully, Archer will jump in and say it's just a joke. I close my eyes and wish for it. The answer to my question is fulfilled after a few seconds of anticipation.

"Start jerking each other off. NOW!" Archer yells.

Jumping to attention, most of the pledges start moving their hands up and down on dicks behind them.

My stomach feels like it's going to drop out of my body. I'm so disgusted. I take a deep breath, reaching behind me. I avoid eye contact with all the guys. Forcefully moving our hands up and down, no one dares to moan or make any noises that signal pleasure. That would make this awkward as fuck. Instantaneously, I feel the pre-cum from the guy behind me getting all over my fingers and hands, so I start to use it as lube. After getting it a little lubed up, I slow down, not wanting him to squirt his load before we get up to the lady.

Reverberating around the room is a palpable sense of discomfort; you can just feel it. I am certain the men in the hooded cloaks have to watch all of this. Picking up our pace, wanting to get this over with, pledge after pledge fucks her in different holes as fast as possible, their eyes vacant.

One guy steps up and straddles her head with his knees on either side and grips fistfuls of her hair. He fucks her mindlessly with his cock, shoving in and out of her throat so deeply that she is a jumbled mess but takes it like an expert. Drool begins leaking out of the sides of her mouth, and she's gagging loudly. After what feels like an eternity, he yanks himself out of her mouth and comes all over her face, scooping it up with two fingers and pushing past her lips until she's sputtering and squirming while he laughs maliciously. Delicately slapping her on the face, he leaps off the bed.

The next initiate steps up and rolls her on her stomach; there seems to be a little slack in the ropes, and he gropes her at her hips and hauls her to his waist. Spitting on his hand and rubbing it on his swollen cock without warning, he plunges into her tight ring of muscle. She whimpers in pain, but as the obedient fuckdoll she is, she doesn't resist.

While the rest step up and have her any way they want, it becomes blurry to me while I'm simultaneously being jacked off and watching guy after guy running a train on this more-than-willing girl. The brutality of it all is astonishing to me.

When it becomes my turn, my preference has always been a hot, eager mouth. Climbing over her body, I get into position, kneeling over her with each leg above her mouth. Battling with my inner persona, I get swept away in the depravity of it all. I seize her jaw with one of my hands, pushing on the pressure points and prying it open. With a thundering gaze, I clench my dick with my other hand and press it into her mouth. Her eyes are stunned by the size of my length as I hit the back of her throat over and over, not letting up.

Right before I'm about to come, I plug her nose with one of my hands so she can't breathe, and her jaw opens more, and I'm able to work my dick further down her throat.

Letting go of her nose, I overflow her mouth with my cum,

and she has no choice but to swallow all of it. After I pop my cock out, I slap it across her cheek, letting her know with my eyes I just owned her mouth.

I find the other pledges uncomfortably standing away from the bed, observing it all, and waiting until we all finish. Not wanting to make eye contact with anyone, I focus on a spot on the brick wall and stare at it for the remainder of the most unhinged ritual I've ever witnessed.

After the last guy barbarically fucks her ass and cunt, thrusting in and out of both and releasing his cum all over her chest, I feel the brothers behind us in hoods gently pushing us closer to the bed.

We form a circle around the bed, and I think the ritual has been completed, but I don't see anyone untying her. She is still blindfolded, and no one reaches to take that off either. She is breathing deeply, obviously exhausted. Cum is leaking out of every hole on her body, and she's covered in it from head to toe. The bed is a rumpled mess, with cum all over it as well; there's even some that hit the floor.

One of the hooded cloaks breaks the circle and stalks toward the bed with pure evil rippling off of him. The woman jolts up to her knees with her hands still secured, now behind her back.

Soundlessly, my heart is pounding in my chest. I'm at a loss for words, wondering what he is going to do.

Carefully, he unsheathes a beautiful knife with a jeweled hilt that is slightly curved at the end, and in another pocket, he takes out a medieval jeweled goblet.

"We appreciate your sacrifice to the brotherhood," he states emotionlessly. Then, he moves directly behind her, clutching a fistful of hair and bringing her back to his chest, which exposes her neck as her face is toward the ceiling. Without hesitating, he slashes her throat from ear to ear.

Rolling her on her side and to the edge of the bed as blood begins spilling out of her profusely, he places the goblet under her neck, filling it to the brim.

"To the brotherhood!" he yells, then gulps the entire amount down.

I'm too stunned to speak or move from where I'm standing. My mind cannot comprehend what is happening before me.

Another hooded figure takes the goblet from his hand and refills it. Looking at us explicitly, he very clearly says, "You will each take a sip and pass it to the next in line, and repeat these words after me: I pledge my life to Alpha Chi until my very last breath leaves my body. I will tell no one any secrets bestowed on me from now on and into the future. Anything that is asked of me, I will fulfill, or I will face a torturous death," he finishes.

One by one, we follow his instructions.

All the hooded figures begin chanting quietly in unison.

"You are now brothers of Alpha Chi!" he bellows.

The hooded figures remove their hoods and reveal their faces. All of them take turns smearing the blood still seeping from the woman's neck over their faces and pounding their chests, still chanting, gradually growing louder. Scanning around the room, all I can think about is that we look like savages. I will take what just happened to my grave. It's appalling, and no one would believe me anyway.

I think about the woman on the bed. Did she have a family? A home? Surely, someone will miss her in this world. I'd never ask any of these questions out loud, but I'm not heartless.

Our clothes are pressed roughly into our chests, causing us to lose our balance and fall backward. I fumble to dress myself after observing and being involved in what just happened, and adrenaline pumps through my veins.

After we finish dressing, gold pins are handed out to us. A gold pin tells anyone who knows the Greek letters what fraternity we are part of and that we are an initiated brother. If you go anywhere in a professional setting or chapter, it is worn on the outside of your jacket.

In a deep voice, one of the hooded figures commands, "Go up

to the common room and wait for the higher-level brothers, who will provide instructions on upcoming steps."

I shudder as I ponder what could be next. The horrors of tonight have drained me. I am slow-moving and disinterested in anything that anyone is going to announce. Everyone trudges up the stairs to the common room, where President Archer is patiently waiting for us with an amused grin.

"Every single thing that occurs in this house stays among brothers and brothers alone. If you breathe the slightest word about anything, you will, without hesitation, be plucked out like a hair on your head, and I don't just mean from the fraternity," he states angrily.

Bluntly, we all get the message of being assassinated. Many former presidents, senators, ranking officials, lawyers, the press, and police departments are covered in corruption.

I walk out of the common room, bewildered. How could my dad possibly want this for me? *Because his son would have access to the best connections money could buy and run any company of my choice.* My gut is telling me the gruesome murder I just witnessed isn't even half of what is going on or what they are going to confide in us.

Fear snakes up my body because now I'm in a position where I have no choice but to submit.

CHAPTER SIXTEEN

CASSIDY

Initiation

Thankfully, for the legacies, there wasn't a long new member period or any type of hazing. Blair and I are getting ready for initiation in our apartment. Honestly, we don't know what to expect. The only requirement we were given was to wear a white dress, white lingerie, and white shoes. Also, no makeup, with our hair flowing naturally, and no jewelry. We were also given a handwritten map telling us where to wait. The map also stated that we would be getting into a black SUV that would take us to an unknown destination. We were instructed to leave our cell phones, purses, and wallets and to come with only our keys to our residence. Blair and I had a good laugh about where we were supposed to put the key since our dresses didn't have pockets. Getting creative, I slipped it into the side of my bra.

Our moms never revealed a single part about initiation; it's a vow you take to only discuss initiation and anything to do with the sisterhood with only sisters.

"What's up with the white?" Blair scoffs while looking over at me. "It makes me look so pale, like a ghost."

We are getting ready in her bedroom.

"No idea; it feels like we are getting ready for our wedding day."

"We look like Virgin Marys," she snickers.

Even though we burst into laughter, I know how nervous we both are.

"Are you ready to head out?" I ask Blair, excitement thrumming through me.

"Yes girl, just imagine we'll be sisters by the end of the day!"

"Like we haven't been already! It'll just be official now." I smirk at her.

Double-checking the key is where I placed it after locking the door, we head out with the map in hand. The map is handwritten with lazy handwriting, and it's hard to make out where to go.

Clapping and jumping up and down, Blair shouts, "Maybe it's really a scavenger hunt!"

I shake my head no with a huge smile on my face.

After walking what feels like a mile in these heels, we come to a secluded lot on the edge of campus. The sun is about to go down, so it's not as hot as it is during the day. Awkwardly, we just stand there, acutely aware of our surroundings. It's eerily silent and getting darker, and the streetlights come on.

Blair tries not to move her mouth when she says, "I see a small black SUV headed this way."

And sure enough, here it comes, pulling up.

"Blair and Cassidy?" a sister in a white angelic lace mask asks.

"Yes, that's us," I tell her.

"Hop in the back," she says.

I open the back door, and Blair and I hop in and buckle our seatbelts. It's a bench seat with a basket in the middle.

The mysterious sister says, "Reach in; there are black blindfolds for you both; put them on as well as the noise-canceling headphones."

With a shaky breath, I reach for mine. Blair winks at me and fastens hers, throwing her headphones over her ears, and I follow. Darkness takes over my senses. My bladder could burst with how nervous I am. My hands and inner thighs are sweating.

The car lurches forward at a normal pace, and then about ten or so minutes later, it speeds up, indicating that we are getting on a highway. I am clueless as to where we are going, but I hope it is anywhere but the middle of nowhere.

A short while later, the car begins to decelerate and move slightly to the right; it must be getting off at an exit. Next, a bump makes my body jump, and my stomach feels uneasy. About fifteen minutes later, the car comes to an urgent halt.

The rear doors are thrown open, and I'm harshly seized under my arms as I'm led out of the car and onto the ground. Another sister holds my hand, and we steadily move toward our destination. She takes the lead, and I follow blindly.

Next, I cross through a threshold and am greeted by cool air, which can only mean one thing—we are in a building. Bumping into a table, I'm pushed on my shoulder to sit in a chair, automatically doing so while I steady my breathing.

A significant amount of time goes by, and then I'm yanked upwards to stand up. I'm tugged by my arm for about twenty or so feet until someone removes my headphones and then my blindfold. Adjusting to the lighting, I blink several times and look around. There are candles scattered throughout the room, and the entire space is draped in white sheets. Sisters in white robes surround me; their hoods are sheer white, making it easy to recognize most of them. All of them are holding a candle, chanting while forming a circle around me, leaving a small opening. Someone comes up and nudges me toward it, and I go and stand silently. Another sister brings a small bathtub and places it in the middle.

Instinctively, my mind works out that we are in a church or cathedral. A sister strides toward me, holding out her hand for me to take. She raises one of her hands, and the chanting stops.

"Today, she leaves behind her life before and will re-emerge as a sister of Zeta Kappa Phi. You will come up purified and live to serve the sisterhood."

She steps into the tub and signals me to follow her. Exactly like a baptism, she holds my nose and arches my head backward, plunging me into the tub. She quickly lifts me back up, and all of the sisters are clapping. We both get out, and towels are given to us.

All of them drop their hoods behind them, and my eyes seek out Blair. Not holding back, she runs over to me and almost topples us both over as she gives me a huge hug. We grin at each other, tears in our eyes, filled with disbelief.

Blair whispers in my ear, "You were the last one, so we can all take off our robes now and wrap this up."

Beaming at her, I laugh and watch the older sisters embrace the new sisters. There is a ton of laughter, hugging, talking, and excitement that fills the room.

Our president informs us afterward that we will be taking a bus back to the sorority house, where we will receive our badges, numbers, and papers, officially making us members.

CHAPTER SEVENTEEN

ARCHER

"You're being paranoid." One of my brothers, Cam, scowls at me.

"You're not being cautious," I chide back at him while tossing a huge black duffel bag into the very back of the van, a loud squeal coming from it. We are in a secret garage located behind the fraternity house.

"Having the new brothers help with the business's workload would take a lot off our plate." Cam sighs.

"I know most of them are legacies, and their family members know about the fraternity being a cover for the illegal business we run, but the newly initiated brothers have no clue. What if they freak out and drop?" I question him.

"Unlikely, for the exact reason you just said. Their families are too intertwined with this."

I rub a hand down my face. "Yeah, you're right." I dismiss the thought.

mouth and stares at mine with doe-like eyes. I slam it down her throat, fucking it ruthlessly, pulling her hair so roughly I'm surprised some hasn't come out of her head.

Cam laughs menacingly. "I'm going to take her ass while you fuck her mouth."

He starts moving her hips up so she's on her hands and knees with her holes on display. She flails her body in every direction, trying to get away, but she's helpless in her state and at our mercy.

Grabbing her ear harshly enough to where there is going to be bruising tomorrow, I tell her, "The more you fight it, the better it is for us and the worse it is for you, and we love the fight." I chuckle.

She struggles as she tries to look back at Cam as he spreads her ass cheeks. He sticks one finger in. "Fuck, she's tight man. I'm going to come so fast with this one," he says as he slaps her hard enough to leave a handprint.

I clutch onto both of her ears and work up a rhythm. The tip of my cock is hitting the back of her throat. She's drooling and gagging all over. Spit is rolling down her chest and onto the ground. It spurs me on even more.

Cam lines up his cock with her ass and shoves himself inside the tight ring of muscle without lube. I can feel her inwardly screaming around my dick, her throat opening up even more to me. I smile, loving the feeling.

Cam doesn't hold back as he sadistically fucks her. He swipes his hand around her tight hole and holds up his hand to me. "Look, I think I'm the first one to take her here." His hand is covered in blood, and he covers his cock in it.

I'm so turned on by the sight of it. I fuck her face, and after a few more thrusts, I spill down her throat.

"Swallow it all, or you'll be licking it up." I grit my teeth at her.

Cam finds his release in her ass, groaning loudly. He pulls out and takes two fingers, and shoves the cum leaking out right back in, causing more tears to spring to her eyes and fall down her face.

"Something to remember me by." He hoots with laughter as he slaps her ass one final time.

We both tuck ourselves back into our pants. Looking around, I can't remember where I placed that piece of tape, and upon finding it after a few moments, I secure it over her mouth, slapping my hand unnecessarily over it.

Cam helps me return her to the bag, and I shift her so I can zip the bag all the way up and launch it on top of the others, hitting the back window to let the driver know the packages are secure and he can go.

"Just a typical Friday night." I clap Cam on the back, and we head back into the fraternity house.

CHAPTER EIGHTEEN

CASSIDY

My alarm goes off at 6:00am. It is finally Sunday, and I want to get ready and look my best before Tyler picks me up. Frankly, I don't know what has gotten into me. Hauling myself as slow as humanly possible out of bed, I slide into my pink fuzzy slippers. I stretch my arms over my head as I make it to my bathroom, willing my eyes to fully open. Turning on the shower and waiting for it to heat up, I grab a towel and take a look at myself in the mirror, eyeing my makeup setup on the small vanity beside it.

The internal debate I have every day is whether to put makeup on. Natural makeup or full glam makeup? There are so many decisions a woman has to make.

After I step out of the shower, wrapping a towel securely around me, I recall that I'm moving Tyler into the fraternity house where I will be surrounded by fine-ass men, and so the decision has been made—yes, makeup! And hell yes to full glam. I rush through my routine as quickly as possible, selecting a cute mid-denim skirt, a tank top, and some white sneakers. Is this reasonable attire to wear when moving? Absolutely not, but I'm going to the hottest fraternity house on campus. Also, I will flat-out refuse to do any kind of heavy lifting or anything that causes me to break a sweat.

In my weekender bag, I toss in some loungewear with a bra and panty set, crossing my fingers in the hope that Tyler invites me to spend the night with him. Our sorority house doesn't allow boys to sleep over, but at the fraternity houses on campus, there is no rule about girls sleeping over or even how many you want to sleep over; you could have the entire class of the freshman girls over if you wanted to.

An unusual, patterned knock comes from the front door. I roll my eyes and smile to myself, knowing it's Tyler. Only he would do something corny like that. I think to myself that I'm actually falling for this guy. He's arrogant and isn't bad on the eyes, and he pleasures me beyond belief. My core doesn't stand a chance when he is in the room; it becomes a weeping mess.

Practically skipping over to my door, I take a deep breath and open it casually.

"Stunning as always, Cassidy." Tyler whistles at me, taking in every inch.

He holds out a hot coffee to me while holding the door open. I'm very much a caffeine addict, and as I take the first sip, I moan at the flavorful taste.

"How do you know my coffee order?" I ask, perplexed, as I stare at the label on the side.

"I may have had some help with that one." He winks and smiles, showing off his perfect teeth.

Blair. That hoebag. What kind of guy texts your best friend for your coffee order? This guy is making me weak for him and has me imagining him naked already.

I hold the door open wider, letting him inside. He walks

through, and I can't help but smell one of my favorite colognes coming off of him: Savage.

I could eat this man up right here. Damn him, he has to smell sexy too?

"We should probably get going so we can move my stuff before it gets too hot," he announces.

"How much stuff do you have?" I ask quizzically.

"Everything is already loaded in my Tahoe," he lifts up his thumb, gesturing toward where his Tahoe is parked, "I just need your help unloading it. The frat house has furniture, and you aren't allowed to bring in any of your own, so it's just a lot of boxes, and of course, I'm on the second floor," he says, clearly annoyed.

"Let me just grab my bag, and we can go," I say, already moving to my room to snatch up my things, excitedly saying a quick thank you to whoever is listening for there being no furniture to move.

"Take your time; watching your backside is one of my new favorite things." He chuckles.

I smirk to myself, secretly wanting to tease, so I make sure my hips move a little more back and forth while I walk down the hall to my room.

When I come back into the living room, I see Tyler scrolling on his phone, waiting for me, and tapping his foot to some song.

"All set. You know you owe me for helping you move," I say with a crooked grin.

Tyler matches my energy. "How about a mind-blowing orgasm?" he teases with a sly grin.

I hum to myself as if I'm taking some time thinking it over. "Make it two." I smile as he follows me out of my apartment, and I turn the key in the lock and lock it up.

Reaching his car, he opens the passenger door for me. Hopping in, smiling while looking down at my legs, I can feel my nipples pebble and perk up as I daydream about how Tyler is going to fuck me this time.

He gets in and starts his car, and we head to Frat Row.

CHAPTER NINETEEN

TYLER

I pull into my designated parking spot in front of the fraternity house. There's a side door most of the brothers use, and the staircase is not even five steps from the door.

I struggle to tear my gaze away from Cassidy. She looks delectable, and I can't wait to have a taste.

All I can think about is ripping her clothes off as soon as possible.

I'm getting hard just imagining her body writhing and moaning under my control through an orgasm.

I bite my knuckles to calm myself down and focus on the pain instead, and talk myself out of just jumping her right here in the car.

I remind myself that I have such a tight schedule. Moving my things into the frat house today is my priority, and I may even unpack a couple of things and get settled in.

"Okay, we'll use the side door. My room is on the second floor, the fourth one on the right," I tell her, turning off my car and getting out.

"Alright, I hope I don't get lost and wander into someone else's room," Cassidy jokes.

"You better hope not either; you won't like the punishment." I glare at her possessively.

"Or maybe I will," she yells as she opens her car door and leaps out, being the first one to head to the back of the car to grab a box.

This woman is going to be the end of me.

CHAPTER TWENTY

CASSIDY

After unloading all of the boxes into Tyler's new room, I help him organize his things. We ordered DoorDash for lunch and ate in his room on his bed. Overall, it was a fun day teasing Tyler every chance I got. I even flashed him a couple of times. Why not? It makes moving a little more enjoyable and less tedious. A few of his brothers met me and shook my hand ever so gentlemanly, including the president of the fraternity, Archer. Tyler seems to admire him for the position he holds, but all I noticed when I met him was that he was a complete tool bag. He hungrily looked me up and down and saw the disgusted look I gave him as he did it. When Tyler glanced over at me as he was talking to him, I quickly plastered a fake smile on my face.

Truthfully, I couldn't get away from him fast enough; he made my whole body cringe, and his ego alone took up the entire room.

More polite comments were exchanged between us, and after

expressing how long of a day it had been, we were able to escape back to Tyler's car, making sure nothing had fallen out and that we got everything. Alpha Chi is situated on a cul-de-sac, and the land behind it extends for miles, encompassing protected areas for endangered animals, ensuring that no one can ever build behind it.

Sweating after a long day, and now with it being dusk out, I'm enraptured by the trees behind the house. Tyler unexpectedly slides up behind me, wrapping his hands around my middle. He swipes my hair that has fallen out of my ponytail to the side, giving him complete access to my ear. He kisses me from the bottom of my neck up to my ear and sucks on it.

His breath is hot and erotic as he whispers, "It's time for your punishment for teasing me all day. You're now going to run as fast as you can in the woods. If I catch you, I get to fuck you however I want."

Startled with a sudden ache between my legs, I look up at him and lock eyes as a wolfish smile forms. I debate what I'm going to do. It doesn't take long because backing down from a challenge isn't something I do.

I squeeze my thighs together with the anticipation of what is to come, not having a single idea, and I love the thrill of it.

Side-eyeing him, I use my entire body weight to propel myself forward, and I take off, breathing hard as I yell back, "I get a five-minute head start for the help I provided today."

I zip in and out of the trees, my legs pumping as fast as they can, and I stumble on a well-worn path ahead of me. I slow, trying to catch my breath, confused and wondering how that could be if these lands are protected?

After what feels like a decent amount of time has passed, my heart feels like it is going to beat out of my chest. The unpredictability has my core pulsing.

"I'm going to sink my teeth into that pretty cunt!" Tyler yells out.

Picking up my pace, still trying to control my breathing, I

glance back. I'm deep in the woods now because I can no longer see the fraternity house.

I trip over something. "Fuck!" I hiss under my breath as one of my knees hits the ground. I peer beneath me, making out what I am looking at, and my flesh begins to crawl as terror streaks over my body. Lying before me is a chain with a large circle at the end, and the other end is chained around the tree.

The color of the chain is deep rust, blending naturally with the fallen leaves and pine needles.

Walking over to it, I notice that it looks like it's been here a while. My eye catches what lies behind the tree; I take a few steps and realize it's a fire pit area with pavers arranged in a circle.

Reaching out, I touch one of the pavers. It's hot, meaning it's been used recently. I back up, fear shooting through me. I'm about fifty feet away when, all of a sudden, a hand slaps over my mouth, and I'm dragged back, connecting with a body that over-powers mine. Instincts take over, and I thrash like a mad woman attempting to get out of the hold. One hand is over my mouth, while the other one is securely wrapped around my chest.

Panic sets in, and small breaths escape me.

"Got you," Tyler throatily whispers as his hands retreat from where they are, and he captures my groan in his mouth. Losing all senses, I intensify the kiss.

He leads my body backward until it hits one of the trees. I climb up his body as he seizes my buttocks with both of his hands, pulling my skirt up to my waist and exposing my panties. He draws me up so that we are face-to-face. He pulls back and looks at me, his eyes bright with excitement. Pulling my scrunchie out of my hair and clutching a fistful, he yanks my head back and exposes my neck to him. One of his hands shoots up and wraps around, gently choking me while he bites at my top, ripping it off along with the buttons. His pelvis connects with mine, and we grind against each other in rhythm. Warmth grows between my legs, and his cock is hard against me. As we explore each other's bodies, ravishing each other's skin, we pull and twist until our clothes are a heap on the ground.

Shaking with need, Tyler wrenches away from me, and his eyes greedily roam over my body.

Growling, he says, "Put your hands above you and hold on to the tree, spread your legs as far as you can, and don't fucking move."

Without hesitation, I position myself exactly as he tells me to. My clit is swollen and throbbing with need.

Tyler gingerly skims his fingertip between my legs from back to front. Stopping at my clit, he kneels, and his tongue replaces his fingertip moving in and out of me. Capturing my bottom lip with my teeth, I close my eyes and fuck his face ruthlessly as he expertly moves one of my legs over his shoulder, and that allows him to go deeper.

As he pulls back from me and looks up with his lips drenched with my cum, he smiles darkly at me and picks up his pace.

I see stars as I get that rush through my body. Shamelessly, I scream his name, cum coating the inside of my legs and his face.

"Taste yourself." His hand wraps around my jaw as he pins my body against the tree, groaning as he kisses me, dizzy from the orgasm.

"That's one," Tyler says playfully.

I feel his length on my abdomen; it's hard and erect again.

"I'm still owed one more." I place my hand on his chest, play-fully pushing him away from me; his body barely moves.

"I am here to serve." He chuckles.

He kisses me fiercely before he asks, "Do you trust me?"

Without thinking, I answer, "Yes."

He flips me so my face is against the tree and my back is to him.

"Put your hands behind your back," he demands.

My hands move behind my back rapidly as he pats his pock-ets, trying to find something. Silence spreads over us for a second, and then I feel the plastic wrapping around my wrists; he is zip-tying them together. I cry out from the tightness of them.

"Fuck, I love seeing you like this," Tyler says as he hauls me back and pushes me forcefully to the ground, gripping my hips back so my ass is in the air. One of his hands holds my face down, firmly securing me.

He pushes two fingers into my wetness. "I knew you'd be ready for me."

I yelp at the unexpected intrusion. He lines himself up and slowly pushes himself in all the way to the hilt. Groaning, he pulls out all the way, then quickly pushes back in. I moan loudly. He spanks my ass, causing me to shriek at the surprising sting.

He begins to violently thrust in and out of me, and I feel it again. The tingles are washing over me, and it is like an out-of-body experience—like I'm levitating. Just as I am about to come, he withdraws himself.

"Only good girls get to come," he snarls over me.

Rubbing my ass back into him, my body begs for the release, and the feeling of emptiness washes over me.

Tyler spits in my puckered hole and drags his cock from my slit to my tight ring of muscle. "I'm going to fuck you here now, and don't come until I tell you to."

His cock nudges my back entrance as he works his way inside, letting me adjust at first. Then, he slams into me.

I scream out and try to bite back the initial pain.

"Relax, let me in," he soothingly says as I try to relax my body.

Tyler lines himself up and shoves back into me. Again, I scream, the pain overtaking pleasure. His fingers find my clit and begin working it while he starts moving back and forth, gradually building up speed. Satisfaction covers me like a warm blanket. After edging me, I know I'm about to come quick, and the light-headedness takes over.

"Go ahead, be my good girl, and come all over my cock." He groans thunderously.

I scream his name as I come again, my entire body racking with spasms, and he yells mine as his release spills inside of me.

We don't move for a minute, trying to catch our breath. Once we do, Tyler opens a knife and cuts the zip-tie, freeing my hands.

I slowly sit up and rub my wrists. I know I must look like a mess, with leaves and pine needles in my tangled hair. My legs ache in the most delicious way, as do other parts of my body.

Tyler silently hands me my clothes, and we start getting dressed, grinning at each other.

"Please feel free to fill out a survey. I love hearing how satisfied you were with the agreed-upon payment," Tyler says, buttoning up his shorts.

"Who says I'm completely satisfied?" I tsk.

He gives me a horrified look. "Screaming my name while orgasming kind of gave you away."

"Are you sure I said YOUR name?" I giggle.

Jealousy clouds over his face as he says, "You're mine, Cassidy. You have been since the moment I saw you."

"Calm down, Hulk. I don't have the time or the patience to see anyone else," I say, tying my shoes.

"It's official; we're exclusive."

"Seems that way." I grab his hand, and we start walking in sync back to the frat house.

"Stay the night with me," Tyler says more than asks.

"Sure." I grin up at him.

"First, you need a shower before you get into my bed." He laughs.

I playfully shove him, scoffing, "Like you don't."

CHAPTER TWENTY-ONE

CASSIDY

As soon as we get back to Tyler's room, he walks straight to his en suite and starts the shower so that the water can warm up.

He pulls me toward the bathroom as it starts to get steamy and licks my collarbone. I catch a glimpse of myself in the mirror as he trails kisses around the area. I guess I must have nicked a branch or something because I'm bleeding.

"Mmmm, you taste good." He drags his mouth over to mine and intertwines my tongue with his, and my mouth is flooded with a coppery taste.

Why am I so turned on by this? Maybe it's just Tyler that turns me on and makes me hyper-aware of my body.

"Let me taste you," I moan and drop to my knees.

His cock is at full mast and already leaking pre-cum. Sticking out the tip of my tongue, I look up at him and taste him before twirling my tongue around the tip of his cock.

"Fuck, Cassidy, you make me lose all sense around you," he groans, weaving his fingers through my hair.

I take his full length inside my mouth and hollow out my cheeks, moving to the base of his cock to the tip. I moan with pleasure, sucking and tasting him. My nose hits his pubic hair, and the musky smell has me moving my own fingers to touch myself.

Tyler has a fistful of my hair now but is completely enraptured, staring at me. Spreading my labia with my fingers and beginning to play with my clit, I groan around his dick.

"Loosen your throat like a good girl," Tyler whispers in pure bliss, his eyes closed and his head thrown back.

Ever the accommodating person I am, I don't have a gag reflex, and I love being able to stun Tyler into silence.

He looks down at me as his eyes widen, and he holds on to my hair tighter, thrusting and hitting the back of my throat, igniting a fire between my legs.

"That's right, get it nice and sloppy," he says huskily.

Fuck. His words hit me right in my core, and I begin rocking back and forth on my own fingers, playing with myself exactly the way I like it.

"Are you going to come all over yourself?" Tyler begins thrusting harder.

I moan around his dick, and my eyes roll back inside my head. I am almost there. I can feel the tingling starting.

He fucks my mouth roughly, and I am completely turned on.

"Come for me, Cass," Tyler whispers as he spills down the back of my throat, "Swallow it all, or you'll lick it up off the floor."

That sends me over the edge. Letting go, I come all over my fingers, slickness running down my thighs.

Tyler reaches for my fingers and puts them in his mouth, sucking hard and groaning. "I'm addicted to the taste of you."

Then, he takes hold of the back of my head and kisses me, mixing our cum together.

Tyler breaks the kiss, smacks my ass, and says, "Get in that shower; you're fucking filthy now." Giggling, I do as he says. We lather and wash each other with his manly-smelling soap, stealing kisses when we can.

After hopping out of the shower, I begin towel drying my hair and put on the loungewear and fuzzy socks I brought in my bag.

Tyler throws on some gray sweatpants and sprawls out on his bed with the TV remote in hand, aimlessly scrolling through channels. He stops on reruns of The Office, and I laugh, throwing myself on the bed. "I love this show; I could watch it over and over again."

"Me too; it's one of my favorite shows of all time," Tyler says.

We mindlessly watch a few episodes, laughing before Tyler asks me if I'm hungry. My stomach growls in response.

"Let me feed you," he says, kissing and biting my lip. He pulls back and says, "Come on."

Following him downstairs to the house's huge kitchen, Tyler tells me to take a seat at one of the barstools. He casually says hi to a few brothers cleaning up from their dinner and gets to work on making a chicken lettuce wrap for both of us. He cuts them both down the middle, puts them on plates, and hands me one.

"Oh my god," I moan as I take a bite of my wrap.

"Best boyfriend ever, right?" Tyler says with a sly smile, lifting up his eyebrows at me with a mouth full of the chicken wrap.

"Two orgasms plus feeding me? Yep, I'd say so." I can't keep the smile off my face as I say it.

"Did I just find my way into Cassidy Matthew's dark heart?" he says, dissolving into laughter.

I tap my chest. "You might have found it."

"I must have because you didn't object to me calling myself your boyfriend."

"No, I guess I didn't."

"Let's go to bed. Heads up, I really enjoy being the little spoon," Tyler casually says and yawns.

"I actually need sleep to function, so if that's code for something, just know you'll get shut down." I sneak a peek at his reaction.

"I'm told I can be very convincing," he says in a hushed tone.

"Sleep only. I have class in the morning!"

Tyler chuckles. "Alright, alright."

We head back to his room, holding hands and smiling like two people who only see each other.

Jumping into bed and peeling back the covers, I turn off the bedside lamp and place my phone on one of the chargers next to Tyler's phone and my glasses.

Tyler notices it and curiously asks, "What's up with the pink cherry blossoms?"

Scoffing, I state, "They symbolize renewal and new beginnings!"

Tyler kisses me on my forehead before pulling me into him.

"And new relationships," he tells me.

The guy has the body temperature of a sauna, and I'm always cold, so I snuggle in close, firmly squeezing his arms.

I might be falling hard for this guy.

CHAPTER TWENTY-TWO

CASSIDY

Groggily, I open my eyes and reach for my glasses on the nightstand. My eyes snap open because I don't immediately recognize where I'm at. But I feel Tyler behind me, snoring lightly, suddenly remembering I'm with him at the frat house. Instantly, my breathing slows down.

The time on his alarm clock reads a little after 1am. My throat is so dry. I look over at Tyler, and he's sleeping so well. I don't want to wake him, so somehow, I wiggle out of his embrace. I slide my sandals on and head downstairs to the kitchen.

This place is the quietest I'll probably ever see it as I make my way down the hallway and toward the stairs. I head down the stairs, but I can't remember which way is the kitchen.

Oh well, I guess I'll run into it whenever I get to it; it can't be that hard.

I start searching downstairs. There's a hallway with a gate in the archway that looks vaguely familiar, so my body leads me that way, licking my lips. The need for a Gatorade overpowers my thoughts; anything to quench my thirst propels me forward, exhaustion taking over.

The gate is unlocked, so I step through. The house is old, and this must be one of the quirks they never remodeled or removed.

There are multiple doors, and the kitchen has to be back here. I try to recall the floor plan from when we were down here last night, and I'm pretty positive I went the right way.

I try the first door. It's a broom closet, so I quickly shut it. "Ugh." I annoyingly groan to myself.

I head to the next door; it seems like it could be a bigger room since the door after this one is further away. The hallway is a regular, beige color, pretty typical for Greek houses, always with white baseboards.

It's very dark as I open the door, so I search for a light switch on the wall nearest to me, and I hear a sudden movement in the room. I freeze up, unable to see shit, and attempt to squint. I try to make out the room I accidentally came upon. There's not a window in sight, which would explain the darkness.

Suddenly, the hair on my arms sticks up, and goosebumps appear, my stomach dropping in sudden fear.

Scratching.

Whipping my head around and squinting again, I make out these black box-looking things. Could those be dog cages? They are lined up against the walls. It's not uncommon for brothers to have dogs. I love dogs. So, forgetting my need for a drink, I excitedly move toward the cages.

Reaching out, I realize they have sheets over them. Black sheets. I've also personally done this with our dogs when I was growing up. It makes the dog feel more confined in the space and more comfortable, especially puppies.

Deciding on the dog crate closest to me, I fumble around a little bit and pull back the sheet. My eyes have adjusted to the darkness, but I'm only able to see maybe six inches in front of me.

As I pull the sheet back, I gasp loudly and throw my hands over my mouth, jerking backwards and tripping on the ground, falling on my butt in disbelief. The sheet falls back into place.

My mind must be playing tricks on me. I am really exhausted because there's no way this can be happening right now.

Shaking all over, terror slowly seeps through my body. I breathe deeply in through my nose and out through my mouth. I feel lightheaded. *Wake up, Cassidy, this is a bad dream.* I cross my arms, trying to protect myself.

Summoning all the courage in me, I extend my arm for the sheet again. All I can feel is my rapid heartbeat in my throat, and my legs are trembling.

Taking the sheet in my hands, I slowly move it back above the crate and make eye contact with a woman around my age. Her mouth is taped, and her hands appear to be zip-tied behind her back. She's in a huge T-shirt and looks like she hasn't bathed in days. Tears begin to form in her eyes, and she starts trying to form words and sounds, gesturing with her head.

My throat feels like rocks are shoved down it, and I don't even know how to process what I am seeing.

Barely, my voice comes out, not sounding like myself at all. "I'm going to get you out of here." She looks at me and then looks around frantically, seeing the other crates, and I quickly count them. There are eleven of them.

Looking petrified, the girl rapidly nods as if answering the silent question in my head: Is there more of you?

Suddenly, I fully take in the room and slow my breathing, and the smell of the room hits me at once. I look at the cage and notice a little bucket. I gag when my eyes land upon it, knowing what it is, and hope that the woman doesn't see it.

I begin looking around the outside of the cage. There is a lock on the front of it. She starts making noises and trying to get me to look around by making motions with her head.

"Please be quiet," I furiously whisper. "I don't know what the hell is going on or what we are dealing with here."

Directly behind me, next to the door, hangs a lanyard with a key attached to it. I also notice a few light switches. I click the one closest to me, and it turns on a subtle light near the doorway, which is just enough to make out my surroundings.

Practically leaping up and sprinting while losing my balance, I yank it off the hook and rush back to the crate, shaking so badly that I can't get the key in the lock at first.

"Be as quiet as you can. I don't want them to hear us. I'm going to get you and anyone else out of here no matter what." I plead with her with determination in my eyes.

After willing my hands to stop moving, I shove the key into the lock, turning it as quickly as I can, and it opens. The girl crawls out of the crate, readjusting herself and trying to walk. I rip the tape off her mouth, and she jerks back in pain.

"We need scissors to cut the zip tie," I say breathlessly.

"There are knives in the closet," she whispers back to me, looking me directly in the eye, intensely wanting the hell out of here.

I didn't see a closet earlier, and a small shiver goes through me, thinking about how the fuck she knows where the knives are at.

I locate the closet and fling open the door, and sure enough, there is a whole case of knives and other tools, which I don't want to think about. There also seems to be what looks like used sex toys.

I see a few dildos with dried blood on the ends. Either they were used recently, or whoever uses them doesn't clean them. More shivers run through my body as I think about either of those options. I shake my head. *No, don't go there; we have to get out of here.*

Closing my mouth super tight to stop myself from getting sick to my stomach, I start sawing her zip tie to free her.

Finally, it pops open, releasing her.

"What's your name?" I ask her, still whispering.

"Jasmine," she says, rubbing her wrists that look very infected.

They are red, completely raw, with older-looking sores. I calculate that she has probably been here a few days, and I try not to get sick again.

"We have to get the others out now!" I whisper-yell at her.

Turning toward them, I start forcefully throwing the sheets off and unlocking all of the crates. Women around my age fall out of them, breathing hard and landing on their shoulders. They must have heard what was going on. All of them look very malnourished, with a vacant look in their eyes. I know that look, the look of no hope. Jasmine finds another knife, and we both get to work on their zip ties.

All of the girls look to her. She must be a leader among them.

I just stand there, completely in shock, not really knowing how to make myself useful, and let Jasmine take the lead on the women.

"We have to get out of here," I tell them. "Right now!"

Nodding frantically and walking over to me, they form a circle.

"The only way out is through the door you came in," Jasmine says.

"Let's go quickly." I turn around and jog over to the door.

Opening it, I rush out with Jasmine and the girls filing out directly behind me.

I lock eyes on the gate in the hallway that I came through, and all of a sudden, it begins shutting slowly, and I hear the lock as it clicks shut. I gasp when I notice two guys appear behind the gate, smiling wickedly. One guy approaches the gate, pressing his head against it. The gears shift in my mind. He looks vaguely familiar. Then, the realization comes crashing over me. It's their fucking president—Archer.

CHAPTER TWENTY-THREE

ARCHER

A few seniors and I are watching TV in the living room, which is across from the kitchen, when we hear the first noise. I pull up the cameras that are in the room housing the sex slaves, which is a holding area before their next destination.

To my utter surprise, I notice Cassidy stumbling in the room, looking around, and then unlocking the crates while both she and another girl are cutting the zip ties.

"Two of you come with me, and one needs to stay here and make sure none of the younger brothers or anyone else comes past the kitchen," I snarl.

I lead my brothers to the hallway.

"Stay on the other side of the gate the entire time while I deal with Cassidy." I feel for my gun behind my back as we walk.

One of them slams the gate closed, hiding himself behind a wall and snickering.

I stroll up and place my face through the iron bars, leering at Cassidy. Recognition rolls over her face. I open the gate and get directly in front of her, staring her down.

Without hesitation, I take out my gun and whack her over the side of her head. The other girls start screaming but cower back away from me. That's what weeks in this place will do. It made them scared shitless of me. Just how I like it.

Cassidy is sprawled out on the floor, blood trickling out from the wound I caused. I bend over and check if she still has a pulse and inspect the head wound. What the fuck am I going to do with her? I start pacing back and forth, puzzled and at a loss.

A lazy grin envelops my entire face.

"All of you, BACK TO YOUR ROOM!" I yell at the girls, swinging my gun around and reaching through the bars for one of the stun guns my brothers are holding. It's used for cattle. At this point, a gun really shouldn't scare them after the shit we've done to them. But they listen nonetheless, like trained animals, because that's exactly how they are treated here. The place they are headed to is worse than this, and they'll look back on this time with longing and haunting memories, wishing to come back.

Clutching onto each other in fear, they wobble back to their room. One of my brothers, Conner, comes up behind me, coming through the gate. "What do you want us to do?"

"Lock the girls back up the way they were. Call the boss and let him know what happened; we need to get this lot transported tonight to the warehouse in preparation for training and then the auction," I command.

"The auction isn't for another two weeks," Conner exasperatedly says.

"Their training will have to start as soon as possible, and it's up to the boss to tell them when they are ready and when the auction should be held. It could be earlier," I snarl at him.

I pick up Cassidy like a rag doll and take her to the room across from the holding room.

I call this room the preparation room. There's a hospital bed in the middle with straps for arms on the handles and straps for their legs to spread them open, with their ass arched up. There are no windows. First aid kits line one wall, and sponge bath supplies are set up and organized with the navy T-shirts we put all the girls in. It's the fraternity's color, you know, a special touch. Also, there are some additional medical tools and tranquilizers if needed. Typically, we use tranquilizers often, for fun.

Lying Cassidy softly on the bed, I secure her arms and legs in the straps. She'll be waking up soon, and I can't take any chances of her escaping and letting anyone know about this place, especially the new initiates; we have to work them into this business. My mind works at record speed, contemplating the idea I had before, but really, what the fuck am I going to do with her? The crazy idea I had before doesn't seem so crazy now. This has never happened in all the years we have done this; she wasn't a target.

After thinking about all the pros and cons, I could throw her in with this lot and make her disappear forever. That seems like the best option. If I let her go, I would have to take a huge chance, and I would risk the fraternity's secret business and reputation if she ran her mouth; it would be my head on a spike. I shake my head. It has to be this way. I have to make her into no one.

Making up my mind, I text Conner.

Me: Send one of the older brothers up to Tyler's room quietly and grab all of Cassidy's things, including her cell phone. Don't get fucking caught.

Conner: On it.

I need to make it appear as though she left in the middle of the night on her own accord and resolve this matter as quickly as possible. She's seen too much.

Reaching for the fabric scissors, I start cutting her loungewear off her body. She's wearing a baby blue lace lingerie set with her boobs pushed up.

Fuck, she's gorgeous. I run my hands up and down her body. Her skin is unusually soft. Maybe I'll just have a taste. It couldn't hurt to try out the product. Cutting off her bra and panties in one swooping motion, a devious grin forms on my face, salivating while seeing what's underneath.

My dick stiffens in my pants. Working the medical tape out, I double-tape her mouth, not wanting to risk any noise.

Her pussy is bare and spread out before me. I find the remote that controls the bed and push the button that allows the bed to go up and down, choosing the up button so my thighs are the same height as the bed.

I put my face between her legs and inhale deeply, closing my eyes. Fuck she smells sweet. Gently, I swipe my tongue over her center, hitting her clit. I groan. She tastes better than she smells.

Intrigued, I wonder what she sounds like when she orgasms. I slide my tongue in and out of her tight hole, and she squirms slightly.

Fuck, I'm not going to have enough time with her.

Unbuttoning my pants and grabbing my hard dick, I start stroking myself. I'm almost there. Cassidy moans and slowly opens her eyes. I place my hand over her mouth as her entire body starts trying to get away from me. She attempts to throw me off of her, but I secure her tightly. She isn't able to move in the slightest.

I laugh maniacally at her struggle. I love it. I line myself up with her entrance and shove myself all the way up to the hilt, not giving her any time to adjust to me, while I cover her mouth with my other hand. She's writhing all over the place.

"Shut up, you filthy whore; your pussy takes me so greedily," I whisper in her ear while I keep thrusting in and out.

Tears form at the corner of her eyes, and as they fall, I lick up every single one of them.

"I'm going to make you hate me. Watch as your own body betrays you. If you don't shut the fuck up, I'll make it hurt," I growl at her.

She stops sobbing, and now she is silently crying.

I pull myself out of her and attack her clit with my mouth,

extensions; those are Connor's favorite. He loves to pull them straight out, and they usually cry hysterically from the pain and loss of their real hair.

"Believe it or not, the hair is all hers," he says, huffing disappointedly.

I grab the nail polish remover and start working on her fingernails and toenails, removing the polish. We try to remove everything we can before the girls are transported to the warehouse.

We always check for piercings and take out their earrings. Cassidy has 3 sets of diamond earrings in each ear and one cartilage piercing. All of it has to go. I throw them into a silver bowl.

Cassidy realizes what's happening and begins thrashing around again. It takes us about 20 minutes to clean her up. We cut her nails down as far as we can without them bleeding. Getting scratched sucks.

I roughly grab her jaw, forcing her to make eye contact with me. "We are going to unstrap you and put a T-shirt on. If you give us a hard time, this will be significantly worse for you," I tell her angrily as I slap the side of her face just for fun.

Conner looks over at me and nods. "You ready?"

I nod back. "Let's hurry up. I'm tired, and I have an exam tomorrow."

He unstraps her, and I grab a T-shirt and dress her like a doll. We both grab one of her shoulders, and Conner gets a zip tie, and we put it around her wrists behind her back. She listened.

"Good girl." I grin at her and shove my hand under the T-shirt and pinch her pussy, hard. She whimpers.

We lead her over to the holding room for the sex slaves.

I find an empty crate and shove her into it. She cowers on the wall furthest from the door of the crate.

I slam the door of the crate and laugh at the thought of never seeing Cassidy fucking Matthews again.

CHAPTER TWENTY-FOUR

CASSIDY

It has to be four or five in the morning; it's truly shocking how much your life can change in a matter of hours.

How can I go from having every freedom to having been sexually assaulted and put in a fucking dog cage?

I am physically, emotionally, and mentally drained, and I feel like I'm probably having a panic attack. I can't do small spaces, and this still feels like a bad dream.

Where could they be taking us? I heard them talking about some kind of auction.

All I can think about is Tyler, and I hope he realizes what has happened. I hope he finds me before we go to wherever we are going next.

And then I feel sick. Does he know about this? Is he actively involved in doing this to women? Human beings?

I hear the other women quietly sobbing in their crates.

I'm fucking shaking. The world is an evil place. Unfortunately, now I know there are things worse in life than death.

I hear a noise coming from the back of the room from a door I'm assuming leads to outside. It sounds like multiple locks are being unlocked.

I can't help but hold my breath, trying to listen for anything. The other girls seem to be doing the same thing because the room is deadly quiet.

The door swings open, creaking, and two men dressed head to toe in black come inside. I hear a car's engine running. The sun isn't up yet, which would explain why they are transporting us while there is still darkness. The vehicle has to be a decent size if it's going to hold all of us.

Archer comes through the door that is connected to the house, the same door I entered when I stumbled upon this place.

I grit my teeth, seething, while looking at his arrogant face.

"How many?" one of the men in black asks Archer.

"Eleven, plus the new merchandise," Archer growls.

How the hell are they going to transport twelve of us?

"Let's quickly load them in the van. We need to transport them while it is still dark outside and there is less traffic," the man in black says. "We need this to go as smoothly as possible without damaging any of the merchandise."

For fuck's sake, we aren't even women, just property now.

Archer opens one of the crates and roughly grabs a woman who is whimpering; she can't scream since she has tape over her mouth.

She looks like she has been here for days, if not weeks. Completely filthy with oily hair and bags under her eyes, her skin even looks pale and dry; they must not have given them much water down here. One by one, I watch these three men move the women to the van. They save me for last.

Archer unlocks my crate, grabs me from the back of it by one of my arms, and pulls me toward the front of the cage. Then, he grabs both my arms to control me. Instinctively, I begin fighting and resisting. He pulls my hair so hard, jerking my body upwards. I can already feel the soreness in my neck, my toes only touching the ground.

"Fight me, and I'll make this worse for you," he whispers. "I will have all of these men run a train on your asshole and make the women watch." He licks his lips as if he's envisioning it.

He lifts up my shirt in front of all the men, exposing my entire body.

Smacking my ass hard, Archer loudly announces, "Look at this hot new addition. You boys have some fun with her, one of the tightest holes I've ever been inside."

Tears stream down my face. What could be worse than this? I stop fighting, thinking I need to save my strength for what is to come, not fully accepting this as my future, but just accepting the fact that I am on my way to my next destination.

He leads me out to the vehicle, which is a black Mercedes Sprinter van. The windows are completely blacked out. The tint has to be illegal; you can't even see inside.

Leather seats line up in a U-shape around the inside of the van, with the focus being on the center. Each seat has a chain with a designated handcuff to keep us in place. That isn't what horrifies me. I gasp, and an uneasy feeling fills my stomach.

There is a man in black in the middle, sitting on a stool with a woman strapped to a reclined chair while he tattoos the inside of her right wrist.

What the fuck?

Archer puts me in one of the chairs and handcuffs my left wrist.

He bends down and whispers, "No one will ever find you. I just wiped Cassidy Matthews off the earth." He chuckles under his breath.

He slams the back of the van doors and bangs on them twice, and we start to move.

CHAPTER TWENTY-FIVE

TYLER

My alarm always goes off at 6am. I am a creature of habit and live by my routine, even on the weekends. When you love being in control, you take control of all of the aspects of your life that you can. I always grab a coffee at the local coffee shop and hit the university's gym. Usually, I walk there from the fraternity house. I hit my alarm to turn it off and smile to myself when I roll over, looking for Cassidy, but I don't feel her.

Fear shoots through me when I notice her side of the bed is empty. Confused, I sit up and turn on my lamp. I mentally replay the events that happened last night and recall that we went to bed together, happy, wrapped up in each other's arms. I glance over at her side of the bed and the wall where she put her bag and shoes the night before, but none of it is there.

I clumsily push things over on the nightstand, looking for any sign of her and that she was here, and I didn't just dream the whole thing.

Did this girl seriously up and leave in the middle of the night? She didn't even have her car.

There is no way she would risk walking down Greek Row in the middle of the night, actually taking the chance of running into some drunk frat guys. She's smarter than that.

I already figured out she had commitment issues, but after we established our relationship last night, this is pretty out of touch, even for someone like her.

I reach over for my phone that sits on the charger next to my lamp and see a text message from her.

Cassidy: I have a math exam today that I have to study for. Catch up later?

I quickly respond.

Me: No problem

I see the three dots waiting for her response, but it doesn't come. My heart sinks into my stomach.

Cassidy never mentioned having any academic struggles. I don't know why she would need to study at all for the exam or need that much preparation.

Shrugging my shoulders, I change for the gym and throw my sneakers on. Deciding not to get coffee at my regular spot, I head down to the kitchen to grab a coffee. The chefs usually get here early and have the coffee and to-go cups ready. On my way out of the fraternity house, I stop by the charging station, which has laptops, headphones, and extra phones, and snag a pair of the new Sony noise-canceling headphones for the gym. I sync them to my phone, and my favorite Spotify playlist starts as I walk out the door.

Still having a weird feeling about Cassidy, I make a mental note to catch up with her later, but right now, I need to focus on my day, which is set up to be a very long one.

CHAPTER TWENTY-SIX

CASSIDY

The tattooist, sitting in the middle of the back of the van with broad shoulders and seemingly confident in his job, is almost finished tattooing all the girls, and, of course, I am last, sweating with anticipation. There are no tattoos on my body.

Half of his face is a skeleton outline tattoo; the rest of his body is covered by a sweatshirt and pants, but I'm sure he has tattoos all over.

For someone with very broad shoulders, he moves gracefully as he unhandcuffs me and moves me to the middle seat, indicating it's my turn to be forever marked.

On instinct, I fight him off me. Anger clouding his face, he grabs my jaw and presses the tips of his fingers into pressure points on either side, causing instant pain that forces me to sit still and look into this man's eyes. As I suspected, they are dark and show no remorse whatsoever for what he is doing. I guess they have to have that mindset doing this kind of work, knowing where we are headed. He doesn't want to speak to any of us or make eye contact because that makes it real and not just a shitty fucked up job he can go home and complain to his girlfriend about.

Gritting his teeth as if he's forcing the words to come out, he says, "Fight me, *bitch,* and I'll inject you with a drug that will make you so high you'll be in the stars for days, *understood*?" Drops of spit land on my face, and I squeeze my eyes shut as tears begin to fall, and I nod, vigorously shaking.

Getting this tattoo will make me want to slice my skin off the first chance I get, knowing what it means.

I don't even know what he is tattooing on us. The other girls have completely sunk into themselves, looking like zombies and zoned out. People deal with trauma in different ways. Personally, I can't shut down like the rest of them. If anything, I am hyper-aware of my surroundings. My adrenaline is at full blast, and I'm looking for any kind of weakness and the first opportunity to escape.

There is no fire left in most of these women. I have to remember they were locked up in those cages for a week, maybe longer, and subjected to unthinkable things, so they knew or had an inkling this was going to be their fate, and this is probably acceptance of it.

As for me, less than twelve hours ago, I was a normal college student who had been literally plucked from that life.

Jasmine makes eye contact with me. I hold her gaze because I need this connection right now to get me through this. I'm trembling, not because of the pain but because of what this tattoo is going to mean on my body. This is what they do to cattle, not humans. The man with the skull face starts up the tattoo gun, and I feel the tip graze my skin. The burn starts as he goes back over what he just drew on my right wrist. I'm too scared to look at what he is putting on my body.

Instead, I look up and notice the sunlight starting to peek

through the windows, which would mean that we have been in the van for almost an hour or so. We can barely see out the windows; It looks like there are blackout tints on the inside as well.

The tattoo takes less than three minutes.

He unstraps me and puts me back in my seat, handcuffing my left wrist. My wrist is wrapped up in that clear wrap they usually use at the tattoo shops, and the tattoo is bleeding. He didn't go easy on me. It reads "9003."

I hold my breath, trying to process this. So, in this sex trafficking ring, they number the girls. I'm number 9,003? My stomach begins churning, and I have to put my head between my legs. How long have they been doing this? And getting away with it? Pure horror sweeps over my body, and I feel completely ill. They've been able to do this to over nine thousand women.

Chills rack over my body as a memory resurfaces, the woman in the bathroom of the club's secret basement who looked like a dominatrix. I couldn't make out her tattoo, but it's in the same placement as mine, and now I realize it was numbers, too. I squeeze my eyes shut. Those women were sex slaves as well... there against their will... to be used.

The man turns to his toolbox, which contains who knows what else. Slowly, he pulls out and places giant syringes on top. What the hell? Opening another drawer, he places the smallest silver contraptions I've seen next to them. They begin to blink red. He retrieves a remote and a small laptop, plugging in numbers.

One by one, he injects every girl in the neck with the tiny device. Screaming in pain and clutching their necks, they cry harder. It's my turn, and I'm so frozen to the bone in fear that I let my mind drift somewhere else.

After the injection, I do the same, holding my neck as some blood seeps out, trying to wrap my mind around what just happened. Then it dawns on me, and my eyes widen. It's a tracking device.

The van begins jostling around, and I can feel we are on a dirt road. More sunlight seeps into the van, and after about ten minutes, it starts to decelerate, coming to a complete stop.

My heart is in my throat. Full-blown panic. This is it. Our final destination where we find out what is about to happen to us. How we disappear like Archer said to me. I shiver all over.

After a minute, the van turns off, and the back doors of the van swing open, and there are about five men, all dressed in black, waiting for us.

Our tattoo artist jumps out first and vanishes from sight with his equipment. He couldn't get out of the van fast enough. He didn't look at any of us, just scurried away like the rat he is.

One of the drivers that had transported us commands, "I will hand you a girl. Frankie and Jon, you'll have two. Bring them inside to the green room."

We are roughly pulled out of the van by our upper arms. I actually trip while being manhandled, and the man who is in charge of me lets me go down, falling on my face in the dirt. I land hard on one of my knees and can feel the scrapes and stinging start. Stunned by the sudden pain, I just lay there, trying to get my mind to speed up on what to do next. I lift my head up somewhat and try to take in my surroundings.

He throatily laughs at my predicament. I can tell he's a smoker because his voice is raspy. He kicks me in the ribs and shouts, "Get the fuck up!"

I groan from the pain on my side and rollover. The wind is knocked out of me, so as I struggle to breathe, he wastes no time and kicks me again. "You dumb bitch. I said get up!" he yells.

One of the other men, who must be above his pay grade, roughly pushes him and yells, "Don't fuck up the property."

He frustratingly grunts and yanks me up by the collar of my shirt. I'm sucking in air and sweating profusely from the pain on my side. It must be the adrenaline that has me on high alert because I know I should be passed out right now with low to no energy. We start walking—more like being dragged—toward this two-story building. It looks exactly like an old warehouse, and there is nothing else out here. I look around in every direction and see no trees or anything else, probably for miles. There are just some gravel roads that look frequently used surrounding the place. The grass that is there is dead and unattended to.

Even if I'm able to escape, it looks like I won't be able to find help for a while. Knots begin to form in my stomach as the hope of getting out of here dwindles. It's been a while since I've eaten anything, and my guess is it will be a while before we're fed. They probably want to keep us weak throughout this process, so there is less chance of us fighting back, and if we do, we won't have the energy to make a significant impact.

I try to commit everything I've seen to memory, even though it's hard when your stomach is empty and you're mentally, emotionally, and physically drained. I mentally catalog the names I've heard, the details, and the windows that I can see on the outside of the building. This is the only thing that is keeping me remotely sane so I don't spiral or zone out like the rest of the girls.

As we approach the building from a side entrance, a guy in front of us holding on to one of the girls uses his finger and presses down on a keypad. He types in what looks like a four-digit code, and the sliding glass door slides back like a pocket door. While walking into the building, I notice two heavily armed guards. They both appear to be well-equipped, as if they are in the military, wearing bulletproof vests, boots, headsets, and multiple weapons strapped to their bodies.

The security in this place looks insane and unnecessary. There are cameras in every corner, as well as a body scanner. The amount of money it must take to run this place, let alone have been doing it this long undetected, is something I can't wrap my mind around.

We immediately walk through the body scanner, and I'm quickly cleared. Then, we make a left turn and walk down a hallway. It smells and feels like a hospital hallway. Disinfectant floods my nose, and I can't help but scrunch it; it's so overpowering to my senses. Whoever owns this place must like the color white; the floors and walls are all the same color, and it goes on for what looks to be a few football fields in length. The floors remind me of the ones you see at a hospital: the shiny white, with tiny blue and red dots scattered throughout. Perhaps it's fear that's making me imagine things, but this place is definitely larger than a typical warehouse.

After passing about three doors with small, clouded windows featuring small black numbers on top, we finally approach another keypad, and again, the man ahead of me types in a four-digit code. I try to make out what it is, but he does it so fast it is hard to keep up.

Inside the room, an armed guard is stationed to the right, and in the center of the room are approximately twenty cots, each equipped with a simple white pillow and a brown blanket. The cots sit about six inches off the ground. It looks like some kind of prison. The room is white and also smells like disinfectant.

When all of the women that were in the van enter the room, the door slams shut automatically, and a lock clicks loudly. I shudder at the thought that we are locked in here and don't know what is going to happen next.

I recognize the driver, who seems to be in charge, as he throws what appears to be light blue and white hospital gowns on top of one of the cots and beside them, a black empty duffel bag.

"Strip. Everything you are wearing, even hair ties and any jewelry that may have been missed in the bag, and put on one of the hospital gowns." He practically yells at us wickedly.

My eyes bug out of my head, questioning if he's serious right now.

He pulls out a handgun and cocks it. "You have 3 minutes."

Tripping over each other, we basically throw off the T-shirts that were put on us at the fraternity house. Some of the women have piercings or hair ties that were missed, so they remove them with an insane amount of speed. None of us has shoes.

All of the men are gawking at us, not giving us any privacy; some even lick their lips, eyeing us deviously. There is no time to be embarrassed, though. I don't want to find out what happens after three minutes, and apparently, the other women don't want to either. The driver seems like a 'gives zero fucks' kind of guy.

As I yank off my T-shirt and fumble with the hospital gown, trying to secure the ties, he walks right up to me and smells my hair while dragging the gun across my temple.

"I wonder what you taste like between those sexy legs of yours," he growls. "Spread your legs." He points the gun right at the side of my head.

I freeze, shaking all over, knowing I have to do this. It must be some kind of scare tactic to get us all to fall in line. Well, it's working because I'm scared shitless about what is going to happen next.

All of the women change silently, everyone on full alert about what is happening. Their eyes are bulging to the point where they look like they might fall out of their heads.

Taking a huge gulp, I look him in his eyes, grinding my teeth with anger written all over my face, and spread my legs. He takes two of his fingers and spreads my pussy lips and pinches my clit.

I yelp. "Don't fucking move," he growls at me. I whimper, and silent tears form in my eyes. He shoves two fingers into me roughly and curls them just right, hitting my G-spot. Fighting with myself, I can't help but whimper again, and a moan slips out that I try to bite back. He gets my pussy wet and shoves another finger in, fucking my pussy with his fingers without easing up. Then he takes his fingers out and shoves them in his mouth, moaning while he licks every last drop. My legs are shaking at the intrusion, and I'm shivering all over.

"Your fear is delicious," he moans. I go back to tying my hospital gown, and he yanks my hands away. "Not yet, you slut." I'm shaking so badly at this point, having no idea what he is about to do to me. He stands right in front of me, breathes me in again, and twists me so my back is hitting his chest. He forcefully bends me forward with my back completely exposed and the hospital gown barely covering me up in the front. He takes his gun and trails it slowly down my spine, stopping it right at the beginning of my ass. Everyone is watching in silence at this point. He takes his other hand and slides his fingers through my wet slit, coating them, and then shoves two fingers into my tight hole, thrusting in and out. I scream and writhe in pain. He whispers in my ear, "Open up, princess," and he starts working his fingers while moaning softly in my ear. I am paralyzed by fear and completely embarrassed while the women watching turn pale and divert their gaze to the floor, tears coating their faces. He quickly unzips his pants, pulls out his enlarged cock, and yells, "This is what happens when sluts don't listen!"

"No, no, please, no!" I start yelling, trying to get out of his grip.

"Frankie and Sam, hold her arms down!" he yells.

"Not a problem, Rio," the one I think is Sam says, delighted by the show.

As both come forward with huge smiles on their faces, they grab my arms, and one of them shoves my head to the tiled floor. He pulls my hips up, spits on his cock, and pushes it into my ass with one swift thrust.

I scream out and begin crying, trying to squirm away; the pain, the burn—it is unbearable. He holds on to my hips, gripping them so tightly I know there will be bruises there. I hear him growling as his length seems to stiffen inside of me, more turned on by my tears spilling over and fighting it.

He reaches through my legs with the gun and moves it back and forth so it slides up and down my clit, and I cry out. The quiet warning is clear as day: stay still, and you get to keep breathing. I swallow the lump forming in my throat, holding the vomit that threatens to come out, pleading with my mind to go elsewhere so I can block this out. The feeling of degradation and humiliation floods my body.

I feel a warm liquid run down between my thighs. He must see it, too, because I feel his cock jerk inside me excitedly at the idea of my body betraying me.

He starts thrusting harder, and I pray he is about to come and put an end to this agony.

Minutes later, he stops thrusting and moans as he spills in my ass. "Take. Every. Last. Drop. Princess," he says, thrusting one final time.

As he pulls out agonizingly slow, he moves to stand beside me, places his boot on my side, and kicks me over. The other guards must have released me at some point, and now I'm on my back, crying and sweating while he leaks out of me. I am completely deflated, knowing my mind is more bruised than my body ever will be, and I want to sink into the floor.

Stumbling to my feet, my eyes never leaving the floor, I straighten my hospital gown. As I'm tying the strings on the back, Rio says, "The first lesson of the day: don't hesitate to follow orders." He winks at me as he licks the tips of his fingers.

Bile starts forming in the back of my throat, and I have to force my eyes toward the ceiling in order to swallow it down.

Frantically, I look over when my senses come back to me, and I hear noises. I notice a guy they were calling Zane shoving his cock down another one of the girl's throats while holding her nose. She is slobbering everywhere with tears streaming down her cheeks while he's holding onto her hair with one hand to control her. Her face is turning a different shade of color due to her not being able to breathe.

He releases her nose, and she inhales deeply just as he finishes down her throat. Then, he takes his boot and kicks her right in the chest, knocking her backwards like she is nothing. She cowers and crawls toward the rest of the girls, who are standing petrified.

"For today's agenda, we are going to escort you to the shaving room where you will be paired with a nurse, and they will remove all of the hair from your body except the hair on your head. You will also get a piercing, which is up to our discretion and has already been assigned to you on your chart."

Many of the women gasp and cover their mouths. I feel like squirming out of my skin, knowing someone else is going to see very intimate parts of me again. They are slowly removing any modesty or privacy we felt like we had and are breaking us down in every way possible. Puzzle pieces are beginning to form in my mind, one of them being that we are like prized show horses being prepared for someone.

"Next up, we are going to head to the showers where you will get to wash yourself for approximately 5 minutes, no more, no less. Then, we are going to visit the good old doc," Rio says, grinning mischievously.

"If you don't obey and cause a problem of any kind, Sam and Frankie here are going to strip you, then beat the shit out of you and take you to the punishment room, where they will hogtie you and take all of your holes at once. They will avoid your face since those are the money makers, and you need your legs and arms, but I've advised them to break your ribs." He chuckles to himself as if it's an inside joke.

He speed-walks over and stands in front of me, and I can feel his breath as he looks down on me.

He takes his gun and places the tip of it under my chin, tilting my head up, and purrs, "Princess, say 'yes, sir' if you understand."

Reluctantly, with my nose flaring in disgust, I angrily spit out, "Yes, sir." I hear the other women robotically say it as well. Some of them have even put their heads down, focusing on the floor or their feet, submitting completely to the idea that this is their fate and the fear of being subjected to the punishment room.

"Good, I'm glad we have an understanding," he growls, and the other men snicker amongst themselves.

"Line up in front of me. Frankie and Sam, you flank the sides, and Zane, you get the back; let's go!" Rio yells, pointing his gun in those directions.

Of course, I am in the front, limping from the pain. I start to follow him through a door in the back of the room, which again has a keypad. He types in the four-digit code with ease, and it opens. I look up, and over the door is a camera.

We are led through another hallway, where we take a left and walk for quite a while until we come to a door on our right, where he stops and punches in the code.

Instantly, I see about twenty patient beds with stirrups and arm cuffs, and sitting in front of them on chairs are women in scrubs and masks. Beside them are small tables with tools scattered on top, some of which I've seen in my gynecologist's office, but the others look like something out of a horror movie.

The armed guard for this room comes up and claps Rio on the back. "Hey, Rio, rough group today?" His eyes darken, hoping for anyone still fighting.

Rio smirks back and responds, "Not too bad, man; I got to at least taste some of the merchandise this time." He looks back and stares right at me.

Holding back a gag, I look elsewhere in disbelief.

Each woman in scrubs comes over, grabs our wrists, and leads us back to their assigned station.

The woman who grabbed me has short blonde hair and blue eyes that come off devoid of any emotion, and she whispers, "Lay back on the bed, legs in the stirrups, and lift your gown."

The men have formed a half circle, talking to each other and eyeing us to ensure we aren't causing any trouble.

As sneakily as possible, trying not to get caught, I glance at the chart beside her, trying to read anything that is on it. There are bullet points and then an outline of a naked human's body. This one has small red x's on both my nipples.

That couldn't be piercings. What the fuck? I throw my head back on the bed and squeeze my eyes shut in anger.

The nurse jostles me, hands me two pills, and whispers, "Take these. It will help with the pain." I take them immediately, dry with no water.

She turns on the wax machine next to her, and as it heats up, she organizes the tools, getting them ready.

"Lift your arms over your head and don't move, or else I'm

going to have to cuff them," she whispers. For once, I don't resist, and I do exactly what I'm told.

Placing a dollop of hot wax on both of my armpits, she waves her arm in the air above them, willing them to dry for a minute. After both seem dry enough for her, she sets down the paper on top and, with plenty of practice, pulls it as I bite my lip, holding in the yelp of pain from the stinging. Working her way down my body, she waxes my arms, torso, and legs, pausing when she reaches what is between my legs. Double-checking the chart, she places the wax on my bikini line and rips off the paper smoothly. This time, I whisper-shout "AH" loudly.

Zane walks over with a deadly expression and tells me, "Shut your mouth, or I'll put something in it," as he grabs his crotch, taunting me with it.

I turn my head away from him as a mix of horror and disgust washes over my face.

My nurse then reaches for the clippers and starts trimming the hair in between my legs. I glance at the chart again, and there is a triangle on my vaginal area.

The buyers must like a little hair in between our legs, or maybe it's just me.

She begins putting antiseptic on a cloth, and I know what's coming next. I look up at the ceiling with silent tears flowing down my face, knowing I have absolutely no control over my body. They own me. They are going to put holes in my body as they would an animal.

She gets her piercing gun. This is it. She does my right nipple first, and I bite down on my tongue from the sensitivity and pain, and then she quickly does my left nipple. Biting my tongue harder, I taste that familiar coppery taste in my mouth. I look down. Two black barbels.

How unique.

"Okay, great, number 9003 is all set," she shouts, and then throws off her gloves, standing up and tossing them into a trash can.

One of the men rushes over to me and grabs my arm roughly, practically pulling my arm from my shoulder blade.

"How could you do this?" I barely say above a whisper, making eye contact with the woman. She looks at me with sorrow in her eyes. "Some people are enslaved in different ways," she whispers back to me and quickly looks away.

I notice the other girls getting piercings. Some of them are getting them in their tongue, clitoris, outer labia where the metal chain connects, their inner labia, and more nipple piercings. All of them, I realize, are for sexual pleasure.

I can barely stand to watch as they squirm and whimper with pain and, above all, turn red with humiliation.

Rio has his rifle in the front of his torso now, eager to display sternness directed at us.

"Form a line when you are finished; it's time for you to meet the good ol' doctor now." He chuckles.

After everyone is done, we line up, and they open the door with another code. We shuffle our feet with our heads down to another room, where we are made to wait outside.

"One at a time," he says, gesturing us in.

Like always, it seems to be a pattern. I'm first again, and I walk into the most sterile room I've seen, with lights on the ceiling that you would typically see in a dentist's office so the doctor can adjust them to their liking.

One of the evilest-looking men I've ever seen sits on a stool. He is smirking, and his eyes look like dark pits.

"Get on the table with your legs spread as far as they can go," he commands, snapping his gloves on.

I hop up on the table and hesitate for a second about putting my legs in another stirrup. What the fuck is this guy going to do to me? While I'm adjusting myself, completely humiliated, he goes and locks the door.

"You're a pretty little thing, aren't you?" he sneers.

Spread eagle on the table, I begin sweating and taking deep breaths. I feel as though I may pass out.

Beside the table, he has an array of tools that look medieval.

"Untie your gown," he commands, and I shiver and do as I'm told.

He examines my nipple piercings. "Perfect, she did a fabulous job," he purrs. He tweaks one of them, and I whimper and try to squirm backwards, which is impossible since I am lying back in a chair.

He snaps his gloves again, making sure they are secure; I jump at the sound. I'm shivering all over now, and he puts his hands on the inside of my thigh, inches away from in between my legs.

"Are you on birth control?" he asks

"I have an IUD," I tell him shakily.

He nods and looks over at the tray beside us, picking up a speculum. He inserts it into my vaginal opening, holding it open. Then he grabs the forceps and slowly tugs on the IUD strings, pulling it out. It's uncomfortable but not horrible. My back arches, and then it is out, followed by the speculum.

Grabbing some antiseptic pads, he rubs them over my upper arm. Swiftly, I see him snatch a pre-filled needle.

"What's that?" I ask.

"Birth control. You can never be too safe in a place like this." He looks me over, leering at my body.

The injection enters my body, and he rolls his stool back in front of my spread legs, his head inches from me. I can feel his hot breath.

"What a beautiful clit you have. The hood is perfectly symmetric," he whispers.

His finger brushes the outside of my pussy and flicks my clit. Then, he begins gently rubbing it, moaning his approval.

"Give me your wrists," he demands. I stall temporarily, wondering what he is going to do. Then, I think that anything is better than back out there with Rio preying on me. I put them in front of me, and he reaches over and locks them at my sides with padded cuffs.

"I want to see that gorgeous clit swell up and see your face as you come undone," he breathily says.

Oh fuck, be careful what you wish for.

I clench my thighs. This should feel wrong, but by his sensual touches, I can tell he knows exactly what he is doing.

He begins by gently stroking the insides of my thighs and then smacks them hard, making me moan. He shoves his nose right in my clit and inhales deeply.

"You smell divine, and I bet you taste even better."

I am overcome with shock, and I just stay silent because I have no idea what this man is going to do to me. I'm going to collapse at any moment, my body not ready to take anymore.

He takes his thumb and pointer finger and pinches my clit a little roughly, and I shriek, squeezing my eyes shut. Then, he begins gently massaging it. Fuck, this man knows his way around a vagina. I try to fight it because I know this is so wrong.

He rubs my little nub faster and faster. I'm arching my back at this point, overcome by the sensation. He stops right before I'm about to combust, and I flop down disappointed. Then he begins probing me with his tongue in and out of my hole.

"Fuck," I squeal, overcome with pure bliss, trying adamantly to fuck his face, chasing that high.

He goes back to interchangeably rubbing my clit sideways and tongue fucking me. That feeling of euphoria sweeps over me, and the tingles begin in my upper back and melt down my body.

I scream out as my orgasm hits, and he watches with delight as my pussy contracts and spasms. I squirt all over this man's face, and he looks thrilled, licking it all up.

"If you weren't going up for auction, I'd keep you chained in my basement all to myself," he states. "Your vaginal health seems to be intact. I'll just take some blood samples and do a vaginal swab, and you are good to go."

My forehead bunches up in confusion. Auction? My heart races, and my face turns pale; they are grooming us to sell us?!

He ties the rubber band around my arm, sticks the needle in, and fills a couple of vials with blood. Then, he uses that tool to open my vagina and swabs it, putting that in a test tube as well. He marks them with a pen and tosses them in a basket behind me.

My face drops to complete horror as I try to process what just happened and why I let this man even touch me.

I have to convince myself that they are toying with me. Finding some sort of pleasure to be able to escape for even a little bit of time in this house of horrors is how I'm going to be able to cope with this.

He gets up, unlocks the door, and yells, "Next!"

He pulls me out of the cuffs and shoves me into the hands of one of the guards who comes in through another door. I don't even notice who since I am so dazed from that incredible orgasm. I still feel the guilt gnawing at me from enjoying it.

I wait outside the room against the wall as, one by one, the girls filter out with the guards walking in front of us, holding their guns in front of them, silently pleading for us to give them trouble.

We are then shuffled like cattle into this gray cement room with multiple shower heads. "You have 5 minutes to wash up, starting now." Not caring which guard said it, lost in my own anxiety, my feet just lead me under a showerhead, and most of us, including me, have to share one. I feel almost immune to my nudeness in front of everyone.

Ice-cold water hits me as I hop backward, but I don't care as long as I can get the grime and stickiness off of me. There is shampoo and conditioner, so I wash my hair, not knowing when our next chance to shower might come. I carefully wash my body, avoiding my new piercings, as they are sore and inflamed. After finishing, I find the towel basket and grab one, drying off and slipping my gown back on. There are holes in the ground to relieve ourselves, so I do; after gently wiping and seeing all of the blood, I throw it in, unable to look at it any longer. After washing my hands, one of the guards points for me to go outside the room and wait on the wall like before.

After all the women finish up, we are led to a set of stairs and retreat down them for about three floors. All I can do is stagger in whatever direction we're being led to. We stop at another room, and this one has a thick metal door with the smallest window at the top. You would have to be at least six feet tall to look in. They unlock it, and one of them says, "Get the fuck in there."

I look down while I slowly walk in, drenched in shame. To my complete surprise, there are bunk beds, some already filled with women. They each contain a pillow and a blanket, if you can even call them that. They seem so worn down. Same as before.

I pick a bunk and lay down immediately, closing my eyes. Tears start pouring down, and eventually, the blackness takes over.

CHAPTER TWENTY-SEVEN

TYLER

It's Tuesday night, and I still haven't heard from Cassidy. Where the fuck is she? It's like she completely ghosted me after mind-blowing sex and a nice time together. I've never been ghosted before, and I would be lying if it wasn't a total hit to my ego. Anyway, I need to try to catch up with her tomorrow since our fraternity has a chapter meeting tonight, and that is one of the things that is absolutely mandatory. You can't miss it, no matter what.

My day pretty much goes like every other day. I go to the gym, classes, and then return to the fraternity house to play video games with the guys, killing time before chapter meetings. I head to our cafeteria and grab a bite to eat so I'm not starving most of the time since the meeting can go until midnight. There is always a lot to cover, including events, voting on new rules, or just some guy who wants his fifteen minutes of fame and drones on for an hour or so.

One of the rules for attending chapter meetings is to dress professionally. So, I put on some slacks and loafers, paired with a polo shirt, and throw on a blazer with my pin on the outside. I make my way down to the basement where the meeting is held, which is the same place as initiation. There is always one of the older brothers outside of the door. You must perform our secret handshake to be let in and recite the password that only initiated brothers know.

After waiting in line, it's my turn to perform the handshake and say the password, and only then does he open the door for me. Newer initiated brothers sit in the back while the older brothers sit in the front. There is a panel at the very front on a stage facing us. They hold high positions in the fraternity and deliver any kind of news related to events, finances, and well-being as a fraternity. I grab a seat in the back, ready for a long night, and lean back in my seat, trying to get comfortable. I spot Archer right away, already in the middle of the panel, scanning over the brothers. One of the other panel members whispers to him, and he nods his head, gazing intently at him. Behind the panel is a huge projector, so if one of the brothers on the panel has something he wants to say, he can present it. This is where some of the homemade porn is shown. I swear this is the kind of stuff that gets you ready for corporate America; it is so formal.

About thirty or so minutes later, Archer hits the gavel, which signals that chapter is starting. We start with mediocre things, what events we are supposed to be at, which sororities we need to hang out with more and attend their events, and then finally, it is Archer's turn to speak. The president is always the first one to present after the miscellaneous information, followed by the other cabinet members. One of the older brothers, who is still standing by the door, locks it and puts himself in front of it.

The newer brothers sit up straighter, like me, looking around at what is happening. I have this uneasy feeling in my gut.

"As you are all initiated, we need to go over some very serious things that are to remain in the brotherhood. If you repeat anything that is said tonight, you will be killed, including the person you told, and then we will go after the people closest to you, including your family and closest friends. We have people who will make it look like an accident and clean up the mess. We have our claws in law enforcement, the medical field, and any type of lawyer you can think of," he states, looking around the room, daring us to make eye contact or make any sudden movement for the door.

My eyes have his complete attention, and a shiver runs through my body. You could hear a pin drop with how silent it is. What the hell could he be talking about, and why would my dad encourage me to join this? He sure as hell knows about the underground situation they have going on here and obviously have been involved in for quite a while.

"The business that helps finance this fraternity and gives us all the luxuries we have is human trafficking, specifically women, as they bring in the most money. We have a type, and we hunt them down. They undergo an extensive process before an auction ensues, and they are sold to their new masters. Every brother here is involved in this process. There are teams that find the girls, prepare them for transport to our remote warehouse, orchestrate the auction, and get in contact with potential buyers. The benefit for you is that when you graduate, you will be able to be a buyer in these auctions and have a little pet for yourself." He smirks. "If that's what you want."

I try to keep my poker face on, but my mind is whirling with all kinds of thoughts. How long have they been doing this? How are they getting away with this? This is barbaric. Selling humans and taking away their lives as they know them? What are we? Free labor with the benefit of being a willing participant in these human auctions? No thanks. Sweat beads on my forehead, signaling vomit is approaching. Quickly, I swallow it down, scared of the repercussions.

"On the screen, I have put you in teams, and there will be no further discussion. You will do as you're told, whether you like it or not, no questions asked. As for the newer brothers, you will get your additional brand tonight, signifying you are 100% involved and committed to this."

Archer clicks a button on the remote, and on the projector, groups with names underneath them pop up.

I frantically search for my name. When my eyes find it, I see that my name is with the prep group. Awesome. So, I have to aid in stripping them of their lives and looks, treating them like dogs by putting them in cages, readying them for the hell they are about to endure for the rest of their lives at the hands of my older fraternity brothers.

Who wants to be part of this? Sex slaves? Human trafficking? How could it not make you sick? The richest and most successful people obviously get bored and think of doing these kinds of things simply because they can.

The next screen shows the brand that will be placed on our chest, right on our pectoral. It is a triangle with a candle in the middle. Wow, they want to make sure we know we are part of this, so if we open our mouths, the authorities will know we obviously played some type of part in this, but knowing what I know now, there are some seriously powerful fraternity brothers out in this world, and there is no doubt that their reach is great. It wouldn't surprise me if they have the best lawyers on deck and brothers directly in law enforcement, just down the street.

Holy shit. This is going to hurt, and there's nothing I can do about it. I've seen my dad's, but he just passed it off as something stupid he did in college when he was drunk. Not a fucking brand seared into your skin, signifying your involvement in this kind of evil.

"Line up new initiates; older brothers, you are dismissed," Archer announces as he bangs his gavel down, indicating chapter is now over.

I get in line, preparing for this to hurt like hell, feeling like my hands are completely tied. The brothers in front of me scream, and one passes out. Two older brothers have to hold us while we get it done. They don't want anyone trying to run and back out or fall to the ground.

When it is my turn, I turn my chin because I don't want to look. As the brand is seared into my skin, the smell of burning flesh is nauseating, but I take some deep breaths and stand up after it's over, feeling a little lightheaded. It is quickly covered with a bandage and medical tape, and I'm dismissed to go back to my room.

I run up to my room, shut and lock the door, and collapse against it, panic rising to the surface as I scan my surroundings, not trusting this place any longer.

What the hell have I gotten myself into? And how the hell am I going to just go along with something like this? It's barbaric.

CHAPTER TWENTY-EIGHT

CASSIDY

When I wake up, there is no lighting. It's completely pitch black. I hear some of the girls crying or rustling around, unable to sleep as fear takes over their minds. I barely open my eyes, wanting to forget the situation I'm in, which is fucked. Completely and utterly fucked.

I hear the light footsteps of someone going up and down the rows of bunks. My stomach is in knots. Whoever it is, he's obviously looking for someone, and it can't be for anything good this late at night when everyone is supposed to be asleep.

He's down my row now. He's wearing a black hoodie, black jeans, and combat boots. He quietly stops at my bunk. "There you are, princess. You didn't think I wouldn't fulfill my promise, did you?"

It's Rio. Of course it is.

"Fuck you," I grit out. He reaches out and pinches my nipple. I push backward in pain, but I can't go far because my back hits the concrete wall.

"Don't touch me," I angrily whisper and try kicking him with my feet.

"Oh, I don't plan on touching you. I plan on making you shut up with that pretty little mouth of yours," he whispers as his smile widens.

He tightly claws at my ankles and pulls me toward him, where my face is directly at his crotch. He unbuckles his pants, pulls down his zipper, and pulls his already hard dick out.

I turn my head to the side, not wanting to do this. Rio punches me so hard that my head jerks to the other side, and my hair is flipped into my face. I lose consciousness for a moment as my world spins.

"You're going to deep throat my cock like it's the most decadent dessert you've ever had because if you don't, I'll send in the next guard and then the next, and they all have their own favorite holes they enjoy abusing. Then, you're going to swallow every last drop. Don't even think about using those teeth, or you won't have any left," he snarls.

"You're a fucking prick," I seethe, and I spit in his face.

He smiles and wipes it off. "You're right, princess," he whispers in my ear, stroking it with his tongue.

Reaching for his dick, I wrap my hand around it and begin stroking it. It's bigger than a normal-sized dick and incredibly veiny. "Don't make me wait all day; open up, princess."

I open and take him in my mouth, my jaw already aching from the strain. He grabs my hair with one of his hands and forcefully shoves his dick in my mouth until it hits the back of my throat.

I'm gagging and can't move. He begins thrusting painfully, not letting up while tears stream down my face, accompanied by drool.

Go somewhere else, Cassidy. Close your eyes and think of Tyler, Blair, or anything remotely happy to remove yourself from this assault.

"This mouth of yours is one of the best I've had; it's so warm and tight." He's groaning, thrusting deeper into the back of my throat, not even caring that I'm gasping for air. My hands immediately push against his thighs as I try to get any air I can.

He uses my hair to control my head. All I am to him is a hole to stick his cock in and use.

Then he pinches my nose, cutting off what little air I had, and my throat expands. He shoves his cock in further. Resisting is useless; he overpowers me easily, especially with my depleted energy levels.

Right when I feel as though I'm about to pass out, he finishes down my throat, jerking his cock in my mouth and giving me every last drop.

Rio looks at me and wipes my bottom lip with his tongue. "You're in the lion's den now, princess," he says with a wicked gleam in his eyes.

"Fuck you, you piece of shit." I practically snarl at him.

He backhands me, and I fall down onto the bed, tears welling up in my eyes.

"Go to bed, you dirty slut," he whispers. "Next time, I'm going to take a different hole and break you down piece by piece."

I glare at him, shivering, knowing I am already cracking, but I refuse to break, and if I do, I won't show that weakness. That is all I have left in this world that I have been unwillingly thrown into.

CHAPTER TWENTY-NINE

CASSIDY

One of the guards uses a baton and holds it outward, hitting all of the metal bed frames as an alarm clock for us. Staggering awake at the loud, dull sound, I remember where I am, and fear overrides my body. I'm guessing it has to be morning because there are no windows in this shithole.

"Rise and shine, whores; it's auction day, but first, we have to make you presentable," Sam yells. "So we can get the most amount of money for you." He grins deviously, probably thinking about the cash flow that is about to come in, lining his pockets with plenty, I'm sure.

We line up without a fight or a word, knowing what is expected of us and how the process works. We are then led down a hallway and into a room that resembles a beauty salon. I am puzzled by what a nice area this is. They weren't kidding when they said they wanted to get the most amount of money for us. I feel queasy knowing that this is for a master we are going to be expected to serve in any way, relinquishing our body over, including whatever is left of our soul, too.

My thoughts wander to what kind of master will buy me. Will he be kind or cruel? I shake my head. *Don't go there, Cassidy.* I can't think about it, or I'll shrink into myself and give up, completely surrendering to this predicament I've been forced into.

Much like before, there is a woman at each station, wearing a nurse's uniform with a face mask, ready to do our hair, makeup, and nails.

I get pushed into a chair and try to whisper to her to find out what is next, but I quickly learn that she doesn't speak English.

She begins messing around with my hair, making 'tsking' sounds as she goes. She gets the hair foils out and starts putting highlights in my hair. While my hair is sitting, she begins filing and buffing my fingernails and toes. She picks out a light pink for the color. Finally, my hair is ready to be washed, so we head back to the hair washing station, which looks exactly like one you would see at a real salon. There, she not so gently shampoos and conditions my hair using cold water.

Can they not afford hot water in this place? It doesn't seem like they are hurting for money with how much inventory they sell. They put a lot of that money into security, and I wonder if they pay these women. My mind tells me they are as trapped as we are. A shudder runs through my body thinking about being trapped in this place with Rio and the abuse I would probably endure daily if I had to stay. Whatever is out there, whatever master buys me, it has to be better than that guy and what I've gone through here. But I know better than to hope. These men buying us obviously view us as property and will treat us as such.

We head back to her station after she washes my hair and pats it dry. Next, she begins to do my makeup, very dramatically, I might add. She gives me cat eyes with neutral eyeshadow, heavy on the browns to match my hair, making my eyes pop, and tops it off with a very red lip to give my lips the plumpness they really don't need. She layers on the foundation and even inspects the rest of my body, covering up the bruises I've gotten here. Knowing what it has done to me mentally will forever be worse than the physical harm I have endured.

Next, she starts blow-drying my hair with a round brush, giving me a full blowout, and to be honest, I look like a total bombshell, which I know is exactly what they want. I saw the names of the makeup brands, and they don't skimp on that either. They use the best of the best, and I'm sure it pays off like they want it to. Obviously, they have to pay more for a better foundation, as I'm sure I'm not the only one who has to have bruises covered up all over their body.

She leaves for a minute and returns with a completely sheer, white, lingerie-like dress that falls to the mid-thigh. There are no sleeves; instead, there are spaghetti straps with a built-in, see-through push-up bra. It looks like something you would get from Victoria's Secret and wear on your wedding night. It leaves nothing to the imagination. She also hands me the tiniest crotchless white thong I have ever seen. Honestly, there's no point in even wearing it; it looks like floss.

She points to the changing curtain and hands me a pair of acrylic high-heeled shoes that are about 5 inches tall. I put everything on quickly, embarrassed to even look in the mirror, and flush as I come out. I look around the salon, and the other girls are wearing the same thing, with different styles of lingerie in the same sheer material.

Two guards come into the room and smack their hands together. "Alright, it's showtime; let's make some money." They both throw their heads back and laugh like it's one of the most hilarious things they have ever said.

I walk shakily while thinking, *Who the fuck is going to buy me?*

Will it be an old fat man? Will it be a man who beats me consistently? Will it be a man who is into kinky shit and makes me walk around with things in my ass and pussy all day?

I vomit in the nearest trash bucket, and thankfully, no one sees me. I wipe the corner of my mouth, trying not to smear the red lipstick with the back of my hand.

"When does the auction begin?" I ask Zane.

"You're lucky I'm in a good mood tonight, or I'd punch you in your stomach for even speaking to me," he growls, making direct eye contact with me menacingly.

"It starts in one hour."

"Time to go to the holding room, ladies," he yells out, snapping his fingers at us.

We all get in line as we are headed to a hell we won't be able to break out of; there's no escaping this, and my heart beats frantically in my chest. Maybe there will be a small window of escape once I get out of this warehouse; my heart sinks as I think about what I will have to go through before a chance like that opens up.

In the blacked-out room, there are folded plastic chairs, and we each take a seat. There is so much anxiety and nervousness in the room that we can't even speak to each other, let alone look at each other, so we just stare straight ahead or at the floor, waiting for the inevitable, trying to check out mentally before the horrors of tonight happen.

Time passes slowly, and I begin to shake my knee, which soon turns into a shaking of my entire body. It's cold in here, and with what I'm wearing, it definitely doesn't help in the warmth department.

We can hear people entering on the other side of the curtain, and it sounds like a large group as I hear conversations and doors being shut, with sounds like buttons being pushed.

"Please go into your designated room and have a seat so we can begin the auction promptly," someone states robotically over a speaker.

The anxiety has taken over, and my hands are sweating profusely. If my stomach weren't empty, I'd be spilling it all over this floor.

The sounds die down, and I hear a microphone connect. A

voice says over the speaker, "We have a lovely assortment of merchandise for you gentlemen tonight."

"Just for the first-timers or to reiterate the rules if it's been a while since you have joined us," he says, chuckling to himself, "you have an array of buttons in front of you. The most important one is the green one, which will place the bid for you. Remember, we go in increments of ten thousand. Every one of these girls starts out at one million dollars. You are not allowed to leave your encasement until the auction has ended and the girls have been placed in a separate room. You will be able to pick up your purchase in one week. In that one week, we will conduct our training program, and you will continue the training when you come to collect your property."

"Let's begin." He claps his hands excitedly

A red-headed girl across from me is pulled and dragged toward the curtain, and all I hear is, "Starting the bid at one million dollars, two million, three million. Sold."

Minutes that feel like hours tick by, and it's my turn as I am pulled toward the curtain. Immediately, I shield my eyes from the bright spotlights on me. A man is holding onto my arm, guiding me across this acrylic-looking stage.

"We have a rare treat for you tonight, gentlemen. This one just so happens to be a sorority sister plucked from UM. She's a freshman, and you know what that means—a tight pussy with an even tighter body."

My eyes adjust to the lighting, and I see little rooms with green lights on the outside of them. I can't see inside them, though, because they are tinted. They are stacked like a stadium, and there have to be over 100 of them.

The announcer says, "Let's give the buyers a little taste of this special purchase." The guard holding me, who is wearing a mask to hide his identity, pulls me to the side of him and turns me around so my backside is facing the buyers. He steps around and kicks my legs open wide, backing up and pushing my head down so everything is on display, hence the crotchless panties. In a stealth-like movement, he spreads me open with his fingers and dips one inside.

After one finger is in, he shoves another finger in my ass while standing on the side of me.

"As you can see with your own eyes, each hole is intact and tight," the announcer says giddily.

I black out what the announcer says next and tune in to the last part of it: "5 million. Wow, 10 million, gentlemen. 15 million. Sold."

My mouth gapes open, and I shake my head. Is that how much they think a human life is worth?

Suddenly, I am pushed forward toward a catwalk off the stage. I try not to trip over myself, and I don't want to look down to see how high up we are. *Just put one foot in front of the other, Cassidy; keep moving forward.* I try to hold my chin high while I walk to the other side of the stage, where I see multiple bodyguards waiting there to collect me.

Two of them grab my arms and thrust me into a white room, and the door is immediately locked. I see the other girls in the room sitting on the floor with their heads down, and I am pushed down into a kneeling position.

Rio is at the head of the room, and he shouts, "Now, your training begins to become a true slave to your master."

"Every time you enter a room, you will look down while walking and immediately get into a kneeling position with your head bowed until you are told what to do."

He grabs the girl nearest to him by the throat, yanking her upwards. "Can you guess what the words should be that come from your mouth after assuming this position?"

He loosens up on her throat, and she croaks out, "Yes, sir."

He throws her back onto the ground, and she catches herself on her elbow on the hard floor.

"Close, it's yes, master," he says, "You officially have owners now. So, you're property. You have no rights; you have no say in your life or body. You are nobody now; forget your name and where you came from. You will be known as whatever your master deems worthy of naming you. You will do as you're told and not bat a fucking eye," he all but yells at us, daring us to say something against him as he paces the room.

The girl next to me is shivering violently, but like the rest of us, refuses to look up and make eye contact, afraid of any type of punishment.

"Now it's late; you will return to your cots, and your sex training to make you good little whores starts tomorrow," he announces. "Stand up and form a line to go back to your room."

We stand up with our heads down, forming a line that leads out the other side, which I assume is to our part of the warehouse. The guards leer at us, trying to instill fear. They are doing a good job. One of them brushes the shoulder down to the breast of the girl in front of me, and I try not to gag; she flinches, and that was the wrong thing to do. He doesn't waste any time grabbing her by her hair and punching her in the stomach. She goes down instantly, coughing and trying to gasp for air.

"Get back in line," he says, and she scrambles up and gets back in line with tears running down her face.

We all but drag our feet back to our cots. When we get there, we go to the ones we slept in the night before. On our beds are what look like new hospital gowns. I quickly tear off the lingerie, toss it on the floor, and secure the strings on the gown. I get under the light sheet they have provided, which feels like sandpaper, and grab the barely fluffed pillow. Rolling over onto my side, I let the tears silently fall down my cheeks as I pull my knees up to my chest.

What kind of hell are we supposed to endure tomorrow? What kind of training are they going to put us through?

CHAPTER THIRTY

TYLER

I bang my fist against the familiar door repeatedly until I hear rustling behind it. Blair swings it open. She's in her pajamas, wiping her eyes, and her hair is in those heatless curler things.

"What the fuck do you want, Tyler? Has the sun even risen yet?" She all but yells at me.

"It's about to, and I need answers before it does." I scowl back at her.

"What could possibly be so important?" she asks, but then she turns a deadly shade of white. "Wait, is it Cassidy? Is she hurt or something?" Her voice frantically raises to a higher octave.

"I figured you would know about her well-being since she's been here with you," I shout back at her vehemently.

Her eyes all but fall out of her head. "No, I haven't seen her since the morning she left with you to move," she screeches, completely awake now. "I thought she was just staying with you at your fraternity house."

"Let me inside right now," I say as I begin pushing my way through. She can sense my urgency, and she opens the door wider to let me in.

The door shuts, and we move in sync with one another toward the living room, neither one of us wanting to take a seat, fidgeting and pacing back and forth with worry.

"I heard her leaving to help you move that morning, and she sent me a laughing emoji that day at one of the reels I had sent her, and that is the last I have heard from her," Blair all but shrieks at me.

"Cassidy stayed with me that night after helping me move, but then she left before my alarm went off the next morning, claiming she had a math exam to study for," I tell her.

Blair looks at me, horrified, clasps her mouth with one of her hands, and lets out a noise that sounds like a whimper. "I need to call her mom and see if maybe she went home or if they've seen her." Tears form in her eyes as she worries about her friend.

I stand there impatiently waiting. I nod, making it apparent that I am not going anywhere.

She runs into her room, grabs her phone, and it takes her a couple of seconds to find the contact she is looking for. Finally, she clicks it, her hands shaking, and she holds the phone to her ear.

I stand in the living room watching her, my heart beating rapidly, and my hands begin to sweat, so I rub them on my pants.

"Lillian, it's me," Blair says in a calmer voice than I expected, swallowing deeply to hold back the tears.

I can hear a response back, but Blair cuts her off, "Is Cassidy at home with you?"

I know the moment she says no. Blair clutches her mouth again and falls to her knees, whimpering and trying to hold the tears back, but they begin to fall silently down her face.

"She hasn't been back to our apartment in a little over 48

hours," Blair says between deep breaths, trying to get the entire sentence out to Cassidy's mom.

You could hear a pin drop; that's how deadly silent the other line goes.

Blair switches the phone from private to speaker, and I hear Cassidy's mom calmly say, "Have you checked everywhere, Blair? This has to be some kind of misunderstanding. You know Cassidy, she can hole up anywhere when it comes to her studies and lose complete track of time."

"I thought she was with this guy she has been seeing, Tyler, but he just turned up, and he hasn't seen her either," Blair says.

Lillian is silent for a moment. "Do you know her school schedule, Blair?"

Blair nods urgently and whispers, "Yes, I have it memorized like my own."

"Ok, dear, let's try not to panic. I need you to contact her professors and see if she has been to her classes. I'm willing to bet she hasn't missed any of those, and she's probably just crashing somewhere else for the time being," Lillian calmly says to a hysterical Blair.

"I'll go to all of them today and see if she's been to any of her classes," Blair says, running into her closet, not even caring that I'm there, and begins changing into a workout set.

"While you are doing that, I'm going to start heading that way," Lillian says. "I will see you soon, dear."

"Alright, sounds like a plan. I'm sure you are right, and I am panicking for nothing." Blair takes some deep breaths while she starts brushing her teeth and throwing her hair into a claw clip.

"Definitely, Cassidy is the more responsible one out of the two of you, I'm sorry to say, dear. She's definitely somewhere around the campus freaking out about an assignment or something," Lillian says, chuckling.

Blair softly laughs back. "Definitely. See you soon." Blair takes her off speaker, and a few more words are exchanged. I can immediately see the change in Blair, like she was overreacting and being dramatic about the whole thing.

She looks up and becomes startled, making eye contact with me. "I forgot you were there."

I nod empathetically. "Listen, here's the plan. You're going to go talk to her professors, check your sorority house, and ask your sisters if they have seen her. I'm going to go to the student union, check those study pods that are open 24/7, and also check the library," I tell her with authority in my voice, feeling a little better with some type of plan forming to find Cassidy.

Blair continuously nods while holding out her hand and says, "Give me your phone."

I hand it over without a thought.

She saves her number in my phone and sends a text message to her phone.

"We'll keep each other updated and meet back up with what we've found out. I'm also going to be back here in a few hours to meet her mom when she gets here," Blair says.

I run my hand through my hair. "Sounds like a plan. I'll meet you back here as soon as I can." I sigh, already moving toward the door.

With my back turned, Blair says, "Something is wrong. I can just feel it."

I don't look back because my stomach turns, and I am thinking the same exact thing as I shut their apartment door.

CHAPTER THIRTY-ONE

CASSIDY

A foghorn wakes me up abruptly, and I bump my head on the bunk above me. What in the actual hell is going on? My eyes adjust to the brightness in the room. My stomach sinks to the floor as memories flood over me, recalling everything that has happened. Rubbing my head, I turn my body, and my feet hit the floor as coldness creeps over me.

"It's time to wake up, slaves; it's the first day of your training," Rio excitedly yells, walking up and down the line of bunk beds and cots. He stops and thrusts his hips forward while stretching his back. "My favorite day." He grins with pure evil in his eyes. "Line the fuck up near the back door," he says as he holds out his thumb and uses it to point behind him.

I look around and see the rest of the women on their feet, immediately bull rushing to get in line. Due to fear, my feet do the thinking for me and quickly carry me to the designated line. I glance at Rio and look him up and down; he's lined from head to toe in all kinds of weapons, some I've only seen on TV shows, and some I don't recognize. They are instilling fear into all of us. Behind him stands a few familiar guards I recognize, including Sam and Zane.

A full-body shiver racks through my body as Zane slowly walks over to our line. He reaches into his pocket, pulls something out, and points it at a woman who is closer to the front of the line. All of a sudden, I hear a zapping type of noise, and two thin wires hooked to it propel outwards, latching onto the side of her body. She hits the floor instantly, screaming out in pain involuntarily and writhing in front of us, losing control.

Horrified, I realize it is a taser, and my mouth hangs open. I'm completely frozen to my spot in line. Laughing like someone told him a hilarious joke, Zane keeps pushing some button, which I can only assume increases the pain because the woman is squeezing her eyes shut, writhing even more, and screaming even louder.

I watch as a yellow liquid seeps all over the floor around her, and she just lays there, helpless to what is going on. My hand shoots up over my mouth, realizing she has peed all over herself.

"Alright, alright, Zane; we haven't even left the room yet." Rio chuckles and slaps him on the shoulder.

Zane lets up on the taser, walks over to the woman, takes the stick-like darts out of her, and tucks them in his pocket.

She is full-blown crying now in a fetal position, her body shaking all over. He's careful where he steps and kicks her over where she's lying on her back, drenched in sweat and piss.

"Clean it up," he snaps at her. She tries standing and falls back down, splashing the piss all over the floor. Another woman beside her helps her up. She frantically looks around for something, anything to clean it up. Spotting some clothes folded against one of the walls, she begins hurriedly walking over to them.

Zane laughs, and in a deathly serious tone with darkness in his eyes, he says, "Ah, ah, ah, with your tongue." We all look at him in disgust. The woman doesn't know what to do, and she is violently shaking and sobbing.

"Did I stutter?" Zane yells at her. She flinches and jumps down to her hands and knees, looks up one more time, and makes eye contact with Zane. He nods once, his eyes blazing with fury.

My already uneasy stomach threatens to lose its contents right there, but I look away quickly enough. The degradation of this is too much to bear.

"Oh no, you are all going to watch her unless you want to suffer something worse than this," Zane tells all of us.

I turn back around with tears in my eyes, horror-stricken at the scene unfolding in front of me, and unable to do anything.

She laps up the piss like a dog and quickly swallows, trying not to vomit all over the floor.

"Wait, you forgot some." Zane chuckles, and she looks up at him, confused.

He leans back on one of his heels, showing her the bottom of his black combat boot.

My face must show the pure rage I feel because he didn't come anywhere close to walking in the piss; he just wants her to lick his boots clean to further degrade her.

Silently, she begins licking up the bottom of one boot, then the other.

When she finishes, she's kneeling with her head down, completely humiliated.

Zane pats her on the head. "You might make your master happy, slave," he sneers.

Rio clears his throat and chuckles, coming to the front of the line. "Alright, enough of that," he states, even though I know he was thoroughly entertained and probably turned on… the sick bastard.

He throws a new gown toward her, and she takes off the soaked one and puts it on.

"We will escort you to the bathroom to shower and relieve yourselves, and then head to training room one." He begins stalking out of the room, and the women follow in a neat line, everyone trying not to make eye contact with any of the guards for fear of what just happened being done to them.

As soon as we arrive at the bathrooms, I notice that they are just toilets lined up against one wall, without any semblance of privacy. Having to pee so badly, I just hike up my gown at the first available toilet. When I'm done, I flush and wash my hands and get in line accordingly for the showers. There are only five showerheads, so we are forced to take turns washing off the grime from our bodies and our hair.

About ten minutes later, all the women have finished, and we are escorted to training room one. Before entering, the hairs on the back of my neck stand up. Really not knowing what to expect and fearing the worst, we are led inside, where it is dark except for the spotlights directly on the mechanical bull in the middle of the room, surrounded by a tall foam floor.

With a puzzled look, I stare at the guards for some clarification, and they smirk as they leave us in the room.

This man enters in all black, and I immediately get goosebumps, knowing something about this man screams evil.

"I'm Will, but you can call me master today as I will be conducting your first training session." I look behind him, and there is a table of all kinds of tools, but what catches my eye is the different-sized and colored dildos set nicely in a row.

Will, or should I say, master, grabs a basket and says, "Take off your gowns and put them in here. You won't need any clothing today; it will just get in the way."

One by one, we take off our gowns and toss them in the basket, privacy long gone out the window.

"Today, you will be riding that mechanical bull like your life depends on it. Because it does. There will be a dildo placed in the seat that has been specially made for this kind of training," Will says.

"And what kind of training is that exactly?" I blurt out, looking him dead in the eye.

He moves toward me and smacks me across the face so hard my head jerks to the side. The pain and throbbing on my cheek and jaw instantly form, my neck aching from the whiplash-like strike.

"Don't speak unless spoken to, slave," he snaps, "or I'll teach you a lesson you won't forget."

Spitting out a small amount of blood with my head down, afraid to piss this guy off, I tremble with rage.

He pulls me up aggressively by my arm. "Why don't you go first and show the class what they have to look forward to?" He leans into me and cups my breast aggressively.

Then I'm pushed over toward the bull, and he makes a beeline to the dildos. He picks out a big ass flesh-colored dildo, not the biggest, but definitely bigger than any cock I have ever seen in my life.

There is no way that it fits inside of me. He goes over to the bull and secures the dildo where I'm going to have to sit. He turns on some kind of remote, and the dildo begins to vibrate and twirl on the bull.

My eyes widen in surprise, and my jaw practically hits the floor.

"Well, climb aboard." He grins at me with an evil glint in his eyes.

I go over to the bull, taking a huge gulp while holding my breath. I swing onto it right behind the dildo.

"How am I supposed to get it inside of me when I'm not even wet?" I bravely ask.

Will opens a lotion bottle that contains lube and drops a dollop on the tip of the dildo.

"You'll ride this bull and pretend it's your master, and you will come when I tell you to. If you don't put on a show for us, or I'm unhappy with your performance, you will go straight to the red room, the punishment room. I know Rio and his gang would be more than thrilled to have some kind of entertainment today."

Nodding quickly, thinking of how terrible that would be, I begin to sink myself onto the dildo slowly. It is ribbed, and I feel myself stretching further as I lower myself onto it, gasping in pain.

Will comes over, grabs hold of my shoulder, and shoves me down forcefully. "We don't have all day, slave," he says in a tone as if I'm nothing more than dirt on his shoe.

Searing pain racks through me, and I cry out at the unexpected intrusion into my body at full force. Holding back tears, my legs shake, and I feel pain in my cervix. I try to barely move my body while also trying to adjust to how uncomfortable this is.

I turn my head gradually and make eye contact with Will. He smirks, holds out the remote pointed right at me, and pushes a button. All of a sudden, I feel the vibration and movement burst through the dildo, and I try to lift myself up slightly, then back down a few times to get a hold of this new sensation coursing through me.

"Hold on," he says to me as he walks over to a podium that is about thirty feet away. I quickly look down in front of me and see the smallest handles known to man, and I clutch onto them, taking deep breaths in and out.

"I'm going to start it off slow, and then it will gradually get faster. Remember to give us a show like you're riding your master's cock," Will yells over the noise.

I look over at the women watching me quietly with pity and worry written all over their faces, knowing they are next.

Sweat trickles from my brow, and adrenaline courses through my veins, unsure of what to expect. I've been to plenty of bars and watched while my friends got thrown from a mechanical bull rather quickly, and we laughed hysterically about it.

It takes technique to ride one of these things, and I don't think I have it, even with the coordination. But now, being forced into this, I'm going to have to figure it out fast because the last thing I want to be is subjected to the red room or anywhere near Rio and his gang of monsters.

The bull begins to move, and to my revulsion, a loud moan escapes from my mouth. The dildo is curving in a way that is hitting my G-spot with every movement of the bull, as the head of it goes down, almost touching the ground, and jerks up and back. The movement of the bull mixed with the vibrating dildo is hitting me in delicious but different ways. I feel my little bundle of nerves being coaxed with the movement.

My body instinctively begins chasing that high of a mind-altering orgasm. I relinquish control of my mind and let myself escape this heinous place for the time being.

I close my eyes and imagine riding Tyler, letting go of one of the handles and riding this bull like I would a real dick, moving my body in sync with this machine. My moans grow increasingly louder with every thrust of the dildo, lifting me up and down while completely blocking out my senses and the people surrounding me in this room.

I don't know how much time has passed, but suddenly, I feel the white-hot waves of release and small cramps in my lower abdomen, and then the sensation like I have to pee. I let it all go, uncaring. As I let my head fall back and my eyes roll back into my head, I let out a guttural moan as a warm liquid seeps out between my legs.

After what feels like seconds, I come down from my high, slightly shaking and trying to ride out the entire sensation, and I'm pulled back to reality as I realize Will has turned off the bull.

My eyes adjust to the room, and my face turns beet red in embarrassment. I just had one of the best orgasms of my life and squirted all over the place in a room full of people watching me.

I hear Will's boots on the floor and look over at him, waiting for his approval.

He begins clapping. "I'm so glad I videotaped that so I can

show the guys and sell it online. Your master is one lucky bastard," he taunts as he licks his lips.

Pure loathing envelopes my face, and I look him dead in the eye as I snarl, "You disgust me."

"Says the girl that enjoyed herself so much she squirted all over my bull," he snaps back to me.

I let out a huff and raise my body up, eager to get off this thing. Once I am up high enough, I swing one of my legs over and hop off the bull. When my feet hit the ground, I stagger a little bit, feeling lightheaded from the orgasm.

Will cleans up the bull, removes the dildo, and shouts, "Next!"

The women look around with puzzled expressions and hesitations. Wasting no time, Will just randomly picks one, clutches onto her hair with one hand, and practically throws her to the bull while he goes back to his toolset. This time, he picks out this gigantic-looking octopus tentacle, and again, my jaw drops to the floor. I've never seen a dildo that looked like that before. Recoiling into my own skin, all I can think about is how painful it is going to be for this woman in front of me. I see the fear etched all over her face, but like the rest of us, we have no choice in the matter.

Repeating the same scenario I was just put through, Will sets it up, and she jumps on, adjusting herself to the torture she is about to endure.

This continues with the remaining women, each one forced to have a turn. One of them doesn't perform the way Will wants, so he hits a button, and one of the guards practically runs into the room. She is dragged from the room while she screams, violently trying to get out of his hold as she is carted off to the red room. Resisting the way she did, I know they are only going to make her punishment that much worse, and I shiver at that thought.

We are given one bottle of water after we finish the bull riding. I savor it, taking small sips at a time and trying to steal glances around the room to avoid watching these women orgasm. I don't even remember the last time I ate. They wouldn't let us eat anything before the auction; they wanted us to look as thin as possible to show off any curves we may have.

It's impossible to continue like this. I know we haven't been fed in about 72 hours, except for the little bit of water we've been given and whatever I was able to drink in the shower.

I can't remember anything about high school science, but I think we can go longer without food and just water. They obviously know that and are pushing us to our limits, probably just trying to get us to a point of desperation.

Well, any longer, and I am definitely going to be there. I would give anything for something to eat. As if on command, my stomach lets out a huge growl, daydreaming about food.

Hours seem to creep by until we have all taken our turn riding the bull.

Will shouts, "The guards will now escort you to the showers and then to bed."

Four guards, whom I recognize right away by their familiar faces these last few days and the unsettling feeling that creeps into my belly, confidently walk in.

We are led to the bathrooms and told, "You have 15 minutes to shower and do your business, no more."

As I am showering, the door to the room opens, and in staggers the woman we saw who had been taken to the red room.

Since we are all naked, my eyes immediately take in her bruising from head to toe, along with her welts. The only part of her body that isn't bruised is her face, and my body shivers because I catch a glimpse of the blood trickling down her thighs.

She finds an empty showerhead and quickly washes her body, crying out in pain.

I turn my head and focus on the wall, quickly showering and using the restroom.

As if we are robots, programmed or conditioned already from the abuse, we all go to where we were supposed to silently and with our heads down, and line up to be taken to our cots.

When we get to our cots, there are clean hospital gowns that have been placed on top, along with a piece of bread and cheese and another bottle of water. My stomach lurches with hunger. I don't even bother with the gown as I scarf down the food, trying to savor the taste but not caring. I take a few sips of the water and then put on my gown, climbing under the sheet, if you could call it that. It feels like sandpaper against my skin.

Darkness takes over me, and I fall asleep quickly.

CHAPTER THIRTY-TWO

CASSIDY

We are all woken up in the same way as the day before, with Rio taking his baton and hitting all the bunks and stalking up and down the rows, with a look daring us to say anything.

Surprisingly, no one is assaulted or attacked before we step foot out of the room.

Right away, I could sense the guard's anxiety, like they were in a hurry to get us to our destination.

We stop by the bathrooms so we can take care of our business, and are commanded to hurry.

The entire time, I have been trying to memorize the corridors and rooms of this place so I can have a decent idea of the floor plan, but where we are headed today is a new part of the ware-house we haven't been to previously.

The hairs on the back of my neck stand up with fear of the unknown.

We approach a thick iron door with a square window in the middle, and I can just feel the uneasiness growing as we draw closer to the new location.

We are ushered in like cattle, and as if this place hasn't already shocked me to my core in this house of horrors, my whole body trembles at the sight before me.

Lined up in a row are multiple machines with dildos sticking forward, and in front of them are leather chairs that are a Z-like shape where your knees go and your arms rest on the part in front of it.

What in the actual fuck is this?

Will steps out with a huge, evil grin on his face.

"Today, we will be doing anal stretching." He looks around at our faces, waiting for our reaction, the pervert he is. "Your masters will want to make sure they can take you in every hole, and you need to be readily available at any command you are given," he says.

One of the women blurts out, "But I've never done anal."

Will chuckles to himself before saying, "Even better, I can't wait to watch your ass stretch all day and bleed before me."

Zane steps forward then, and Will looks over at him. "To ensure you don't deviate from the training today, Zane is going to be helping me as we increase the size of the dildo throughout the day."

Zane smiles widely at all of us, relishing our frightened faces, obviously looking forward to our pain and humiliation.

"We are going to start with an average-sized dildo and then work our way up, and by the end, your ass should be stretched to be able to accommodate a fist if it needs to."

"And you expect us to just sit in position and take the pain without any preparation or thought of the intrusion into our bodies?" I couldn't help but practically spit out my disgust.

Zane takes a few quick steps toward me and backhands me so hard I fall to the ground, and blood pools in my mouth. I spit it out and glare up at him.

"You're not only going to sit there and take it, but if you move at any point, you will be taken to the red room."

All the women hold their breath, and some start shaking, remembering the appearance of the woman who was taken there yesterday and the aftereffects on her body.

"Go to your leather chair with your ass in the air. Zane and I will line it up and turn the machine on." Will claps his hands once over his head excitedly and hurriedly looks over to us, eyes wide.

We practically run over to one of the chairs. My body is trembling with adrenaline coursing through my body.

I keep telling myself to breathe in and out. Deep breaths. I try to convince myself that it could be worse.

And after the horrific acts I have already endured in a short amount of time, I shake my head, trying not to think about it. I can do this. I have at least done anal a few times, so it wasn't exactly new to me.

As I position myself accordingly on the leather chair that has been custom-made for something like this, I swallow deeply, pulling my hair over to one side over my shoulder, and wait for the inevitable pain.

I picked a chair in the middle and saw Zane working his way down one side while Will worked his way down the other. I hear a few of the machines start up, and a buzzing sound begins to overtake the room. I squeeze my eyes shut in anticipation of what is to come any minute now. Suddenly, I hear some of the women whimper, followed by screams and cries. I can't bear to look over at them, too afraid of seeing the pain etched on their faces. I keep my eyes and head pointed directly in front of me, focusing on a spot on the wall.

I feel a hot breath on my back, grazing and making its way up to my exposed neck. "I can't wait to watch you take this cock in your ass until you scream." I knew it was Will.

I shiver, but I know better than to try to squirm away.

I feel a lubed finger push into my ass. It isn't painful, just uncomfortable and unwanted. Then, he adds a second finger, and they begin thrusting back and forth, fucking my ass. He pulls out of me, and I hear a squirt from a bottle—more lube. He jams two fingers into my ass. "I think you're ready," he whispers in my ear.

I can hear the machine sliding up behind me as it lines up.

Goosebumps appear all over my body as I feel the nudge of the tip of the dildo's head line up with my back entrance.

This sick fuck was enjoying every second of this, making it unbearably slow; he was getting off on my fear. I tried relaxing my body, knowing it wouldn't hurt as much if I wasn't clenching, but I couldn't help it.

Will pushes the dildo in slowly, inch by inch, while I whimper and squint my eyes, shaking from the intrusion. He must feel like it is in a good place because I can feel him move behind the machine and turn it on. The buzzing begins, and it starts slowly thrusting in and out of me. A scream escapes my lips from the all-encompassing burn I feel rack through my body, but of course, the machine doesn't let up as it thrusts in and out at slow speed. I am feeling lightheaded from the pain. What if I pass out?

Breathe, Cassidy. You cannot pass out; what if they send you to the red room? Rio is sitting there, probably eagerly waiting for me.

I firmly grip the sides of the chair where my elbows are supposed to be, holding on for dear life as this thing shoves inside of me, willing my mind to go elsewhere.

I think about math and the equations I was doing in my algebra class, which allows me to take some deep breaths and lighten up on grinding my teeth so hard.

I feel a small stream fall down my thigh, which I can only assume is blood.

If this is the smallest dildo they are using on us today, and I can barely take it, how is my body going to be able to handle more?

I look over at the woman to my right, and you can tell she is in an awful lot of pain. Sweat streams down her face.

I whisper to her, "Take a deep breath in through your nose and exhale out through your mouth; your body needs to relax."

She looks over at me with fear in her eyes and nods, doing as I tell her.

Will, not missing anything, stalks over to me and snatches my chin upwards, stretching my neck at a painful angle so I'm looking at him. "Don't fucking breathe in the other's direction, or I will take you off this thing and fuck your ass on the floor in front of them. Understand?"

I can do nothing but try to nod at him to show that I understood.

This fucking hell hole. I want to burn this place to the ground.

"Alright, since Cassidy has decided to offer advice, we are going to up the size sooner than we normally would," Will announces.

I can feel the other women's anger directed at me. My face blushes, feeling responsible for even more pain they are about to endure.

The machines click off, and Zane and Will go around snatching the dildos off. My body sags in relief, but I know it won't be for long.

I chance a glance over by the toolbox-looking thing where they keep all the sex toys. Will has a whole handful of flesh-colored dildos that are rimmed, and the head on them is huge, practically double in size compared to a normal dick, and they have a slight curve. They have to be at least seven or eight inches.

Perspiration begins to seep through my pores because my adrenaline increases at the thought of it plunging inside of me.

Trying more breathing exercises that I picked up at a yoga class I used to attend, I attempt to relax my body and mind a little bit.

Zane and Will split up and begin attaching them to the machines. When they get to my machine, I can't help but clench up as perspiration forms on my brow.

"Back up toward your machines where the tip is touching your ring of muscle," Zane shouts.

I hesitate for a moment, glancing down at my shaking legs, but I do as he tells us, willing my body to stop shaking so I can line up with the dildo correctly.

Will walks down the row and squirts lube onto the tip of the dildos, carelessly flicking his wrist so more lands on the women's ass cracks. As soon as he's done, he flips the button on the machine, and it turns on. The screams and painful sobs that follow will be seared into my mind for the foreseeable future.

Zane reaches my station, and I hold my breath, feeling my erratic heartbeat. He puts the lube on his fingers, spreads it on the outer rim of my hole, and coats a generous amount on the dildo.

"I want to hear the wet sounds of your asshole taking this so well," Zane whispers to me, and he reaches between my legs and flicks my clit. "Maybe I'll pay you a visit tonight and slide my cock in your filthy hole just to make sure it's stretched properly."

He slowly nudges the head in, and I hold back tears, clutching the chair, ready to embrace the pain. I can do this. He continues to slowly slide it in, and just when I think my body has taken it all, there's more to go. I brace myself in agony. More sweat beads on my forehead, and my breath quickens.

Next, he reaches down and turns the machine on. It feels like I am being split in two. I grab onto the armrest for dear life, begging for the pain to go away and praying this would at least be over quickly.

Then Zane does something with the rest of the girls because the screaming seems to simmer down, but I can't look around. My eyes are squeezed shut as I focus on my own pain.

He attaches a clit sucker onto me, hitting the exact spot with one swoop. They know what they are doing. They are trying to train our minds to associate immense pain with pleasure.

Moans escape my mouth at the sensation. I narrow my mind on the clit sucker, and my hold on the armrest eases up. My body relaxes a bit, leaning into the pleasure forming from the suction on my clit.

I arch my back because the slight movement causes the sucker to shift a bit, and I would be lying if I said I didn't enjoy that feeling. Chasing that feeling of euphoria has always been one of life's greatest pleasures.

I've never had an anal orgasm, but I know from my friends and watching homemade porn that they are intense.

I'm not sure how much time has passed, but I know it has to have been more than an hour of this overwhelming stimulation. It definitely feels that way.

I can feel my G-spot being stimulated through my anal wall. The dildo repeatedly moves in and out, and the clit sucker is still going.

Will and Zane pace through the room, awaiting our reactions.

The dildo penetrates deeper than I've ever experienced before.

I feel chills all over my body, and a wave-like rippling feeling starts in my toes, moving all the way up my body. Suddenly, I feel a tickling, tingling sensation deep inside my G-spot.

My vision doubles as I moan louder, and I scream as the anal orgasm takes over my body. Cum gushes down between my thighs in increments I have never seen or felt my body do before. The clit sucker lets me ride the high until the very end.

I am so dazed that I don't hear the person approaching to shut off the dildo machine and remove the clit sucker.

My whole body shakes with that out-of-body feeling, and I am soaking up every bit of it.

Will pets my head and says, "That's my girl." Then, he dumps a cold bucket of water over me.

Yelping out from the cold, I come back to my senses and surroundings. I turn around on the chair and slump forward with my face covered in shame and exhaustion. Some of the women are still silently crying, and I just had the best orgasm of my life in this place. Crossing my arms over my breasts, trying to fight the coldness over my body, I keep my eyes down, ashamed of what had just happened.

That doesn't last for long because Zane takes me by the arm and throws me against the opposite wall. I land awkwardly on my side, and when I look up, I'm tossed a water bottle, which I catch and quickly open, drinking the whole thing in two gulps.

After finishing my water, I notice several women sitting to my right; there are only a couple left on the machines.

Their goal is to get us to orgasm, and then we are rewarded with water. I can't help but think about food as my stomach lets out a growl. I am starving.

Minutes pass by, and the other two women finally join us on our side of the wall.

Will stands in front of us. "We still have one more item we need to complete for today's training."

A woman huffs out, "Our bodies are exhausted, and we are starving. What more could you possibly subject us to?" She immediately realizes her error and clamps her mouth shut with both hands, her eyes widening in horror.

Will smirks and snaps his fingers, and Zane, like the hound dog he is, scoops her up and drags her out the back door.

The rest of us can only stare, knowing where she is headed—the red room.

Will begins walking back and forth in front of us with his hands behind his back. "As I was saying, there is one more thing we have to complete today, and that is more anal stretching."

Biting my tongue, I look down at my feet. I wanted to say: What the fuck have we been doing this whole time?

I glance up and notice Zane moving the machines back into a closet and rolling out these narrow, ottoman-looking things with individual foam pads attached to them. If I had to guess, we're supposed to bend over it and rest our knees on the foam pads.

Everything here seems custom-designed, as I have never seen any of these things before, even at a sex store. As much money as they make from us, it is not like they can't afford it.

"You may go to your station, arms and elbows resting on the ledge with knees on the pad. Your knees need to be back far enough where your ass is in the air," Will says.

My body is sore in places I've never been sore before. I can barely lift myself up, and honestly, I want to crawl over, but I have too much pride, and I don't want them to have the satisfaction of seeing how much pain I am in.

"I've given you a command, slaves; what should be your response?" Will yells.

"Yes, master," we all say without hesitation.

I don't know what to expect. I mean, how can it get any worse at this point? I know better than to ask that question, especially in a place like this with these deranged men.

We assume the position they told us to get in, the anticipation sinking in for what is to come next. It is pure torture, and they love this part. I can see the bulges in their pants. They don't even try to hide that they are turned on by this.

Again, I am in the middle, so all I hear are gasps as they work their way down the line, both together this time. There are no screams, so I send a silent thanks up for that small mercy.

Finally, it's my turn. I hear lube being squeezed from a bottle and hitting my ass crack, quickly followed by a finger, and I can't help but jump due to the soreness and sensitivity from what had just happened.

I'm quickly punished with a loud and hard smack on my ass, and I swallow back a yell.

Then, I feel something being inserted into my hole. It is not exceptionally large, and I can feel two fingers pushing it in, but within seconds, the fingers retreat, and whatever it is stays put.

Then something is hooked up to the end of it, but again, there's not much pain.

After a few more minutes, Will and Zane take their places in front of us, looking around. Will has a remote.

"You all have a balloon in your rectums attached to an air

pump, and we're going to steadily inflate them with air in order to stretch them out fully," Will announces.

All I can hear is my heartbeat quickening in my ears as my body fills with worry.

Will clicks a button, and the balloon begins to inflate. It's not much, but it is a completely different sensation from the dildo machine. All I want to do is push it out of me. It is so uncomfortable. But I know better. I know if I don't do this, they will gladly cart me off to the red room.

The inflation increases, and I look down. My body begins to shake and sweat. This isn't pleasurable at all, just painful.

I don't know how much time has passed, but I can feel my legs tingling and going numb.

After some more time has passed, the balloon finally deflates, and I exhale, not realizing I was holding my breath the entire time.

Almost collapsing with relief, I feel a presence behind me as the balloon is pulled out with a wet plop. I don't even have the energy to look and see who did it.

I must have fainted because when I come to, I'm in my cot in the gown with two pieces of bread beside me and another bottle of water. I scarf down everything.

Moments passed by, and I let my body succumb to the darkness, allowing parts of my soul to go with it.

CHAPTER THIRTY-THREE

TYLER

Blair: Cassidy's mom is here. I think you should head to our apartment.

Me: Ok, on my way.

Blair: Just a heads up, the police are on their way over. Her mom is filing a missing person's report.

Me: 👍

Speechless, I move swiftly to my car. I have been frantically asking all my fraternity brothers if they saw her leave the house that night. Not surprisingly, all of them claimed to be sleeping and never saw her, shrugging me off.

I remember us falling asleep around 11ish. I had looked at my alarm clock at some point after we popped down to the kitchen to grab something to eat.

My stomach feels like it's going to come out of my throat at the thought of making a police report on my girlfriend as I drive over to her and Blair's apartment. I must've beaten the police here because I don't see any police cars in the parking lot.

I walk up the stairs to their place, and just as I am about to knock, a frazzled-looking Blair swings the door open.

"I just had a feeling you were outside," she says, moving to let me in.

I take in my surroundings and see a middle-aged woman sitting on their couch, silently fidgeting with her hands. She looks like an older version of Cassidy; she is stunning, even with silent tears streaming down her face.

I don't waste any time and walk right up to where she is sitting.

She stands up abruptly, and I hold out my hand. "Hi, I'm Tyler," I tell her.

"Blair filled me in on who you are; it's nice to meet you. I'm Lillian. I wish we were meeting under better circumstances," she says stiffly.

I nod, not knowing what to say.

"The police should be here any minute," Blair states.

I look over at her. "Any luck today?" I ask, and she shakes her head, trying to hold back more tears.

She's trying to hold it together for the police statement. I can tell she's planning to break down after.

Who could blame her? She and Cassidy were more like sisters than friends.

The police spend hours asking us questions, uniquely repeating the same questions to see if our answers change. My answers come out robotic. I feel numb all over, still in denial about Cassidy being an actual missing person.

Lillian escorts the police out, and she and Blair completely break down together. Feeling uncomfortable and out of place, I wait patiently before saying my goodbyes and ask them to stay in touch if they hear anything about Cassidy. After many promises telling me they will, I head to my car.

Mindlessly, I drive to my fraternity house. As I pull into the parking lot, I realize I don't even know how I got here safely. I drove on autopilot.

I blink and look around a few times, trying to get my bearings.

As I walk up to the side door of the house, Archer comes barreling out, knocking into me, and I am thrown off balance, almost falling on my ass.

After such a mentally draining night, I shout out at him, "Watch where the fuck you're going, man!"

Immediately, he straightens up and glares at me. "Be careful who you're talking to."

"I really don't give a shit, Archer. I am not in the mood, and you are obviously drunk." I try to step around him to get to the door.

A couple of other brothers come from the other side of the house to see what is going on.

"Still crying about your girl, Tyler?" Archer sneers. "She was just a warm hole; you'll find another."

My spine tingles, and anger spreads through my body as I jerk back toward him. "What the fuck did you just say?" I growl.

"I said you're going to have to find another hole for your dick; she's a ghost now." He leers back at me, snapping his fingers and chuckling.

Not thinking, I lunge for him, and some of the brothers grab hold of me and pull me back. One brother tries to push him into one of their cars to get him away from me.

Anger contorts my face as I try to get free from the brothers holding me back.

"Don't do anything stupid," one of them whispers to me. "He's the president; don't forget who you're messing with."

Realization of the mistake I made hits me, but then I am overtaken by confusion at what Archer said.

I stand frozen as Archer laughs hysterically with two of the older brothers as they jump into an Audi Q8.

Pure terror races through my body, and I stare in Archer's direction, my gut twisting, knowing he knows what happened to Cassidy. There is no way he could be that evil?

Coming to my senses, I shake my head, and the guys who are holding me let me go.

Quickly, I mentally check off how it would be impossible for Cassidy to just disappear like Archer implied. She is a student at the school, a sorority sister, for Christ's sake.

From my understanding, we only sell women in more vulnerable situations, not those with connections, or in areas where people would notice if they were missing.

I slowly walk up to my room, my mind in a different place.

Cassidy is missing, but missing people can be found. This is just a misunderstanding. Information will come out, and she will be back soon.

I fall asleep trying to comfort myself, but deep down, I know something terrible happened to her.

CHAPTER THIRTY-FOUR

CASSIDY

I can barely open my eyes, and as soon as I do, my body throbs with pain and soreness. Instantly recalling yesterday, I shut my eyes, trying to block out the memories.

"Hurry the fuck up, ladies!" one of the guards yells at us.

Groaning, I pull myself up into a sitting position, allowing my eyes to adjust to the spotlights above us.

A woman who slept on the bunk above me, Chelsea, I think, hops down inches from me and whispers, "I don't know how much more my body can take."

I look at her with pity and a sense of helplessness. "What other choice do we have?" I whisper back.

"No fucking talking." Rio must have seen us and rushes over, slapping Chelsea across the face. I hear the sting echo in the air and wince.

She quickly clutches that side of her face with both hands, crying out.

My body goes rigid as I quickly get into the line forming at the door to the hallway.

Trembling while standing in line, all I can think about is what the red room would be like with Rio.

Fucking pigs. All of them. The internal rage churning in my stomach grows each day I'm in this place and with these people. I have stopped questioning how they could do something like this and have concluded that they are just pure evil.

The door opens after the code is entered, and we are led to the bathrooms again to relieve ourselves and take showers within the allotted fifteen minutes.

I scrub my body aggressively, wanting to get the feeling of dirtiness off me.

When I'm done with my shower, I move toward the line forming to take us to the atrocities that await us today.

We are given another bottle of water and a piece of bread while we walk to a room we have never been to. I scarf everything down in minutes.

Rio smirks over at us while we wait to be escorted into the room. He holds out his hand. "Undress and hand me your gowns before entering."

We listen to and follow his instructions without giving him any pushback.

As we walk into the room, I take in the black walls and the concrete floors with crimson stains. It's dark, and I can only see a little bit in front of me.

My stomach almost heaves up the little I have in it, knowing those stains are old blood from other women before me.

We are shoved toward one of the walls, forced to stand side by side as Will stalks forward, coming into view.

"When you enter a room, how should you be positioned, slaves?" he sneers.

Automatically, we all kneel with our heads down, looking at the ground.

"If you enter one of my rooms again, doing anything but kneeling like this with your head down, you will be severely punished. I will beat this into you until it becomes as natural as breathing," he growls.

He flips on the lights that shine on the back side of the room. I dare not look up or sneak a glance, but my stomach flips with anticipation.

"Today is day three of sex slave training. Today's lesson is about flogging." I can hear the smile in his voice. "You each will be assigned a guard to help me with your training today; they have volunteered." The guards snicker as he talks.

My stomach flips; they are all sadists, and I know they more than jumped at this opportunity.

My head is pounding with stress because I already know Rio will be my guard. He wouldn't miss an opportunity to inflict pain on me of any kind. For some reason, he has zeroed in on me.

My hands begin to sweat with anticipation; I rub them on my thighs. Who hasn't dabbled in a little BDSM with a boyfriend or at least heard of the term flogging? A memory barrels through my mind of me buying a beginner kit with my high school boyfriend, thinking it would be fun and add a little spice to our relationship. The flogger that was in the kit was small and harmless.

I am sure it is vastly different here, more extreme. A frown forms on my face, thinking of the potential possibilities.

"Look up, slaves," Will instructs, snapping his fingers.

Our heads pop up in unison. My head instinctively rears backward, and I have to prevent myself from shifting my body backward to try to get as far away as possible from the sight in front of me.

Wooden pillories are lined up in a row against the other wall, all of them stained with blood. Old blood, new blood, all of it seeped into the wood.

One of the women starts heaving. She vomits everything that

was in her stomach directly in front of her, narrowly missing her knees and feet.

Will turns a shade of red I have not seen from him before from pure anger.

He begins stalking over to her, but one of the guards beats him there, cutting him off with his dominating body. He gets behind her and puts his work boot on her back, pressing his weight on her. Her body is pushed down and almost touches the vomit.

"Put it back where it came from while keeping your hands behind your back." He glowers down at the back of her head.

Shaking violently, the woman opens her mouth and begins wrapping her lips around the chunks on the ground, swallowing them while gagging. After she finishes with the bigger pieces, she sticks out her tongue and licks up the liquid from the floor.

She almost vomits again, but shakes it off and quickly laps up the rest of it.

I couldn't watch much of it, but it was so silent in the room you could hear the slurping and swallowing noises, and that was enough to make me gag multiple times.

"Good girl," he says as he swats her ass a few times.

Without missing a beat, Will continues, "As I was saying, your training is flogging today, and you will be hooked up to one of the pillories behind me."

Letting curiosity get the best of me, I side-eye the wall to the right and notice all kinds of whips, floggers, chains, and other various items hanging there.

Some of them look like they came right out of medieval times. I know they can't inflict extreme damage to our bodies since we have already been purchased. It wouldn't be a good look for them as the sellers.

However, they could cause a significant amount of pain in places hidden from public view. Bruises, scrapes, and cuts can be hidden under clothing. Most would heal and cause minimal scarring.

Will walks down the line, opening the pillories. Our wrists and heads will be confined, leaving us in a bent-over standing position, completely exposed.

"Please pick a pillory and position yourself accordingly," Will states as though this is a normal everyday thing to do. I guess for him, it is.

I drag my feet over to one at the very end, as far away from the wall of whips as possible, slowly placing my wrists in the wooden semi-circles and then my head, resting my neck on it. It seems like the perfect height. I look down and notice they can be adjusted on the sides if not.

Hurriedly snapping it shut and locking it down, Rio rounds on me where I can see him, brushing his fingers along my jaw. His eyes look wild as he leans in inches from my face. "We are going to have so much fun today, princess." He moves behind me where I can't see him, and I try to stop my body from shaking so much. I don't want to give him the satisfaction of how terrified I really am.

He runs his hand over my butt, down my thighs and calves. "So smooth, but not for long," he whispers.

"You sadistic asshole!" I whisper-yell at him.

He spanks me hard, and I wince at the pain. This is going to be the least amount inflicted on me today.

"Guards, please grab the leather floggers with the leather knotted handles. Ladies, you are in luck. We are starting with an easy one, and we will work our way up," Will shouts, clapping.

I hear footsteps shuffle over to what I call the Wall of Terror. I can shift my head slightly to the right and left, but not all the way, so I'm only able to see the guards move over there quickly, selecting their floggers.

Rio moves around me so he is standing directly behind me.

"I'm not going easy on you today, princess. In fact, I want to mark your pretty skin as much as possible," he whispers in my ear with venom in his voice.

"When flogging, you want to hit the buttocks, upper thigh, and back. Those are your main points of target," Will instructs as he walks back and forth like some kind of deranged professor.

Rio lightly grazes the leather flogger over my backside; I can feel the multiple leather string-like pieces, and goosebumps break out all over my body.

Whack. I let out a whine-like sound as the flogger hits the back of my thighs, feeling the sting directly after the hit. It's not as bad as I thought he was going to strike me the first time, but I know this is going to get progressively worse.

Whack. Pause. Whack. Pause. Whack.

Rio delivers a series of hits on my shoulders, lower back, and butt.

My body instinctively tries to move forward away from the pain being inflicted on it, but the pillory holds me in place, pushing back against my chest, not allowing me to move anywhere.

Rio huffs as he hits me harder in other places on my backside.

Whack. Whack. Whack.

I cry out, wanting to fall to the ground, but the pillory holds me upright in place. I can't even get on my knees. I have no choice but to stay standing. My wrists are straining against the wood, and I know there will be marks there as well.

My skin is on fire. Tomorrow, I will be covered in bruises, probably worse.

"Your skin reddens so nicely for me," Rio says, sucking on his teeth with approval.

I grit out a "fuck you" under my breath.

He must have heard it because he delivers absolute agony on my backside. The pain is unbearable, and I scream out.

My senses are heightened rapidly and at an all-time high. All I hear around me is the other women being beaten as well, crying and weeping for the guards to stop, which only makes them hit with more ferocity.

"Time to switch it up, guards; please take your leather floggers and place them in the black bin, and grab the black rubber floggers," Will commands.

Will walks over to me and inspects my backside. Then, he gets directly in front of me, and I see the bulge in his pants.

"I might need you to help me with this later," he whispers to me, grabbing himself.

I shudder, thinking of how he will abuse my mouth.

Rio returns and lightly caresses the backside of my body with the rubber flogger. The pieces feel longer and thinner, more painful.

He does not hold back this time.

Whack, whack, whack, whack.

Losing count of how many times he has hit my body, I feel lightheaded, as though I might pass out from the pain. I feel the small abrasions as the cool air hits them all up and down my body.

He keeps going, making sure to hit the cuts that have formed, deepening them.

I am going to vomit from the pain, but I stifle it down, knowing what would happen if I were to.

I try to will my brain to go elsewhere and not think of the pain being inflicted on my body.

Suddenly, Rio takes the handle of the flogger and roughly rubs it between my thighs, hitting my sensitive clit, still sore from yesterday.

"You're so wet from this," he says in a low tone, grinding himself against me so I can feel his arousal.

He could not be further from the truth. I am completely dry.

Suddenly, he shoves the handle up inside of me, and I scream at the unexpected intrusion. He begins brutally fucking me with the handle, eliciting more screams from me. He laughs and keeps going at a fast pace.

Deeper and deeper, he drives it into me. I am sure he has hit my cervix; I feel cramping. My entire body goes limp, and right before I am about to black out from the pain, he pulls it out of me and starts whipping my back in a quick pattern. My survival instincts kick in and keep me from blacking out.

I curse to myself, wanting to black out so I can escape the pain.

"Time is up. We will move to the final flogger, the horsehair flogger." I can just hear the grin in Will's voice. "Guards, remember we stick to the backside only. No marks are to be made anywhere else," he instructs them.

I hear more shuffling over to the wall and then the floggers being tossed carelessly into the bin. The guards clap each other on the back, snickering at each other as if this is some kind of sport, complimenting each other's technique.

The sick fucks.

Rio returns and puts himself at eye level with me, pure malice in his eyes as he says, "You're going to love this one." He shows me the long horsehair flogger, with tiny barbs scattered throughout the hair and a leather handle. He strokes it, and I flinch at the sight of it causing cuts to his hand, but he doesn't wince. No, not Rio. He gets off on any type of pain infliction.

He slowly walks behind me.

My body is trembling with suspense. He soaks in my fear and is far from impulsive, wanting to enjoy every moment of this.

He brushes the flogger over my shoulder, letting it hang beside my neck where it strokes the top of my breast. Then, he does it to the other side.

My hands shake uncontrollably, and my teeth begin to chatter.

He whacks me across my back, and the warm spray of blood steadily drips down my back. I yell out from the unimaginable pain, kicking my legs back and forth, trying to sit down, but my hands and my head are held tightly in place. My hands tingle as they go numb from trying to squeeze them through the holes. I have no choice but to keep myself upright.

Again, he hits me across the back in the opposite direction than before, and I feel the blood spray and drip down my back. I am screaming now without holding anything back, animalistic sounds coming from my mouth that I have never heard before. Tears freely flow down my face, wishing for it to stop.

"Mmmm, I am the artist, and you're my muse; your blood will

coat the floor of this room when I am done," he yells, more to himself than to me.

Then, he whips both of my thighs, and the horse hairs wrap themselves around them, the barbs sinking into my skin.

Finally, the pain is too much, and the darkness overtakes me.

CHAPTER THIRTY-FIVE

CASSIDY

Gradually, I open my eyes to bright lights shining over me, and my hands and ankles are bound on a table.

My eyes spring open. I am in a hospital room.

Did someone save me? Am I out of the house of horrors? Did I dream up the entire thing? Tears begin forming in my eyes.

That hope is abruptly snuffed out as the doctor who checked me in days ago walks in the door. I gasp.

I look down at my body. I am naked with just a white sheet over me. I see the wires connected to some type of machine that is checking my heart rate and other vitals, I am assuming with the multiple wires.

Then, I notice the IV.

Fuck, what is happening?

The doctor ends the silence and the crazy possible scenarios that are running through my mind.

"You lost quite a bit of blood from the flogging, so we had to conduct a blood transfusion."

"How long have I been here?" I croak out, my throat dry.

"About twelve hours. Don't worry, you won't miss today's training." He grins savagely.

I can barely move my head; it hurts everywhere.

"I have bandaged up the cuts along your backside and put some antibiotic ointment on them to reduce the risk of infection, and I also have given you liquids through the IV," he continues.

"About another hour of liquids, and you can join the rest of the women for day four of your training," he says happily like I'm on my way to Disney fucking World.

I lay there motionless, not knowing what to do or say. He checks the monitors, squeezes the IV bag, and then leaves without another word.

I have to try to get out of here. I look at the cuffs and try to reach them with my mouth, but they are secured tightly with buckles.

Heaving myself painfully over to my right hand, I use my teeth to bite at the cuff, pulling it as hard as I can, even with the searing pain on my back. My teeth tingle as they cling to it.

To my utter surprise, it loosens.

My heartbeat starts beating erratically. The machine begins beeping frantically, and I stop what I am doing, but no one comes running in. Holy shit.

I quickly begin biting at it again, and it loosens enough so that I can slip my hand out.

I roll over and get to work on freeing my other wrist, working my fingers through the buckle, perspiration forming on my head and my hands.

It loosens, and I slide my hand out. I sit up and groan in pain, rubbing my wrists.

I get to work on my left ankle and free it, then my right ankle, and the cuffs fall to the floor.

Gritting my teeth, I rip the IV out, and blood starts trickling down my arm. I run to the sink and drawers, throwing open the cabinets to find the medical tape. I tape up my arm at lightning speed, understanding my time is limited.

I duck down and move toward the door. There is a small square window at the top, and I don't want anyone to see me, already hoping that no one heard me.

I sigh, remembering there is a lock on every single one of these doors, and I don't know the code.

Holding my breath, I try the handle. To my surprise, the handle moves down. My stomach is in my throat as the realization hits me—I could escape. This could actually happen, and I could get out of here.

Slowly opening the heavy door, I peek my head up and down the hall.

Empty.

I creep out of the room and turn right.

Walking turns into full-blown running, looking for an exit like a madwoman; I take turns left and right, weaving toward any door or staircase that could lead me out of this place, looking up for any kind of signs with arrows or words.

I see a guard up ahead, and I skid to a stop, rushing behind a divot in the wall and urging it to swallow me up. I cover my mouth to stifle my heavy breathing and wait a few moments before peeking my head out.

The hallway is clear, and I take off again, some of it looking familiar. I see a door about a hundred yards away, and it looks different compared to the other doors.

Trusting my gut, I sprint toward it, trying to stay on the balls of my feet to prevent noise.

As my hand touches the handle and I feel the coolness of the metal, a force knocks into my side, and my feet lift off the ground as I fly through the air, landing hard on the other side of my body on the tiled floor.

Rolling over, groaning in despair and agony, I hear footsteps approach me.

I open my eyes, and Rio is crouching down, smiling at me.

"I thought it would be fun to watch you try to escape, princess; it was very entertaining," he taunts.

He grabs my chin, forcing me to look directly at him. "All that hope squashed and shoved right back down."

Anger washes over me, and without thinking, I say, "You're a piece of shit," and I spit in his face.

Still smiling, he sluggishly wipes off his face. "I cannot wait for training today; we are going to have so much fun together. He moves to grab my arm, and I push my body in the opposite direction, sliding on the floor and trying to get away.

He chuckles. "I love it when you fight me; I get bored so easily these days."

He snatches a handful of my hair close to my scalp and starts dragging me through the halls.

I desperately claw at his hands to try to get him to release my hair to stop the throbbing pain.

He is unbelievably strong, and with such little food provided to us, I feel weaker than ever. However, I don't give up; my stubbornness won't let me show any kind of weakness to him.

We reach a steel door where he types in a code and walks us through; I am still thrashing as he throws me to the floor roughly.

I get my bearings and look around at where he has brought me.

This room is bigger than the others, huge.

There are multiple beds set up, with four tall metal poles in the corners, and two women sit propped up on each bed. One woman lies on the bed, hooked up to a metal spreader bar, with her legs stretched as far as they can go, and her ankles are in cuffs with links attached to the poles. Her hands are stretched back above her head into handcuffs attached to the upper poles.

A guard is stationed at each bed, standing beside it.

There is another bed with a woman hooked up to the spreader bar, without a guard, and I swear my stomach completely bottoms out, knowing what is coming. My feet automatically move in that direction.

Will scoffs at me, narrowing his gaze with an annoyed expression. "You're late."

Feeling depleted, I don't even have a snarky comeback for him.

All my hopes of escaping this place have gone down the drain. To be so close to freedom and then have it taken away in the blink of an eye is depressing as hell.

My body aches, but not as much as my mind and my heart.

This place reaches inside you and pulls out your soul in the darkest and most depraved way, holding it prisoner. I will forever be part of these walls, alongside the other women.

Slowly, it has chipped away at me little by little until, finally, there is nothing left. I feel hollow.

I look up and notice Rio taking the position as the guard beside the woman attached to the spreader bar and me.

There is nothing left this place can claim from me. It has taken my body in every conceivable way, my mind, and now my will.

"Today is your fourth day of training. Your masters will expect you to be able to eat pussy as well as you can suck cock. You will be expected to actively take part in threesomes and orgies regularly, as I know your masters all have, how shall I say it, compulsive sexual behaviors." Will chuckles and continues, "You will also be expected to satisfy another partner while being fucked by another person or two at the same time." Will pauses for a dramatic effect and keeps going, "The slave on the spreader will be eaten out first, and then you will switch." He looks around. "Begin."

We are all already naked. Even the guards shredded their clothes before Will finished speaking. Rio begins stroking himself.

I have experimented with and kissed girls as a teenager, but never further than that. They want me to make her come? What if I can't?

I move slowly onto the bed and get in between her legs, which are spread as wide as they can go. She looks me in the eyes and nods, telling me with her body language to go ahead, offering me consent even though we don't have a choice in the matter.

I am on my knees as I bend forward, taking in the scene. I can see every part of her pussy. I send a quick prayer of thanks that I have spent a lot of close-up time with my own, getting to know my body thoroughly and what turns me on.

I am just going to do to her what I typically like and see if it works. I graze my fingers over her center, lightly touching and rubbing. I see her clit, and I put it in between my fingers and rub it while gently pulling it. She lets out a whimper.

I take my thumb and move it side to side over her clit, and I get another reaction from her; she twitches and lets out a slight groan.

Continuing to move my thumb back and forth over her clit, I take my other hand and easily slide one finger inside her, working it back and forth.

Then, I slide two fingers in, moving them faster. She arches her back, enjoying the pleasure.

I feel myself getting wet between my thighs while watching her. This is turning me on.

I decide to remove my thumb from her clit and press my face closer, sticking out my tongue, and I begin moving it up and down her clit while still sliding my two fingers in and out of her. My ass is in the air as I lap up her juices.

She is moaning loudly now. "Don't stop," she pants. "I am almost there."

I feel movement behind me, but I pay no attention, too focused on wanting her to unravel before me. My legs are kicked apart, and a hand shoves my shoulders down, pushing my breasts into the mattress, and my face is completely in this woman's legs.

I don't stop pleasuring her. I replace my fingers with my tongue and fuck her with it, and my fingers go back to working her clit.

Suddenly, a cock is slammed inside me, and I can feel him all the way up to the hilt as his balls smack against me. I know it is Rio, but I really don't care. I am so turned on from eating her out, and I need a release, too. Rio grabs hold of my hips and begins thrusting into me more roughly, pulling his cock all the way out and then shoving into me with all his strength. At one point, I'm pushed so far forward I'm struggling to get air in, but I don't slow my pace.

She grabs onto my hair and starts fucking my face, moaning, "Yes, yes, yes!"

I am dripping at this point; I am so aroused. She screams as her legs clasp my head, and she comes all over my tongue. I lick up every bit of it, tasting her. She throws her head back, completely dazed, watching Rio fuck me from behind.

Just as I am about to come, Rio stops and pulls out, pinching my clit so hard to stop me from coming.

"You bad girl, you aren't supposed to come yet," he taunts as he unbuckles her.

"Time to switch. Cassidy, jump on the bed, now!" Rio yells.

I lie on my back, and Rio fastens my arms to the cuffs on the poles and my legs to the spreader bar. Then, he fastens a ball gag to my mouth.

"Look at you, princess, ready to be eaten." He licks his lips. "When she makes you come, I don't want you screaming anyone's name but mine, so I will be fucking you after she brings you there."

I glare at him, daring him to fucking do it. He chuckles, pinching my nipple so hard it feels like it's going to rip off. "I own your body until your master comes to claim you."

The woman bends low and starts doing the exact same thing I did to her. The caressing begins, getting the lay of the land. Then, she begins flicking my clit, moving it back and forth and lightly up and down. Then she blows on it, which feels so fucking good since I am already wet as hell down there.

She puts two fingers inside me and begins fucking me while

licking my clit. I watch as Rio lines up behind her, squirting lube all over his dick and onto her backside.

I look in horror as he slams into her backside without warning and with no prep. She can't help but scream out, and I feel it on my pussy. To my surprise, she keeps licking and probing my hole, fucking me with her tongue while Rio fucks her ass.

I can't help it; I start moaning, and my eyes roll back into my head as I arch my back and come all over her tongue and face, squirting everywhere.

I come back down from my high, and Rio has pushed the woman off the bed. His cock is fully erect and hard as a rock as he slams into me and rips off the ball gag. He takes the spreader bar and lifts it to where it is almost hitting my head, attaching it to something. There must be some sort of clip there. My pussy and ass are on full display, my thighs touching my chest. He lifts my hips slightly and continues slamming into me. He doesn't have a small dick by any means, and he is going so deep that it hurts and feels good at the same time.

They would be happy to know the training is working.

Closing my eyes, chasing the feeling of euphoria, I am almost there again. I can feel another one coming.

Rio slaps me hard in the face. "Keep your eyes open, and say my name when you come."

Inner turmoil surges through me at having my tormentor and rapist making me come and wanting me to say his name as I do it. There is no way.

But what is the alternative? Piss him off and get sent to the red room for a day? No thanks.

I have no choice, and it sickens me. He is making me hate my body while my body is betraying me.

The waves start racking my body, and I know I am about to come. I chase it and let my body go. I scream and come all over Rio's dick while saying his name.

Not letting me enjoy this tiny escape, Rio jerks out of me and comes all over my face.

He undoes my arms and says, "Clean your face with your fingers and lick them clean."

Defiantly, because I truly feel broken and like there is nothing else they can do to me, I say, "No." He hits me over the head with so much force I feel my teeth rattle.

"Do it," he snarls.

Will appears and pulls Rio off me. "We can't put marks on their faces; we will be punished."

"I want her in the red room tomorrow for disobeying a direct command," Rio tells Will.

"Sure, sure. We will finish up here, clean up, get the girls to bed, and I will send her to the red room first thing in the morning. Or you can pick her up from her bed and save me the hassle," Will says calmly.

"I'll come collect her first thing in the morning," Rio growls.

I blanch and tremble all over, my imagination running wild as to what will be waiting for me tomorrow.

Will ushers me and the other woman to a wall by the door and hands us an apple, some bread, and a water bottle. I finish it quickly while looking at the other girls still performing on the beds.

I hear one girl cry, "I can't get her off, I'm trying everything!" A loud whipping sound envelops the room, and she cries louder.

"Get her off, or you'll have a severe punishment," the guard threatens her.

She starts eating the other woman's pussy like it's a Thanksgiving meal.

The moans and groans are so loud in this room that I am surprised it did not distract me, but I was so aroused with pleasure that I was able to block it out.

Trying not to think about the red room, fear races through my mind. I hold my knees to my chest and begin rocking back and forth. I cannot lose my mind in this place; it is all I have left. My mind wanders to my family, Blair, and, most of all, Tyler. I miss them so much that my chest aches.

After the last group finishes, we are escorted to the bathrooms and then back to our cots. Sleep does not come immediately due to the anxiety of thinking about tomorrow, and I toss and turn in my cot. Hours pass by before rest wins out, and I close my eyes and pass out.

CHAPTER THIRTY-SIX

TYLER

"Have you seen this woman?" I ask the bartender at a local bar.

He shakes his head, not giving me the time of day.

I lean over the bar with the picture in my hand. "Please just take a good look at her picture and tell me if she's been in here in the last few weeks," I ask again, my voice getting more stern.

He drops his rag from cleaning up the bar, getting ready for it to open, lets out an irritated sigh, and finally gives the picture his full attention, fed up with me.

"No, I haven't seen her man. Check the other bars around campus," he tells me, and gets back to his task.

"But I have checked over twenty bars in this area, and they've said the same thing," I grumble, more so to myself because the man has gone back to acting like I don't exist, wanting me to leave as soon as possible.

Storming out of the bar, I slam the door in frustration and make my way to my car parked out front.

I jump in and let out a yell, consumed with defeat, and bang on the steering wheel.

Everywhere. I have checked everywhere. Local bars, local hangouts, and other fraternities and sororities.

No one has even seemed to recognize her photo. How does someone just disappear like this without a trace or scrap of something left behind?

I have even posted missing persons posters all over campus, trying to gather any information I can.

I reach for my phone and make my daily call to the person who can relate to what I'm going through right now the most.

It rings, and I wait.

"Nothing today, Tyler," Blair says cryptically.

"You already checked in with Lillian?" I ask hopefully.

"Yes, you know I call her every morning, and nothing has changed in the investigation. The police have no leads. It is as if she vanished into thin air," she tells me in an exasperated tone.

"That isn't possible!" I yell, shaking my head in disbelief.

"Apparently so," she says on the verge of tears.

"I'm sorry, Blair, I didn't mean to upset you. I know you are hurting too and are desperate for answers," I say soothingly.

She sighs. "It is ok. I am barely making it through each day. I had to drop some of my classes because I just can't pull myself out of bed most days."

"She wouldn't want to see you like this, Blair; you have to keep fighting."

"I'm fighting to hold on, and it's barely by a thread," She cries.

I recoil, knowing how she must feel.

"I'll call you tomorrow," I tell her, and she just ends the call.

I have managed to keep my grades up and stick with my routine, but my mental health is at an all-time low. This obsession with trying to find Cassidy has consumed any extra spare moment I have.

From the moment I met her, I knew she was going to put a lasting imprint on me, but this was the last thing I expected to happen.

CHAPTER THIRTY-SEVEN

CASSIDY

Groggily blinking my eyes, barely opening them, not wanting to adjust to the bright lights yet, I take in the soreness of my body. Every day is a new ache, bruise, laceration, or exhaustion.

Before I am even able to move my body to get out of bed, my throat is seized, and I am wrenched from my cot and thrown up against the concrete wall.

My brain has not even registered what is fully happening. My head hits the wall with a loud smack, and my vision is instantaneously foggy.

I open my eyes to see who is cutting off my oxygen—Rio.

His nose is touching mine as he roars, "How did you pull this off, you fucking cunt!?"

I scratch at his wrist that is holding my throat, trying to get any air, and failing, but he tightens his grip, lifting me off the ground. "Your new master is demanding to have his property now, and I'm not quite through with you yet."

He lets me go, and I sink to the ground, holding my stomach. I curl over, trying to calm down, and take in deep breaths. I really thought that he was going to kill me—a couple more minutes, and he could have.

He kicks me in my ribs, and I hear a crack, doubling over.

I spit at his feet. "Fuck you," I say, laughing maniacally. "Now you'll have to find a new toy to play your sick games with."

He looks directly into my eyes, and all I see is darkness. "Sometimes the unknown is worse than the place you're currently in."

My body shudders all over, knowing he is speaking the truth. I wonder if he's met my master or, at the very least, heard of him.

He hauls me up by the back of my gown like I am some kind of rag doll and propels me ahead of him. "Go," he growls.

I will be glad to never see this asshole again. Am I supposed to know where to go in this shithole? Apparently, he assumes so.

He quickens his pace, grabbing onto my arm and wrenching on it so roughly I swear it's going to come out of the socket.

We stop abruptly, and he takes something shiny out of his pocket. I recognize the handcuffs and fight as hard as I can out of his grasp, not wanting to be at his mercy.

He snatches my bottom lip, bringing it to his lips. "Please keep resisting. I would love to give your master a reason as to why we are making him wait.

Then, he bites my collarbone so hard it pierces my skin just enough to leave indents of his teeth, blood rising to the surface.

Reluctantly, I place my wrists in front of me. Shaking his head at me, I roll my eyes as he positions my hands behind my back and fastens them tighter than he should.

"Ow, fucker," I hiss as it pinches and rubs uncomfortably on my skin.

Typical dick.

He starts guiding me to what I can only assume is the front of the warehouse. It resembles a traditional waiting room at a doctor's office, minus the secretary, making this officially the most fucked up place I have ever been to.

Dread fills my stomach. What will my master look like? Will he be brutal or show mercy and treat me like a pet of some sort? Sadness consumes me as I hope for the latter of the two.

I try to hold my head high. I'm leaving this fucking place. It did not break me. Almost, but not quite.

At the front of this waiting room stands a guard I have never seen before, and he is talking quietly to another man dressed in a perfectly tailored beige suit.

You can feel the power oozing from the guard; he must be the guy who runs the place.

I take in the man in the suit. Medium build, over six feet, with blondish brown hair and glasses.

He looks up as he sees me coming. This place has really fucked with my head. Desperately, I scan over him, looking for any sort of comfort or human connection compared to what I have been subjected to here.

He glances hungrily up and down at my appearance, and his lips quirk up in disgust.

I have not seen myself since the auction. I am sure I look like a crazed woman being released from an asylum.

He returns to whatever he is doing on his phone and says to no one in particular, "Let's go. The jet is on the tarmac, ready for takeoff."

Someone from behind me takes hold of my other arm, and we begin following the man in the suit. I glance up at my new holder, and he looks normal besides the earpiece he is sporting.

I'm placed nicely into the back of a blacked-out Cadillac SUV. The earpiece man slides into the driver's seat, and my master sits in the passenger seat.

I feel like a little kid being outside and taking in all the sights.

Embracing the sunlight and the feeling of the fresh air, I want to cry, thinking I would never get out of that place.

The drive is silent, and not long after we leave, we turn onto a narrow road. At the very end of it, I see a small airport. On the tarmac is a massive jet, and as we get closer, I can hear the engine has already been started. Someone stands at the bottom of the extended staircase on the side of the jet, wearing a uniform. It's probably the pilot. We pull up as close as we can, and I am removed more delicately than I have been in a while and escorted up the stairs to an empty seat, the guard buckling me in.

My master walks in ominously and sits in the row beside me, taking the farthest seat away, still typing away on his phone. Chancing it, I steal a glance at him.

"Martin," he blurts out.

Confused, I am unsure what to say, so I stay silent.

"That's my name, but you will address me as Master unless I specifically instruct you to call me by my first name," he tells me, not bothering to look up at me.

After taking off, the unbuckle light comes on, and he comes over and unlocks my handcuffs. "There is a bathroom in the back of the plane; please shower and dress in the clothes set out for you. I expect you to look presentable. There are hair tools and some makeup in there as well. You have one hour," he says as he pulls me up from my seat.

Not knowing what to say, I respond quietly, "Yes, Master." I start heading to the back of the plane. Relieved is an understatement. I'm eager to take a hot shower and feel like myself again.

I reach the bathroom door and turn on the lights, scared to look at my reflection, but I make myself do it anyway, wanting to get it over with.

I see myself in the mirror, and my jaw drops at the woman looking back at me. My face is thinner, I have bags under my eyes, and my hair is tangled and matted. I slowly take off the hospital gown I have been accustomed to wearing and inspect my body.

I gasp as I see the bruises, welts, and healing scratches on my backside.

My throat has the newest bruises that look grotesque. I could try to cover some of it up with some of the makeup in here.

First things first, I start the shower, letting it heat up until steam forms.

I moan internally. I've missed a hot shower. Before this, I would have thought nothing of it, but now it's a small luxury.

I hop in and notice the nicest shampoos, conditioners, and soaps from France, recognizing the French words on their labels. They smell amazing. This guy has to be rich beyond belief.

I use every single one and finally step out, sighing deeply and feeling refreshed. It felt good to wash away old blood, bodily fluids, grime, and other things I'm not entirely sure about, but I know that some scars from that place I will never be able to wash away.

I get to work with a blow dryer and curler while also applying my makeup, trying to cover up all the bruises that would be visible with clothes on, focusing on my throat.

I look over at the outfit hanging in the little closet in the bathroom. It is a little black dress that's going to hug all of my curves, and it's so short that I'm afraid if I bend over, my ass will show. Sitting underneath it are black high heels with red bottoms.

There are no undergarments, which makes sense since the dress has a plunging neckline. But no panties? I shiver at the thought.

I finish getting ready and look at myself one more time in the mirror, shaking slightly at my new reality.

Telling myself I can get through this, I open the door and move back to my seat on the plane.

My master hasn't moved, but he notices my presence as I take my seat, still not looking directly at me.

"I hope you like steak and potatoes because that's what they are about to serve us," he says.

My mouth salivates at the thought. The flight attendant wheels out our meals, and the aroma reaches my nose. I have to fight back the urge to jump on the table and shove my mouth to the brim.

A table slides out from the wall beside me, and a plate is placed in front of me with silverware. The flight attendant then serves us the meal. I look over at Martin, and he's looking at the meal, and then looks over to me. "You may eat."

I try to be as mannerly as I can muster as I cut every bite into small bite-like pieces, and I can't help the moans that come out of my mouth as the steak melts on my tongue; it is cooked to perfection. The only thing that is missing is a good glass of red wine. As if reading my mind, the flight attendant places wine glasses in front of us, showing the bottle to Martin. He nods, and she fills them both to the halfway point.

I gulp that down. Only having minimal water for multiple days, I would have gulped down anything they put in front of me. I barely even tasted the red wine; it just hit the back of my throat.

I finish my meal, wipe my mouth with the napkin, and lean back, feeling completely satisfied.

Martin looks over at me with an eyebrow quirked and laughs.

"You must really like steak," he says to me.

"You could say that." I chuckle back.

"Dessert will be served at my house; we will be descending there in about fifteen minutes," he announces.

I simply nod once, not knowing what to say as we embark on my prison. Martin doesn't seem that bad. Maybe I lucked out and got one of the better masters who just wants companionship.

As the plane descends, he steps ahead of me and offers me his hand, and I take it as he helps me down the stairs, careful not to trip in these heels.

I take in his mansion, or should I say compound. There are three different houses with huge gates, some made of iron and some of concrete. Some people like their privacy; I cannot fault him for that. The landscaping is lush and full of vibrant, colored flowers, and the lawn looks well-kept. I try to commit my surroundings to memory and see if anything looks familiar. For all I know, we could be in an entirely different country.

Moving through paved pathways, dimly lit by motion-sensor lights, we walk beside one another to the mid-sized home.

We pass through another antique-looking iron door, and it opens into a beautiful courtyard, where the front door to the home awaits.

Martin opens it with a wave of his hand. It must be a smart home that is chip-activated. I look up, and there are cameras scattered all over the place. I am not entirely surprised.

Walking into the home, it is a very cozy Victorian feel. There is exposed brick on one of the walls in the front room, featuring large leather cigar sofas and a thick burgundy wool rug in the center, alongside an old-looking fireplace.

Suddenly, I stop walking. Martin notices and looks at me as he says, "The kitchen is right through here. Do you like chocolate or strawberry?"

Suspiciously, I answer the opposite of what I would normally say, "Strawberry."

He smirks and heads through the double oval archway. Cautiously, I follow him through and gasp in awe at the beautiful kitchen.

I take in the green cabinets, marble countertops, and the two islands in the middle, each with a beautiful butcher block atop it. This place looks like a home you would see in Architectural Digest.

He opens the fridge door and pulls out what looks like a strawberry cheesecake, freshly made on a serving dish, and places it on the island nearest to him.

He slides open a drawer and reveals two spoons, waving them in my direction, then points with them to a barstool in front of him. "Sit."

Without hesitating, I move to sit down, and he glides a spoon in my direction.

"This was freshly made today by my private chef; it is one of my favorites," he informs me, casually leaning his hip into the island, already poking the spoon at the cake.

Copying his movements, I bring a spoonful to my mouth and close my eyes, savoring the delicious taste as the sweet strawberry flavor bursts on my tongue.

"Oh my god," unexpectedly falls out of my mouth, and I quickly move my spoon back toward the cake for another bite.

Martin chuckles. "Tell me your name."

Apprehensively, I take him in for a moment and say, "They already told you my name."

"But I want to hear it from you," he replies softly.

"Cassidy, but my friends call me Cass." I have no idea why I shared that personal information with him.

"Hmm, well, Cassidy, tell me what you were studying in school."

"Statistics," I tell him promptly, perking up as my passion spills over as if this is all normal.

"So, I take it you must really love numbers?" He raises his eyebrow at me.

"You could say that."

"Do you want something to drink? I always like milk with my cake."

"Milk is fine."

Martin sets off to a different side of the kitchen, and I watch as he opens a cabinet door with glass paneling. I can see that this is where the crystal is on display. He plucks two beautiful glasses and fills them both with milk precisely at the same level, taking his time.

Holding the cold fancy glass in my hand, I down the milk straight away, not letting up for air as I gulp it down.

Placing the glass down in front of me, I notice Martin sipping on his.

"Do you want a tour of this place?" He grins in a friendly manner.

"Sure," I respond indifferently, still feeling really unsteady about this entire situation, but at a loss for what my new life will hold.

He looks at me darkly and vehemently says to me, "Is that any way to reply to your master?"

Color drains from my face; is this a Jekyll and Hyde situation? Not wanting to upset him further, I obediently say, "Yes, Master, that would be very kind of you."

He sets off walking me around his house, or rather, his museum. There are seven grand bedrooms, five and a half bathrooms that any woman would eat her left arm to have, a theater, a gym, and a library.

At the end of the tour, we make our way back to the kitchen, and the wine must be hitting me because I feel a little buzzed, and my vision is blurry.

"I haven't shown you my favorite part of the house," he says coyly.

"Well, you brought me back to the kitchen, so I've seen it."

Martin throws his head back and laughs. "That is most people's favorite part of the house, but it is not mine."

Not wanting to say the wrong thing, I stay silent.

"No, not the kitchen for me; it's the wine cellar," he says with a twisted grin on his perfectly shaped face, pointing coolly to an older-looking Italian door with brushed glass that I hadn't noticed before.

He gazes at me, his eyes devoid of emotion, which I haven't seen yet. Fear washes over me.

Sauntering arrogantly over to the door, I follow him, indulging him in this tour that I could give two shits about. I just want to get some sleep. I convince myself that this is just another room, and I need to go since I plan on escaping at the first opportunity, and therefore, need to familiarize myself with every inch of this house.

Swinging open the door, he says, "Ladies first." His expression is deadly, eyes glinting full of excitement

Straightening my spine, I manage to muster courage I don't

feel. This seems off, but in the back of my mind, I attempt to calm myself down; he could just be a wine enthusiast. After all, it is a wine cellar.

As we descend on a black iron spiral staircase, my mind drifts to Martin, reasoning with myself that he is an extremely attractive, fit older man who comes off as charming if you are into that sort of thing.

And he buys women to keep as his property.

He made me forget that fucked up character trait for a moment.

Hardening my expression, I steadily walk down the steps, not wanting to fall.

The light is very dim, and I take in the fact of how far this underground cellar really is. The coldness trickles through me.

"I custom-built this so I could ship the finest wines from across the world and store them down here."

He rattles on about the different countries the wine he owns originated from, and I zone out, not meaning to. The wine has hit me in a way alcohol never has; it could be because I went without it for a while and had barely anything on my stomach for days. Everything is swaying. He cuts me off on the staircase, now leading the way down the stairs, and I weakly follow, worrying about being able to physically stand much longer, let alone walk for however long down here.

"I own a few vineyards in Europe and produce my own wine as well," he continues as we reach the concrete floor at last. There is a wall near me, and I flail my hand out, reaching for it, attempting to balance myself and stop my double vision.

Martin comes over to me and looks me over with genuine care in his eyes, "Are you feeling alright?"

"Yes, yes, I am fine. It must be the wine and the speed at which I drank it after not having a drop of alcohol for so long," I explain, pushing him away from me in case I vomit.

"You don't look so good," he says, leering over me.

My legs give out underneath me, and I fall clumsily to my

knees. Soon after, the rest of my body goes slack, and I stare up, panicking and puzzled at what is going on.

Martin towers over me, straddling my head as he bends down, laughing. "We're going to have so much fun together," he purrs as he captures my lip with his teeth and bites down firmly.

Everything turns black.

CHAPTER THIRTY-EIGHT

CASSIDY

The agony throbbing in my arms pulls me from the darkness, bringing me back to the present. I sluggishly open my eyes, not wanting to see the mess I am in now. Facing it head-on, I frantically take in my predicament. My stomach sinks as I come to. My arms are suspended above my head with my wrists tied into an intricate knot and attached to an elongated hook hanging from a metal rod that extends to each side of the room, anchoring me.

A cool breeze brushes my skin, and I suddenly notice that I am naked and exposed.

Looking down, I see that the tops of my toes are barely brushing the floor. That is when I glimpse the multiple drains in the floor, coated in a nasty, rust-colored substance that matches the splotches on the walls. There are no windows, and the walls appear to be deteriorated concrete, suggesting that this place has been here for a while, something you would see if you stripped away a building to the studs.

Sheer panic consumes me when I look over and see a leather apron hanging with rubber boots alongside it and a table of assorted tools, pliers of all sizes, a hammer, axes, a chainsaw, and other tools I do not know the name of. All are spread out in a neat line with sharp or jagged edges.

At least my torturer is organized. Wow, what a relief. The tools are clean.

My arms feel as if they are going to rip out of their sockets. I must have been out for a while. Suddenly, it all floods back to me in a jumbled mess—leaving the warehouse, meeting Martin, going into his house, eating dessert, and touring the home.

It was all a setup to catch me off guard and believe his façade. But why? Why show any type of kindness and then inevitably hold me in a place I knew was a possibility?

It is all part of his ruse.

The heavy footsteps outside the concrete door grow louder as they approach. One by one, the assortment of locks is unlocked, and Martin strolls in, whistling to himself.

"Hello, my dear Cassidy," he croons in a calm but terrifying voice.

I swallow a lump in my throat as sweat beads and slips down between my breasts.

He walks over to me and yanks on the rope, pulling my arms from my body further, and a loud cry is wrenched from my lips from the shock of the pain. My skin is crawling from the evil aura he gives off.

"You can give me the silent treatment now, but you'll be really talkative here soon when we begin, pleading for me to stop." There's a danger lurking in his eyes, accompanied by a twisted grin.

"Begin what?" I startle, my voice cracking.

Martin pats me on the head before grabbing my face harshly between his hands, possessively growling, "You are mine. I own every inch, every crevice of you. You are breathing because I allow it."

He turns his head, eyes focused on the table of tools, and gestures to them with a sick smile on his face; silence ensues as he studies me, waiting for a reaction.

"You can't expect me to think you're going to use those on me," I whisper, shaking in disbelief, uneasiness spreading through my stomach.

"Cassidy, how many times do I have to remind you? You are my property, and I will do whatever I damn well please to you." He brushes his hand up and down over the tools, savoring my anticipation and fear.

I release a shaky breath as his eyes roam over me.

Martin selects a long wrench and comes back over to me. While standing in front of me, he drags it lightly from my wrists and over my nose and mouth, pausing on my right breast.

Cupping underneath my breast and yanking it toward him, he latches on, sucking and biting down on my nipple. Fighting every instinct not to cry out, I squirm, trying to get away from him. At last, the burn wins out, and I let out a guttural scream as he bites even harder until his teeth are under my skin and blood oozes out.

Tears drip down my cheeks, completely at his mercy, wiggling relentlessly, wanting to block this out or, at the very least, focus on the other pain in my arms.

Martin laps at the blood pouring from my nipple, erotically licking, sucking, and pulling on my entire breast.

"As I was saying, I own every piece of you. You are nothing more than the plot of land I bought yesterday." He leans back and continues dragging the wrench down my navel, stopping at my pussy. He takes the wrench and drags it between my legs, lifting it to his nose and smelling it. My core pulses as I brace my body for the inevitable torture.

"Ahh, just what I thought. What a sweet smell." He then licks the wrench, tasting my juices.

"You taste divine," he purrs in my ear.

My blood runs cold as my head spins. Resuming the mental torment, he carries on stroking the wrench down my body until he gets to my toes, tapping every toe on both of my feet as I am paralyzed with dread.

"Why are you doing this?" I bravely blurt out.

"The question you should be asking is, why not? When you are a man like me who has the world at his fingertips, I want what others cannot have, cannot even fathom. Human flesh. The total power over another person, knowing that at any moment I could take your life if I so wish it."

Reeling at what he just said, my stomach coils, and I ask, "So there have been others you have done this to?"

He throws his head back and laughs heartily. "Oh, my dear girl, there have been many, many others. Men, women, children. Specifically, whatever I am craving at any given moment. My appetite knows no bounds, and it is insatiable," he taunts.

"All of this is some kind of sick game to you from the moment I met you?"

"Oh yes, I love filling your stomach, getting you comfortable, having you under the impression that kindness is going to be bestowed on you after what you endured at the auction house, and then having you wake up here. It is always the same, and the delight that washes over me knowing it was all premeditated and I was the puppet master the entire time, it's unmatched," Martin joyfully reveals.

"You're a sadistic fuck," I snarl, shaking my head at him.

"Oh, Cassidy, I am just a wealthy man who gets bored with his wife and can come down here and let this little persona of mine out of his cage. I get off on pain. In fact, I wish I could bottle it up and bathe in it."

I'm frozen, but I must keep him talking. He is a narcissist and loves talking about himself, so I will just play the part of ignorance, which I am sure he will just eat up.

"What kind of pain?" I wince, not wanting an in-depth answer from him.

"Every kind, but physical pain is what really does it for me. I love watching blood flow from another's body from what I inflicted. I have been obsessively going through scenarios about exactly what I want to do to you tonight since you have been sleeping, and I haven't come to a decision yet."

"Sleeping? You drugged me!" I spat at him angrily.

"Same thing. You were quite fond of the milk." He shrugs indifferently.

I think back to the glass of milk he gave me. He was across the room when he grabbed the glasses. He could have crushed anything into the glass and had it prepared before I even got there.

Just like an innocent lamb, so naïve for the slaughter.

"Look at your tight little body." He lays his hand on his bulge, stroking it up and down. "We really are going to have the best time together." He nuzzles the side of my neck, inhaling deeply

"I doubt that," I snap back.

He goes over to his tools of torture again, walking back and forth, causing chills to break out across my skin.

My hands are numb, having lost all feeling, and my head hangs down, wishing my mind could drift away from here.

Martin selects surgical-looking pliers. They are silver and appear to be about two feet long.

Holy fucking shit. This guy really does get off on extreme torture.

Sucking on my bottom lip as firmly as possible, I try to prevent myself from shaking.

"I love inflicting pain on others. The screams, the crying, the fear, the helplessness, and the begging, all of it gets me off in a way nothing else does," he whispers more to himself than to me. "I spend all day in the OR, operating on patients that are asleep and can't feel the pain I'm inflicting."

Of course, I would get a sadist as my master.

He clasps the top of a metal chair and tows it over until he is sitting about three feet in front of me. He props one of his ankles on top of his thigh so that he can rest the pliers on his lap.

"The goal is not to mar you just yet. You are my new plaything. I want to extend my time with you as long as possible. I wouldn't want to mess up that pretty face of yours, at least not for a while," he claims. eerily calm. "I will extract piece by piece from you until you are broken down to the point you plead with me to take your life. The fire will eventually leave your eyes, and it will give me immense pleasure. And so, the cycle goes on."

"I will kill you!" I shout, not knowing where that bravery came from as it glided through my lips.

He laughs maniacally. "Many have tried throughout the years, but all have failed. You are at my disposal and have no leverage here." He waves his hand up and down, motioning to the predicament I'm in.

"I don't know how you and this organization have gotten away with this for so long, but I will burn it to the ground," I boldly shriek at him.

"Oh, my dear, you do not know the half of it and all the powerful people behind it. We get away with murder while people sit on death row." He snickers.

"Enough of the small talk; let's get started, shall we?"

He advances on me, with deviance coursing through him. Holding up the pliers, he opens and shuts them, letting me see how sharp they are and boasting a huge smile. Circling my bruised nipple, it slices into me, and I cry out, tears forming in the corner of my eyes before falling freely down my cheeks. He licks the trail of tears before they reach my chin. I resist the urge to scream out. I don't want to give him that power, but it only encourages him further.

The blood slowly drips down the length of my body, and he watches it with the precision of a predator.

Taking a step back, he absorbs the sight before him and sets about undressing.

His socks and designer shoes come off first, and he puts them on the chair next to his belt, pants, and custom-made dress shirt, all neatly stacked in a pile.

I gawk at him and his mannerisms, anger rolling through me at what he just revealed to me about himself.

He's stark naked before me. I inspect his entire body, noticing that it is toned to perfection. I'm puzzled as my mind plays with the idea that I would say he's good-looking for his age. If I had to guess, he's in his late forties or early fifties, and he is over six feet tall.

He reaches for the pliers that he placed next to the chair and struts over to me; he scans the floor, and I follow his eyes. That is when I see the chains and steel handcuffs about two feet apart from each other.

He lunges for one of my legs, and I desperately fight him with everything I have. I'm still feeling the aftereffects of the drug still running through my system, grogginess making my movements slower. Martin manages to lock one of my ankles down, and I kick out with my remaining free leg.

The bottom of my foot makes contact with his chest, and he laughs boisterously, loving every second of this. He snatches at my other leg, reaching out and failing to grasp it a few times. Frustration envelops his face, and he looks at me with danger lurking behind his eyes. After some time, he secures my other leg in the locks. I am spread out before him. Defeat overtakes me, but the little act of defiance causes my lip to quirk up, making a promise to myself that I am going to make this anything but easy for him.

I grit my teeth. "Go ahead, do your worst."

"Ah, ah, ah, Cassidy, not yet." He wags his brow at me as he circles me, and a myriad of emotions seem to cross over his face.

Abruptly, he halts in front of me with a manic grin. He looks relieved, as if he has made up his mind about what he intends to do to me.

One of his hands locks onto my foot, and with skilled precision, he opens the pliers slightly and snatches my second toe, pushing it up.

"No, no, no!" I scream with my entire chest, terror overwhelming me at what he is about to do to me. My eyes widen at the sheer horror of it all.

Like the surgeon he is, he lines up the pliers on the base of my toe, waiting for my reaction. My mouth hangs open, but no words seem to form.

Swiftly, he cuts it from my foot in one motion.

I throw my head back, and a glass-shattering wail erupts from me as blood spurts out from where my toe was. My vision becomes hazy, and everything fades into blurry shapes.

Beaming at me, he reaches down and gathers some of the blood in his hand and lathers it all over his cock, jerking it a few times to smear the blood all over himself from base to tip.

He works his cock harder as he practically sprints behind me.

A sharp pain explodes from between my legs, and I scream out in all-consuming pain as he pushes himself past my entrance.

Even if I make it out of this alive, this man and this place will forever be etched into my skull.

"I've been looking forward to taking your pussy since I laid eyes on you at the auction," he groans, loving the sounds of my suffering. "That's why I had to come collect you early. I couldn't get this image out of my head," he says as he fucks me so roughly I know I'm tearing.

To him, I'm only a fuckable statue.

Tears fall from my face, and my screams have been rendered silent. I can barely breathe, desperate for this to be over with.

My inner walls are stretched to the limit as the foreign feeling of having this man brutally fuck me registers.

I try to escape mentally, but the pain in my foot is unbearable.

A loud scream escapes from my mouth, and it only spurs him on even more as he clutches my hips tighter and then pulls out as he releases his semen, the ropes of sticky liquid hitting the back of my body.

My core feels raw and battered. Appalled at what just happened, I stare down at the floor, focusing on my toe.

Humming to himself with satisfaction, he goes to a door I hadn't noticed before and pulls out bandages and a suture kit.

Bending down, he hoists my foot on a stool as he pulls over another chair to sit on. His expression is unreadable as he begins suturing the hole where my toe used to be.

Flashes of blood obscure my view, each throb causing more discomfort.

My hands aren't the only thing that is affected by numbness.

I don't know any purpose for me here other than to satisfy his twisted desires.

Finishing up with my foot, he works on the cut on my nipple, cleaning it with saline and bandaging it.

This monster.

I'm surprised I haven't blacked out yet.

He finishes with all my wounds and reaches up, untying me. I fall hard to the floor and slump into a fetal position; exhaustion and soreness take over my senses. I fall asleep immediately in my own blood.

Without saying a word, Martin leaves.

CHAPTER THIRTY-NINE

TYLER

It's chapter night for my fraternity, and I don't even have the energy to go. This is the last one before winter break. My family has organized a week-long trip on our family yacht to the Bahamas, and I am looking forward to relaxing and spending time in the sun. We leave in two days.

When it is Archer's turn to speak, he makes it quick and tells us to follow him, and I silently oblige his command, getting in line.

He takes us to a part of the fraternity house I have never been to before and explains the fraternity's illegal business operations. I try to block most of it out because it sickens me.

We move from each room, looking at the cages that are clearly made for animals and the hospital-like room for the preparation of the girls.

I act interested and walk through each room with fake excitement and curiosity.

In the preparation room, I spot something in the corner that catches my eye.

My stomach recoils; no, it can't be. It's just a strange coincidence. Vomit threatens to spill out of me.

Hanging back in the room until all the brothers exit, my heart thundering in my chest, I look around to double check that there is no one else in here and the door is shut.

I hold the item in front of me; it's an iPhone in a black case with pink cherry blossoms on it. I have only seen one other like it.

Swiping the phone hurriedly, I pocket it in case someone were to come back in.

My heart flutters as Archer comes in seconds later. "Get lost?" he asks suspiciously.

"I was just taking it all in." I grin at him, faking my excitement.

When we are finished, I rush up the stairs, taking two steps at a time as I make my way to my room, shutting my door and locking it immediately. I pull out the phone from my pocket, and sure enough, there's a picture of Cassidy and Blair on the lock screen.

Shock overwhelms me, and the phone tumbles out of my hand accidentally.

"No, no, no." I slump over, putting my head between my knees. Sickness rises up my throat, and I run for the small trashcan next to my desk, throwing up all the contents I had in my stomach.

Suddenly, a memory plays in my head about the encounter with Archer calling Cassidy a ghost.

Anger races through my veins, and I punch the wall next to me, leaving a decent-sized hole.

The feeling of helplessness floods me. Archer was right. How will I ever find her? They keep everything anonymous; there are no written records.

Pulling myself up, my mind whirls with scenarios of what Cassidy is enduring right now.

The darkness of pure grief over never seeing her again goes through my mind because that is the reality; she could be anywhere with who knows.

She has vanished without a trace, and there's nothing I can do about it.

CHAPTER FORTY

CASSIDY

As I come to consciousness, my foot is throbbing in pain, and between my legs feels broken and battered.

I'm strung up in the air again, my wrists tied securely to the hook like a creature awaiting slaughter.

Martin is right; he is going to be my undoing. He is going to break my soul along with any dignity I have left.

Marching in with a wicked look on his face, eyes filled with malice, he grips my chin tightly, igniting all my senses. "Today is going to be more fun than yesterday." He releases my chin, slapping my cheek a few times.

My heart flutters for the inevitable, more torture and assault on my body.

"We can skip the theatrics today and advance to the main part of the show," he states with brutal honesty as his face warps into perverse pleasure.

"If you have a wife or any type of family, I wish they knew what kind of monster you are," I spit, having no idea where that came from, but it is too late now because it's out there.

His eyes brighten, and he bursts into a fit of laughter, doubling over as he moves over to the table of tools.

"Oh, my dear girl, with the right amount of money and resources, you can hide just about anything, including a double life. Hiding this part of me comes easily. Blending in with society is a bit harder, but I have had plenty of practice."

His hands roam over a silver pair of sharp scissors that are longer than the typical kind you buy at the store.

Walking over to me with his hands behind his back, holding on to the scissors, he leans over at a ninety-degree angle and licks my pussy, taking his time.

Muffling my groans at the pleasant feeling, he leisurely removes his head from between my thighs, coating it with wetness.

Martin hums his approval at the taste of me, leering at my body as my head lolls backward.

"Shall we begin?" he asks as if I have a choice in the matter.

His hand drifts softly across my neck. My eyes tighten as I brace for the pain that is about to start.

He is scarily at ease as he holds the scissors in front of my face.

Methodically, he brushes my hair out of my face and behind my shoulder, taking his fingers and maneuvering the loose strands behind my ear.

Unsure of what is going to happen next, sweat beads on my forehead and under my arms, signaling that vomit is approaching as my nerves unsettle me.

With clinical precision, I hear the scissors open, and lacking any hesitation as any doctor does, he severs the top of my ear with one swift clip.

Feeling unbelievable agony at my cartilage being removed from my body, I scream in crippling pain as blood falls freely down the side of my face, dripping onto the floor.

My body flails, begging for my wrists to be released so I can scurry away from this cruelty.

At some point, he moved behind me and is now prodding my other entrance.

I register the uncomfortable feeling as he thrusts into my tight ring of muscle without any preparation.

My stomach coils as he latches onto my wounded ear harshly. A loud cry tears through me from the intrusion.

Leaning into the pain, I become completely immobile; I am a prisoner to this man. He moves his body side to side so his cock can hit different angles in my ass, pushing himself deeper and deeper into me.

He's still gripping my severed ear, and his breathing becomes increasingly excited by the torment he inflicted on my body.

I hear him groan, and I can feel his cock getting larger and larger inside of me until he releases spurts of hot liquid.

After a few more thrusts as he comes, he leans in, nipping the top of my shoulder before he whispers, "Your catatonic position only arouses me more."

"Keep it up," he taunts, smacking my backside hard enough that a huge pop-like sound erupts through the room.

I feel utterly powerless, sorrow overwhelming me at the depravity of the hell I'm in.

With blazing soreness lingering in my most intimate areas, I lower my head, submitting to the wickedness of my existence.

CHAPTER FORTY-ONE

CASSIDY

Startling awake, I find myself in a new room. From what I can see, it appears to be a bedroom. Chains rattle as I try to stand up. I look down, noticing that I am chained to the bed. I also take in the fact that I am naked again, with my arms and legs secured tightly. It feels like I was heavily drugged. As I strain to open my mouth, I become fully aware that something is in it, and my jaw is aching from the stretch. There's a ball gag strapped around my head.

Wriggling my body to no avail, I throw my head back in frustration.

Where has he taken me now? I take deep breaths in and out of my nose, doing my best to soothe my discomfort.

Organizing my thoughts, I try not to spiral, taking in my surroundings. The room is dimly lit. There are no windows, and the door is solid wood. The heat is unbearable; how can there be no air conditioning?

I lay there for what seems like hours before the door creaks open. My gut drops as Martin saunters through the door.

"She wakes!" Martin exclaims in a high-pitched tone. "You have been out for twenty-four hours. I had my men transfer you here." He motions to the room.

Even though I'm scared, I glare at him, no smart remarks, as my voice has been stolen from me.

Quickly looking at my body, I see I have been cleaned, and new bandages have been placed on my wounds.

Bile rises in my throat, and I squeeze my eyes shut, willing it to go away. I think about how Martin or some guard bathed me, the unwanted touch repulsing me.

A loud horn blares, and we begin to move. I have no idea where this bedroom is located. After a few minutes, Martin starts touching me between my legs. "I am going to fuck you in every hole while we are gone." No matter what, I can't fight my body's reaction to his touch, which happens to be pleasurable.

Wait. Gone? What does he mean?

And that is when I feel the up and down motion propelling us forward. My body is drifting up and then back down ever so slightly.

On edge, I gulp my anxiety down as much as the ball gag will allow me. I clench my core, recognizing we are on a boat. But with Martin, I'm sure it's more than likely a yacht.

CHAPTER FORTY-TWO

TYLER

Sitting on the deck of my family's yacht with an old-fashioned in my hand, I take in the sight of the ocean as we easily cruise over the waves.

My mind is still on Cassidy, and there has not been a day that I have not thought about her, thoroughly envisioning plans on how to find her.

Unexpectedly, my dad joins me, sitting down across from me on one of the many custom-made sectionals on the yacht.

I tilt my head as I gaze over at him. I'd consider my father a handsome man. He has a sharp jawline, salt-and-pepper-colored hair, and is muscular for his age. We share a lot of similar features.

Questions whirl through my brain about the fraternity, holding back anger for not being told the truth about it. I feel disgusted by the memories of being conditioned to rush, thinking it was just a normal fraternity experience. I don't even know where to start; there are so many questions.

I admired the man before me. There was nothing I wanted more than to follow in his footsteps, attend college, join his fraternity, and go on to medical school. Be the legacy he could be proud of.

I can't help but look at the man before me and see him entirely through a different lens after finding out about the illegal business behind the fraternity. He put up a façade, and no one knew the difference. He was alongside me, pushing me to be a part of something so corrupt. He lacks all morals for human life and involved me in the most grotesque way.

Bravely elevating my voice, I say, "Dad, there are some things that came up in the fraternity I wanted to talk to you about."

"Like what, son?" he asks, giving me his full attention.

"This illegal business they are heavily involved in that has been going on for who knows how long. Actual human trafficking? I can't stomach it. How could you be part of this?" My hands shake, demanding an answer.

Sighing, he looks over at the ocean in deep thought before he answers me, "Tyler, it is more common around the world than you think. There are some incredibly powerful people wrapped up in this. Your brothers, for one. There are countless connections and positions you would never even dream of that you will be able to select from.

"Yeah, but at what cost, Dad? How do I just turn a blind eye to this and not say anything?" I lean forward, hitting this next point with the most seriousness I can muster, "Human beings are being auctioned off as nothing more than sex slaves, wiped of their identities and rights." Instantly, I put my hands on either side of my face, trying to wrap my head around this and willing my dad to comprehend the severity.

"Listen, just keep your head down like I did and get through it. Man up and stomach it. Do as little as possible, only doing what is asked of you, and do not involve yourself with any of the slaves; take your emotions out of this." The words roll off his tongue nonchalantly.

"They told us the brothers who have graduated can take part in the auction; they can truly buy sex slaves for their own gratification. You aren't tangled up in that side, are you, Dad?" I ask, afraid of the answer.

"Of course not, son," he scoffs, brushing it off. "I am in love with your mother, and that is nothing but a dirty business. I own a prestigious medical practice; what would be the need for me to involve myself in that?"

I nod my head, feeling relieved by his answer. "I didn't think so, but I had to ask."

"Dad, I have this friend who rushed with me. She went missing, and I found evidence in the fraternity house; I am positive she was trafficked and auctioned off to a brother. There's no trace of her anywhere; she has completely disappeared. Is there any way to find her?" I plead with desperation.

"Tyler, you cannot go near any of that. Whoever she was sold to, that is the end of it. If you are caught seeking information on her, you could be punished. What are you going to do? Take away another brother's slave? That kind of offense is punishable, shamefully in front of the brotherhood, and could result in death," he informs me.

Tears form in my eyes, but they don't fall as I hang my head in defeat. Staring off into the ocean, I grieve the woman I fell hard for. Had the circumstances been different, I might have even loved her.

CHAPTER FORTY-THREE

CASSIDY

As I lay in bed in silence, all I can think about is that if I get the chance, I am jumping off this boat. I'll embrace death like it is a long-lost friend. I really couldn't care less if sharks get me or I drown. I am not going to let this man have control over me and torture me like this and then eventually kill me. I would rather do it myself.

I hear the locks on the door, and Martin enters, carrying head-phones with him.

He goes to the dresser beside the bed and pulls out sex toys. The shapes are unique but look like dildos.

"You will lay here with a vibrating dildo in your ass and your pussy," he says animatedly. "I'll be watching the show from up there." He points to the camera. "With the noise-blocking head-phones, the only thing you will be able to focus on is the orgasms that sporadically overtake you." With amusement dancing across his face, he sinks his teeth into his bottom lip and lustfully whispers, "I will be fantasizing all day about the sweet taste of your cum, impatiently waiting to come clean up your creamy thighs with my tongue."

The trauma of all of this causes my mind to zone out because Martin snaps his finger in my face, and a quick squeal escapes my lips.

Resuming his task, he hums a tune as he lubes up both vibrators. I see that both have remotes. He will be controlling the intensity of my pleasure throughout the day.

Great. Can't wait for the next impending torment.

The most I have ever orgasmed in a day is maybe two times.

He wants me to go an entire day filled with multiple orgasms? I will be physically drained and extremely sensitive afterward.

My legs are spread wide as he dips his finger inside of me, curling it, making contact with my G-spot. He starts to prepare me by stretching me with his fingers. He fucks me with his fingers moving them in and out of me, making it wet. Rubbing the vibrator up and down my slit, he pauses at my clit and lightly moves it from side to side, igniting my arousal. Then, as slowly as possible, he glides the vibrator into my pussy, and it goes in easily.

Next, he lines up the anal vibrator, reaching back for more lube as he coats my rim with it. Jutting a finger in, he swirls it around inside of me, stopping me from clenching and allowing me to relax at the unwanted intrusion.

My body complies, enjoying the sensations as he clicks a button on the remote. Turning them both on, a soft vibration begins.

Fuck me sideways. This sensation of feeling full and the vibration overwhelms my senses. I am going to come fast.

He turns up the vibrations. I writhe on the bed, unable to control myself.

"Oh, I almost forgot," he says as he slides the headphones on, careful of my damaged ear. He leaves the ball gag in place.

Before he even leaves the room, my body seizes up, and my muscles contract and spasm, and I come hard.

Slapping the inside of my thigh, he openly praises me, "That's my good girl." He shakes his head with amusement in his eyes and promptly exits the room.

The vibrators don't turn off. I am so fucked. Literally.

Unable to fight my body no matter how hard I try, escapes me, growing louder as the orgasms flow through me at an alarming rate. There must be some sort of limit. Seriously, how many times can someone come in a day?

CHAPTER FORTY-FOUR

TYLER

"Mom, please calm down. I'm just going down to the engine room like I always do. You know I love checking out the mechanics and any upgrades the staff has made," I tell her.

"Honey, I just want you to be careful. It's so hot down there, and you know how your father doesn't like anyone in that area of the yacht. It has always been forbidden and completely off limits to most of the staff members," she chides.

"Well, you caught me, but like I said, it's not my first time down there. I just like to hear the mechanics; it stills my warring thoughts."

She rolls her blue eyes and throws up her hands, surrendering to me. "Fine, I won't say anything; just be quick about it."

Descending the stairs, I open the thick, steel, white door to the engine room, which features a small, textured glass window that doesn't allow you to see clearly what's on the other side. Loud sounds wash out everything around me, even the ocean, and I love it. It allows me not to be in my head. It's the same concept as a white noise machine for me.

As I walk around the engine room, an unfamiliar door comes into view. This must be part of the upgrades they worked on during the yacht's renovation last year.

Cautiously walking up to the door, I hesitantly reach for the handle. I try to open it, but it won't budge because it's locked. That is strange. Gently, I press my ear against the door, and all I hear are ear-piercing moans.

Assuming it is some of the staff that have snuck off and wanted a quick fuck, I inwardly chuckle to myself.

Listening again, I only hear one person continuously moaning; it sounds like a woman, but it is hard to make out with the engine directly behind me.

Searching around the room, I find a key holder located on the wall beside the door I entered, with three sets of keys hanging from the hooks.

I start to think better of it. Disturbing her would not be the best idea, especially if she is about to reach her climax, but my intuition takes over, as well as my dick, and I convince myself that I will only take a peek.

Hurrying over to the key rack, I grab the first set of keys closest to the door. I try them out, but they don't fit. The same thing happens to the keys in the middle.

I take a deep breath as I hold the final set of keys in my hand. I place it in the lock and turn it, and it clicks. Nervously, I set my hand on the door and push, barely cracking the door open, and I hear a clunking sound.

Spinning around, I notice a set of keys fell to the ground because I did not secure them on the hook.

Sporting a bulge in my pants, I open the door.

The sight before me makes all of the hair on my arms stand upright, and goosebumps flow over my entire body. There, lying naked on the bed, is someone I thought had become a ghost.

CHAPTER FORTY-FIVE

CASSIDY

As I tremble through another orgasm, the door gradually opens, and my stomach recoils in disgust, expecting to see Martin. To my utter shock, I take in the familiar face before me.

Am I hallucinating?

My eyes widen, and my heart is about to leap out of my chest.

I frantically shake my head at him in disbelief, but also with a sense of panic.

He is totally stunned and unmoving, as if his body has frozen at the mere sight of me.

His face pales like he has seen a ghost.

I direct my head to the corner where the camera is located, trying with everything in me to warn him.

Not wanting to shift his gaze from me, he steadily turns his head to what I am wiggling my body toward.

The camera shows a green light when Martin is watching and a red light when it is off.

I lift my body as far as I can off the bed, the chains tearing into my wrist, but I don't care. We don't have much time before Martin turns on the camera.

Tyler must sense my urgency because he sprints to the side of the bed, looking me over, not sure where to start freeing me.

He makes a decision and unhooks the ball gag first, then rips the headphones off my ears.

I spit the extra saliva that had pooled in my mouth away from him. Now, I will be able to talk.

"What the fuck are you doing here?" he all but whispers.

My gut twists, and I take in his facial features.

Subtly, they are somewhat familiar, and it crashes over me. Martin and Tyler. They are related, but how? I jerk back from him instinctively, speechless, and silence fills the room.

Tyler blurts out, "I have been looking for you everywhere. I refused to give up on finding you."

Another thought dawns on me. Tyler is wrapped up in this. He knows about the illegal business the fraternity is involved in.

"How could you be entangled in this barbaric trade? Tyler, human beings are auctioned off as sex slaves?!"

He deceived me the entire time we were together. I thought he was a good person.

"Tyler, your uncle or maybe even your dad bought me at the auction," I croak out.

With harshness in his voice, he firmly says, "No. No, that is not possible." He backs away from me, his back connecting with the dresser, and it wobbles due to his distress. "My dad would never do something like that. He's a doctor. He cares for people in need."

"You have no idea who he really is underneath that mask he presents to the world," I spit out, throwing my head back and groaning since the vibrators are still on.

Tyler's eyes widen as he notices the tails of the vibrators hanging out between my legs, and his mouth drops open.

That is when he does a quick scan of my body, taking in the chains around my wrists and ankles.

"Please, you must leave now. The camera... Your dad turns it on every hour or so, sometimes less than that, to watch me."

"There's no way in hell I'm leaving you like this," he states, determined to rescue me from this.

"You have to until we can formulate a plan," I say hysterically, begging him. "Please, please just put the ball gag back on and then leave."

Not wanting to move, I can tell his mind is racing with alternative options.

"Go! Go now!" I raise my voice in agitation.

He snaps back out of his trance and places the ball gag gently in my mouth, securing it in place.

Tyler lightly kisses my forehead. "I promise you, I will be back and get you out of here."

Tears manifest in the corner of my eyes at the feeling; it has been so long since I had any sort of affection or care of any kind, and I know Tyler means it.

He leaves, rushing from the room and shutting the door quietly.

Throwing my head back on the pillow, I let out a sigh of relief.

But it's short-lived, as the color drains from my face when I see the headphones beside me. My stomach drops as I shake my head side to side violently—no, no, no!

CHAPTER FORTY-SIX

TYLER

I all but sprint back to the main deck, stopping at one of the walls hidden from view. I straighten up and roll my shoulders, calming down in case I run into my parents or any staff members.

How the hell is Cassidy here, of all places? My dad fucking bought her? After he blatantly told me that he has never been involved in the human trafficking business?

I just witnessed it with my own eyes, and Cassidy is my dad's personal sex slave. Pure, unfiltered anger tunnels my vision, and my fists clench.

I am going to kill him. He's a monster, not a loving dad and husband that he portrays to the world.

A psychopath. The reality of it unnerves me, and the picture of who I thought he was disappears.

Closing my eyes and blocking out my surroundings, I meditate as I think of the ocean, calming myself before walking out of here.

After a few minutes, I stroll to the main living space and nonchalantly take a seat and lean back.

"Sir, is there anything you would like to drink?" a staff member asks me, interrupting my thoughts.

Shaken out of my stupor, I blink a few times. The waitress is blurred out of my vision as evil thoughts rack my brain.

Not wanting to cause a scene, I reply, "Whiskey neat."

"Right away, sir." She turns on her heel, heading for the kitchen.

I try to organize my thoughts and wrap my mind around killing my father. I didn't think about the repercussions that would come from the fraternity for murdering a brother and stealing a sex slave.

They would use all their power to hunt me down and kill me without thought.

The need to free her from my father overpowers the consequences. I won't be able to live with myself if I just sit back and do nothing.

How in the world am I supposed to do that?

Another thought occurs: is my dad really raping her? Forcing her to do unimaginable things? I saw the bandages all over her, but didn't want to upset her further.

I drag my hands down my face, having a challenging time understanding how a human being could be put through this torture.

How am I supposed to act normal around my family when my girlfriend, who is my dad's sex slave, is chained in a room at the bottom of this yacht?

CHAPTER FORTY-SEVEN

CASSIDY

Unable to stabilize my breathing and rapid heart rate, hope soars through me at the thought of gaining my freedom back after seeing Tyler. Another orgasm slips through and sends me over the edge with exhilaration. Arching my back this time, I relish the high and ride it out fully.

After the last of it, my mind returns to what just happened.

Tyler. My Tyler. Here on the same yacht as me.

Another thought materializes: Martin is Tyler's dad.

Nausea rises up my throat at how fucked up this entire situation is.

Observing Tyler's reaction when he saw me and the genuineness he showed when he said he had absolutely no idea about his dad's involvement in this brings me comfort, but not for long.

When Tyler found out about the human trafficking, why didn't he walk away?

Was he just going to turn a blind eye to it? Or was he going to participate in helping facilitate it?

Distrust courses through me. I should never have gone over to the fraternity's house. Now, I'm a victim because of it. Letting people into my heart is so rare for me, and I did that without a thought for Tyler.

Suspicion over the situation and Tyler's participation in all of this makes me wary.

But what choice do I have? He is my only chance.

At least four orgasms and a few hours have passed by before the door swings open, and a drunk Martin staggers in.

He quirks his lip mischievously at me.

"You clearly had a great day," he states, without any kind of emotion in his voice.

Not reacting to him since I know it turns him on, I refrain from shifting my body and proceed to glare at him.

First, he pulls the remotes for the vibrators out of his pocket and turns them off. My core pulses as I close my eyes, the fatigue taking over.

Delicately, he moves to remove the ball gag but suddenly pauses, seeing that the headphones are to the side of me.

Confused, his lips turned down.

"How did you get these off, my resourceful girl?" He bends over me as he shakes his head, making light of it, and unbuckles the ball gag, withdrawing it from my mouth.

He reaches his hand out, quickly grabs a small towel, and wipes off the drool on the sides of my face. Noticing I have relieved myself on the bed, he yanks the sheet off underneath me and cleans between my legs.

"Tonight, my dear, you rest. You have earned it after your performance today. Tomorrow is a new day."

Opening one of the cabinets, there is a small fridge, and he brings a cold water bottle to my lips. I slurp it down along with a few purple grapes he hand-feeds me.

My stomach growls. I am still hungry.

After dabbing my mouth with the towel, he strides out of the room, vacant of any regard for me.

I close my eyes, and sleep comes easily.

CHAPTER FORTY-EIGHT

CASSIDY

A hand encasing my mouth awakens me from a deep sleep. Going into survival mode, I attempt to throw off whoever is doing this to me, forgetting about the chains holding me back. The person closes the gap between us in the darkness, and I stop fighting when I realize it's Tyler.

"Cassidy, you have to know I had no idea about any of this—the fraternity, the human trafficking, and my own father. They just disclosed it to all of us and threatened our lives and families. The whole thing makes me sick."

I glower at him, desperately looking for any truth in his words. "Honestly, these last few weeks have made me question everything," I spit, turning my gaze away from him.

He places a hand over his heart. "Look, I have no idea what you have been through, but I'm sure it has been a living hell. You can believe in one thing—I am getting you off this boat and as far away from these people. The yacht is scheduled to dock in the Bahamas tomorrow. I'll get you to that island, and you can make a run for it. You can relocate to any island of your choice and start over. I am sorry that is your only choice, but you can't risk these people finding you."

"Hell would have been better than where I ended up, Tyler. Death would have been better," I tell him bitterly.

He searches my eyes. Not wanting that to be entirely true, he whispers, "You don't mean that."

"With every fiber of my being. You have no idea what we have to go through. We're tortured, assaulted, abused, starved, auctioned off, and then put through training on how to be the best sex slave," I say incredulously.

I deflate at the thought of all the pain I have endured. Not knowing what to say to make me feel better, Tyler says, "My parents always go to Atlantis on the first day. They have lunch and dinner there and lounge by the pool. I am going to say I am sick and get you the hell out of here."

"Come with me," I choke out.

He searches my eyes, wondering if I mean it. "If you don't want me to, I'm going to have to go my own way; they'll kill me for this."

"Come with me; we can start over together," I say more confidently this time.

"You know I'd follow you anywhere, Cassidy. You have left an imprint on my heart I haven't been able to shake since laying eyes on you," he says, stroking my hair.

Tears freely fall down my face. I haven't felt a loving touch in a long time.

"You need to go." I shove his shoulder back away from me. "If your dad wakes up and turns on the camera, this plan all goes down the drain," I say, afraid of the chance of escape slipping through.

"Yeah, I will. Just give me another minute to look at you. I thought I had lost you for good. It feels surreal that you are standing in front of me."

"I'm not the same person you met; I am damaged in ways you will never be able to make sense of," I state, my face downcast, grieving the woman I was before all of this.

"I could never begin to comprehend the horrors you have gone through. All I can do is be there for you as you heal and be a shoulder to lean on. I care about you deeply, and I see a wonderful future in front of us." He looks at me with hope in his eyes.

"I need your help to get me out of this prison. Your dad is not the same person you know him to be. I am not your dad's first sex slave," I beg him, and he blanches, taken aback by what I said.

"I will. I promise. We will look for a boat tomorrow that is going directly to Turks and Caicos and start over.

The realization of that hits me like a ton of bricks. I ache to go back to my former life, but with the risk of my life and my family's being so high, my hands are tied. They will hunt us all down.

My heart plummets when I think about not being able to see or talk to my family or Blair again.

All of them will wonder what happened to me and if I am still alive every day.

Misery eats at me as I fight the urge to sob unsuccessfully.

"For both our sakes, you have to stop crying. We can't risk them overhearing you," he whispers, stroking my back.

He sighs, more to himself, peering over my body. Not being able to read his face, I can't make out if it's with longing or pity.

The odds against us escaping unscathed are low, but my backup plan is simple—Martin will not take me back alive.

I have come to terms with that choice, and I intend to keep it to myself.

"I'll be back tomorrow as soon as I can." Tyler squeezes my arm reassuringly.

I just nod my head weakly, nervous for what is to come.

CHAPTER FORTY-NINE

CASSIDY

I wake up to soreness below the waist, broken and battered.

There isn't a clock down here, so I don't know what time it is or how long I have been asleep. Martin has pre-planned everything, down to breaking my mind and body.

Turning my head to the right, I see Martin sitting there in a wooden chair, studying me with interest.

Startled by the sight of him, I recoil.

"Hello, dear. I thought we could start the day with something fun," he purrs, malice looming in his eyes.

"No thanks," I retort, scowling at him.

He throws his head back and laughs maniacally, relishing the fact that I can't do anything and I am at his mercy.

He walks over to the bed and circles it, licking his lips hungrily as uneasiness rolls off me.

In precise movements, as if he has done it so many times that it has become a habit, Martin removes his shoes, socks, and custom-made suit, along with the tie, cufflinks, and his expensive-looking watch, folding them flawlessly to avoid wrinkling his clothes.

Climbing onto the bed, he straddles my face. His cock and balls dangle directly over my nose and mouth, brushing against me.

A look of possessiveness washes over his face, and he snatches my cheeks with a firm grip.

Clutching his cock with his other hand, he drags it up and down over my lips.

Grinning as he unlatches my face, I turn away from him, appalled at the degradation.

"Rise and shine; you have cock to suck," he taunts as he slaps me across the side of my face.

Riled up by his demand, with my eyes portraying a dangerous mixture of repulsion and boldness, I lock eyes with him, spitting out, "If you put that thing anywhere near my mouth, I'll bite it off."

He seizes both my cheeks again, pressing them together so hard they are touching one another inside my mouth, my teeth cutting into them. "Try it. I will remove every single one of your teeth with the pliers I have stored away in my bag right now while you are wide awake with no sedation. You are already aware of how much I love inflicting pain. Blow jobs would be infinitely better with you being toothless."

Grumbling my disdain at having to suck him off while chained to the bed, I open my mouth, allowing him entrance, readying myself for something I can't prevent from happening.

"I will be away for the day and need the release. He shoves his balls into my mouth first. "Suck them greedily." He moans as I do. "That's it; get them nice and wet, you whore. You are enjoying every moment of this."

His cock stiffens and sweeps across my nose. He adjusts his

legs further apart so he can stuff his balls in my mouth as deep as they can go.

He pulls his balls out, and I swallow as he prods his dick on my lips, wanting access to my mouth.

I hesitate at first, and that was the wrong thing to do. He grabs a fistful of my hair, wrapping it around his hand and pulling it so hard my head is off the pillow. Pain shoots up my arms from the strain of the chains.

"Never hesitate again, or the punishment for it will be excruciating," he growls.

Automatically, my mouth opens wide, and he plunges his dick into my mouth, hitting the back of my throat.

My lips are extremely dry from dehydration and are chapped and cracked. They split open, and I can taste the blood as he vigorously thrusts in and out of my mouth while still gripping my hair tightly, forcing me into the ideal angle.

His musky scent exuding from his pubic hair makes me want to gag.

Martin grasps the sides of my face and forces my head up and down his cock in rhythm with his thrusting, using my mouth as nothing more than a warm hole.

My neck starts cramping and feels like it could detach from my shoulders.

Reaching for the headboard, he tightens his fists around the top of it and widens his legs as he grinds my mouth, pinning me down, allowing him to go further down my throat. He is moaning so loudly now. I choke around his cock, feeling light-headed because I can't take in any air. Tears mixed with slobber roll down my face. I scream around his cock, but only gurgling sounds manage to come out.

He doesn't stop or bother glancing down at my state, only worried about his own pleasure.

Just as I am about to pass out, hot, sticky cum spurts out of him in streams down the back of my throat, coating my tongue and cheeks, tasting the salty flavor. Positioned the way I am, I am forced to swallow it.

"If you don't swallow every last drop and lick your lips in appreciation at what I have fed you, I will turn you over onto your stomach and fuck your ass raw with anything I see lying around," he says aggressively.

Thrusting one more time into my mouth, I suck it greedily, closing my eyes and pretending it is a lollipop until he is clean of any cum on him.

My face is tender, and my jaw is going to bruise.

"Threatening you seems to help; you follow instructions better. I will see you tonight, dear. Don't wait up for me. I love the thought of you waking up to my dick somewhere inside you." He raises his brows at me as he dresses himself meticulously.

Fastening his watch, he looks at the time and speedily steps out of the room.

CHAPTER FIFTY

TYLER

Rushing to eat my breakfast this morning, I fidget with my silverware, anxiety crawling over me. I get dressed and pack a small bag, leaving my identification items behind. I sneak into my mom and dad's room and pack some of my mom's clothes for Cassidy.

I wait in my room, sitting on my bed and nervously checking my watch every minute. As planned, I told my parents I wasn't feeling well, and they made sure to tell me I could meet up with them later for lunch if I felt up to it.

Afterward, they took a small boat from the yacht to the island. I decided to wait an hour to be sure they didn't come back for any reason. I double-check the small backpack, ensuring I have everything we need, and stuff some extra money at the bottom.

At long last, with the bag in tow, I head down to the engine room as relaxed as I can, not wanting to draw any unwanted attention.

Throwing open the door, I see her staring off to the side, looking even more lifeless than yesterday. What happened?

"We don't have much time," I yell at her, getting her attention. "I'm going to unplug the camera and unwind the chains that are knotted to the bed."

Sprinting over to the camera, I look over it, find the plug, and angrily yank it from the wall.

Next, I rush over to Cassidy, bending down beside the first set of chains holding her down. Spinning the chains around, I recognize them to be tied in boater's or sailor's knots. I detangle them as fast as I can, and somehow, I manage to get them all. She is free.

CASSIDY

"Hurry, Tyler, he is going to come back for me. We don't have much time if we want to get out of here unseen," I hurriedly tell him.

I coddle and rub my raw wrists and ankles, whimpering at the torn skin.

"Get dressed," he demands, throwing clothes at me.

Not bothering to look at them, I throw on whatever he gave me as quickly as I can.

My legs falter as I stand upright, the blood rushing through them since I haven't moved them in over forty-eight hours.

Tyler bolts over and clasps onto my arm, allowing me to lean my weight on him. He uses his other hand to help me put on my pants.

"Well, well, look what we have here," a teasing voice behind us says.

We both whip around in panic.

"It's not what it looks like, Dad. This is the friend I was telling you about," Tyler pleads with him.

An emotionless Martin walks over to him and punches him in the nose, and Tyler goes down on the floor, holding his face in his hands as the blood rushes from his broken nose.

"You are not leaving this room, slave. And if my son wants to take turns with you, well, that is his decision." He shrugs.

He lunges for me, and I fall backward, scratching and hitting him like a rabid animal. I refuse to be his prisoner again.

"Tyler! Get up! Tyler!" I am screaming at the top of my lungs as tears form in my eyes. Martin slings me over his shoulder like I weigh nothing and leads us back to the bed, setting me down. He reaches for the chains, and that is what triggers a fire in my eyes. I fight Martin as much as I can, hitting, biting, and scratching at him, just hoping to make contact that would give me time to escape his grasp on me. The back of my head connects with his stomach, making him double over as he gasps for breath; holding on to the wall nearest to him, he attempts to stand upright, but the wind is still knocked out of him.

He gets ahold of himself and shouts, "You fucking bitch! You will pay for that."

He stumbles toward me, blocking the only pathway out of the room. I move backward, frantically looking for anything I can use as a weapon around me. He manages to get inches from my face, and then he spits on me.

"You're nothing but a slave, and it seems as though you need to be taught another lesson." He jerks his hand out, wrapping it around my throat and choking me as he hoists me off the ground.

I pound on his arms to let me go, helplessly hoping he will release me as I run out of air.

Bang.

Martin falls to the ground, and I look up to see a shocked Tyler standing behind him with a metal rod.

I hold my throat with both hands, kneading the soreness. Locking eyes with Tyler, he wordlessly reaches for the small bag and gives me his open hand, letting me decide whether to take it.

There is no decision to make; our lives are dependent on escaping together.

I clasp Tyler's hand as if it is the only thing keeping me in one piece, and we head to the door, hopping over Martin's body.

Letting go of Tyler's hand, I turn around and kick Martin in the face, ribs, and dick over and over as if I'm possessed.

Tyler wraps his arms around my waist and hauls me away from Martin. "There's no time for your anger to take over; we have to go!"

Sheer panic ripples through my body as I realize I forgot one crucial detail of my escape. I yank Tyler by his wrist and turn to face him.

Bile lingers in my throat as I all but shriek, "They put a tracker in my neck. We have to get it out now!"

Tyler combs his fingers through his hair roughly as he paces back and forth. "Okay, okay, we can figure this out."

He stops, and I look over at where his eyes land. It is a small toolbox.

Hurriedly, he sprints over to it, going through the drawers like a madman. When he finds what he is looking for, he runs back over to me.

My body is shivering uncontrollably as I see what is in his hands: a switchblade that looks relatively new and a pair of pliers that have seen better days.

"This is going to hurt, but you can't move or make a sound," Tyler states, looking me in the eyes.

I nod as tears form in the corners of my eyes.

He doesn't hesitate as I wordlessly pull back my hair on the side of the neck it's on.

"It's a tiny scar, but I see it," Tyler informs me.

I feel the cold metal of the blade sink into my neck, and with his fingers, Tyler spreads the wound open.

Feeling faint, I bite my lip so hard that the bitter taste of iron seeps into my mouth as I reach for Tyler's shirt to steady myself.

That's when I feel the pliers digging around in my neck.

"I see it, but it's a little deeper and blinking red, just a few more seconds." He huffs.

Whimpering, I squeeze Tyler's shirt, trying to remain upright.

"Got it," he murmurs.

I sink into his arms, and he pulls a rag he must have grabbed from the toolbox and places it on my neck.

"Apply a lot of pressure for as long as you can," Tyler says.

I feel the blood trickling down my neck.

He takes hold of my hand, and we begin to ascend the stairs, running in sync with each other as Tyler leads the way.

Panting, Tyler lowers his voice to where only I can hear. "Up ahead, there is a lifeboat that can take us to shore. I'm going to maneuver you down to it." He stops abruptly and clutches both my shoulders. "If for any reason I'm held back by someone, leave and don't look back."

I nod, confirming I will do as he says.

As I lift my head up, the lifeboat is only feet away from us.

True to his word, he lowers me into it first, tossing the bag in the back of the boat.

Tyler climbs down the ladder, skipping the last step, as he jumps into the small boat and begins working on the ropes that will lower the boat into the water. His hand slips up a few times, trying to hurry as his hands shake with the uneasy feeling of being caught.

As the boat finally makes contact with the water, Tyler revs up the engine and throws the throttle as far back as it can go. I flail, losing my balance but catching myself on one of the sides.

"Sorry!" he shouts, glancing over at me to see if I am okay.

I situate myself after taking in the sun, and I see the island straight ahead of us.

Daring to look back at the yacht, I jump when I see Martin holding onto the safety bar at the very front of the yacht, watching us. He turns around to throw things at the captain while screaming at him. After Martin leaves the captain with no choice, they jump into the smaller boat and trail behind us, gaining momentum.

Tyler doesn't even bother with the dock as we reach ankle-deep water. We throw ourselves out of the boat, clutching each other's hands with the bag strapped over Tyler's shoulder, and make a run for it.

Tyler knows his way around the island; I have never been here. Chancing a glance behind us, I see Martin's boat docking as the captain grabs the ropes to secure it. Martin jumps onto the dock and barrels after us.

Sprinting while weaving in and out of people, Tyler spots a cab, and we dash over to it, throwing the door open so roughly it starts to shut. Tyler clutches the door open with one hand and throws me across the seats, leaping in as he closes the door. Tyler shouts at the driver, throwing his arm in front of him and signaling to go. "Drive, just fucking drive!"

The taxi driver stares back at him, calmly asking, "What's the rush, man?"

Martin makes it to the door of the cab, and his fists connect with the window as he reaches for the handle.

Without thinking, I launch myself over Tyler and slam my palm down on the lock on the door, beating Martin by seconds from opening it.

"Go, go quick!" Tyler raises his voice, shouting at the driver again.

The driver stomps his foot on the gas pedal, and we take off with Martin refusing to let go of the handle. He doesn't have a choice as the car speeds up, and he tumbles over the concrete.

Tyler and I lean back against the seats, sweating profusely and breathing heavily.

"We did it," I say, sinking more into the seat.

"Yeah, we did," Tyler says as he winks at me and grabs hold of my hand, giving it a squeeze and kissing the back of it.

"Take us to the other side of the island, where there are boats headed to Turks and Caicos," Tyler directs the driver, tossing a few hundred-dollar bills his way.

The man nods enthusiastically, his smile widening. "Right away, sir." He steps on the gas, moving the vehicle faster along.

After about forty-five minutes going in and out of traffic, we pull up to white docks with smaller boats, not yachts, with rooms below deck.

Our driver gets out of the cab and walks over to where the captains of these boats are standing. He strikes up a conversation and gets a few of them laughing.

He hurries back to the cab, informing us, "There is only one boat heading to Turks and Caicos, but it is going to cost you a pretty penny, my friends—one thousand American dollars."

Tyler says too quickly, "That's no problem." He unlocks his door, opening it wide. Still holding my hand, he drags me out of the vehicle, and I stagger at the abruptness of it.

Our driver points out the boat, and Tyler counts out the money. He spots the captain standing in front of it and hands the money over to him. "We need to leave right now," he rashly tells the captain.

Nodding once, the captain motions us to board the boat. Once we're on, we make our way to the main cabin in the back of the boat. Still worrying that Martin will catch up to us, I peek out the large windows of the boat.

As the engine starts up, the captain does a quick once-over. My eyes spot Martin as he exits a vehicle, running while searching up and down the row of boats.

Our boat slowly starts to move forward, and Martin's eyes zone in on it. He sprints in our direction. "Tyler!" he shouts. "You can't do this to yourself!"

He stops at the end of the dock, contemplating jumping and

taking a chance on trying to land on our boat. He looks down and examines the length he would need to jump to make it.

In that amount of time, he makes a colossal mistake in his hesitation, and it is too late. The boat is too far from the dock. He would have to swim, and there is no chance he would be able to swim fast enough to reach our boat.

Letting out a breath I feel like I have been holding for weeks, I wave to him and give him my award-winning smile.

Martin is furiously pacing the dock, kicking the air, and screams, "You fucking bitch! I will find you if it is the last thing I do!"

I sit back on the couch and glance at Tyler, concerned he is having second thoughts about the choice he made, but he is sporting a wide smile.

"What are you smiling for? You just left your entire life behind to start over with me in a new country," I ask incredulously.

"I told you I was going to do whatever it takes to make you mine, Cassidy Matthews." He smirks at me as he takes hold of my shirt. Pulling me to him, he kisses me passionately, running his fingers through my hair.

THE END

EPILOGUE

CASSIDY

3 months later

I roll over in the most comfortable bed to face my husband as the ocean breeze washes over us, smiling with immense happiness.

I survived.

I am a survivor.

Tyler is still fast asleep as I tip-toe out onto the balcony, taking in the vast ocean before me.

It was hard at first, starting over, but we made it together, healing alongside each other.

Somehow, we've managed to remain undetected by the fraternity, but we have emergency bags packed just in case. I think we will always have that worry in the back of our minds.

Tyler started a fishing charter business shortly after we got here; he enjoys meeting new people and tourists from all around the world.

It took me a little longer to be comfortable leaving our home, fear etched deep in my bones from my time in captivity. I recently started a part-time job as a hotel receptionist at a local hotel. So far, it has been great for my mental health to interact with people again.

For the first month, I wouldn't let Tyler come near me, but he has been so patient, and we've taken it slowly and gotten back to where we were before I was kidnapped.

Recently, after feeling a sense of safety, I sent Blair a postcard in a code we used when we were younger. She hasn't written back yet, but I check the mail every day with anticipation that it will come. I know she will relay the information to my mom, and this is how we will have to communicate for now.

Tyler sneaks up behind me and wraps his arms around my stomach, still naked from sleep. "Come back to bed," he tries to coax me, whispering in my ear while pinching my nipple through my sheer top.

I groan. "Only if you promise to make it worth it," I tease him.

He lifts me on the railing of the balcony, shimmies my boy shorts off, and spreads my legs wide with his hands. Dropping to his knees, he kisses my inner thighs simultaneously. I throw my head back, closing my eyes in ecstasy. He kisses my clit, barely sticking out his tongue as he slides it back and forth over my slit. Then, he licks and sucks his way down, sliding his tongue inside me and pulling it out at a slow pace, savoring me.

He begins fucking me relentlessly with his tongue, and moans leave my lips shamelessly.

Right before I am about to come, he lifts me up by my ass, one cheek in each hand, as our chests are pressed together. I feel his length, fully erect, bobbing between us.

He hoists me up against the wall of the house and locks his lips on mine, kissing me like he is trying to steal the breath from my lungs. I kiss him back just as hungrily, warmth growing between my legs as I open myself up more to him.

He slides himself into me easily and adjusts himself so his cock can hit the right angle. Not taking long, he sets about thrusting in and out of me while my back slides up and down the wall. The friction causes pain, while Tyler gives me pleasure. The best of both worlds.

Suddenly, he stops, removing himself from inside me as he carries me over to the bed, splaying me out in front of him.

"Knees to your chest," he commands as his eyes darken.

I obediently follow his instructions, a thrill of the unexpected washing over me.

"Look at you with both holes on display for me."

He spreads my ass cheeks and spits on my hole. Moving his face down, he licks around my rim, slowly building me up. Edging me. Then he slides his tongue in and holds it there, bringing one of his fingers to my clit and flicking it back and forth. I squirm at the overwhelming sensation.

Then, he begins fucking my ass with his glorious tongue as he works my clit over and over.

The waves of pleasure engulf me, causing a small cramping in my stomach. As I open my mouth and scream his name, I squirt all over his face.

He licks up every bit of it and then climbs on top of me. He bends one of my legs to rest on my stomach and slides into me. He fucks me into the bed relentlessly, determined to make us come at the same time, grunting with each thrust.

He hits my G-spot at the right angle, and the pleasure is so immense I feel as though I am going to explode. We yell each other's names at the same time as he pulls out of me and comes all over my chest and face, marking me as his.

Sliding my fingers through it, I take two of them and suck them eagerly as he watches me intently.

"I love you, Cassidy, but I have to know... Would you change anything about our life?" he asks softly.

I ponder over this for a moment, and then bitterness consumes me as I say with venom lacing my tone, "I absolutely would."

"And what is that, my love?"

Locking my wild eyes with his, full of revenge, I say, "I would burn Alpha Chi to the fucking ground."

ACKNOWLEDGMENTS

There are so many emotions you go through when writing your debut novel. I have been a book lover ever since I could put words together. My nose was and still is always in a book. Never in my wildest dreams did I ever think I would write one. Well, I did it!

A big thank you goes to BookTok and all the friends and supporters I've made since starting my account two years ago. All of you cheered me on, and I could not have done this without you. I have had so much fun getting to know you and talking about our favorite thing: books. I am so thankful for this community because, for the first time in my life, I feel like I fit in.

My biggest thank you is to my husband. When I told him my crazy idea of reviewing books on social media and making videos, he was my cheerleader and pushed me to do it. Then, when I told him I was thinking about writing my own book, he was front and center with overwhelming support, even when I doubted myself multiple times. Marrying you is by far the best decision I have ever made.

To my beautiful children, Owen, Grant, and Chloe. All of you are a huge reason I took a leap of faith and pushed myself to write my book. This has always been a dream of mine since I was a little girl, but I always thought I was not qualified, and it seemed out of reach. I did this to prove to all of you that no dream is too big and that your dreams may change throughout your life, but don't ever think they aren't achievable. The impossible is always possible, and it does not matter how old you are; you can do anything if you persevere.

To my incredible parents, what a journey! You both have had a front-row seat to all my successes and all my low points in life. No matter what I have done, you have always been more supportive than I could have ever dreamed. I strive to be the parent you have both been to me. This year has been the hardest year for me, and both of you wrapped your arms around me and got me through it. There are no words for how much I love you both.

Thank you to my editor, Taylor, who has been so much fun to work with! You were the first one to read my book and provided me with nothing but support, kindness, and honesty. If you are in the process of writing a book, I cannot think of a better person to work with. Taylor went above and beyond and guided me through it.

How could I ever not say thank you to my best friend Zuley? Girl, you have been right beside me throughout this entire process. Cheering me on and helping me make decisions since we both know how indecisive I am. Honestly, the best part about making a TikTok was meeting you, and I know I tell you that all the time, but it is true. I love you, and I cannot put into words how much our friendship means to me.

Lastly, I want to thank Sky Blu, the author of one of my favorite books of all time, In Love with the Devil. This book would not have happened if it wasn't for you. You answered every question I had and held my hand along the way. You are an amazing person, and I am so lucky to be able to call you a friend.

If you would like to follow me on my social media accounts:

TikTok: @kristaturnerclark
Instagram: @kristareadsmore

Printed in Dunstable, United Kingdom